Sin & Seduction

ALLISON CASSATTA

Dreamspinner Press

Published by
Dreamspinner Press
5032 Capital Circle SW
Ste 2, PMB# 279
Tallahassee, FL 32305-7886
USA
http://www.dreamspinnerpress.com/

Sin & Seduction
Copyright © 2012 by Allison Cassatta

Cover Art by Allison Cassatta

ISBN: 978-1-61372-679-2

Printed in the United States of America
First Edition
August 2012

eBook edition available
eBook ISBN: 978-1-61372-680-8

This book is dedicated to
the friends and fans who have
continuously supported me.

Thank you.

ACKNOWLEDGMENTS

Thank you to the amazing staff and editors at Dreamspinner Press. And I would like to add a special thank you to Emmie and Lori for loving Dorian Grant for who and what he is and for helping me keep him real despite my urges to turn him into a big ol' mushy boy. As always, a huge thank you to Jessica Murchie for proofreading all my work and giving me constructive feedback.

AUTHOR'S NOTE

Dear Readers,

In this book I've created a fictional club—just outside the French Quarter in New Orleans—where a lot of questionable activity takes place. That's not to say I've seen this type of behavior in any of the New Orleans nightclubs or gay clubs I've visited. I'm not trying to stereotype or assume this kind of lifestyle comes with being gay. It may for some, but certainly not all. It is important to remember this is purely a work of fiction.

Thank you,
Allison Cassatta

1

THE last place Dorian Grant wanted to be on a Friday night was standing in a marshy field in the middle of fuckin' nowhere, watching the ape of a man he'd hired as his head of security beating the bloody hell out of some poor schmuck. And all because said schmuck *tried* to screw *him*—Mr. Sadistic Narcissist, of all people—out of a couple bills.

It wasn't the money. Dorian Grant didn't give a shit about the money. He didn't have to. He'd been born with a silver spoon in his mouth and a few to spare. It was the trust, the respect. That asshole had thought he would put one over on the crudest "businessman" in New Orleans, and he thought Dorian wouldn't do shit about it.

Wrong!

Dark brown eyes narrowing with rage, Dorian looked over at Angelo—who stood almost seven feet tall and laughed in the face of the three hundred pounds—and said, "Hold him down, dumbass. He gets away, I'm kickin' the shit outta ya!"

The threat should've been amusing, considering Dorian stood less than six and a quarter and barely hit two fifty. Granted, most of those pounds were muscle. Still, nobody ever had the balls to laugh at Dorian Grant, because what he lacked in size, he made up for in temper, and when that temper exploded into a full-fledged tear, no one was safe, not even a man whom he'd known for almost twenty years, a man who doubled him in size.

Angelo dropped the wooden Louisville Slugger he'd been toting and wrenched the schmuck up from the filthy ground. The land on the swampy edge of Lake Pontchartrain, just outside of Slidell, belonged to Dorian's family. It'd always been the safest place to do business because no one in his right mind set foot on that spot of land. It was useless, wasted, and abandoned, and perfect for the kinds of crimes Dorian and Angelo committed out there.

No one to witness the shit, and the gators always took care of the evidence.

The half-beaten dumbass, covered in mud and blood, fisted Angelo's long black ponytail, thinking he'd pull three-hundred-plus pounds of muscle down to the ground, then maybe make an escape.

"I don't fuckin' think so," Dorian said as his fist imprinted the three carats of clustered diamond ring on his middle finger right in the side of the guy's face. Blood erupted from the wound. The victim—or would that be the perpetrator, in this case—fell to the ground, coughing and wheezing and shit, spitting blood all over the grass and Dorian Grant's designer Italian boots. "Motherfu…. Boy, ya pissin' me off right fast, ya know? I might've let ya beg your way out of this one, but now—"

"Please, Mr. Grant," the guy sniveled. "Please, let me go."

"Oh, hell no! Look what the fuck ya did to my damn shoes!"

The loser's blood was already on his brand new Armani suit jacket and now, *now* it was all over his shoes! Thank God he'd gone for morbid and picked black on black, otherwise he would have to make a pit stop at his house on the East bank before heading over to Sin & Seduction. Too many hours had already been wasted screwing around with the dude on the ground. He wouldn't waste another second cleaning up. The cure to his mood waited at the club, and by God, he intended to get there quick.

Dorian looked over at the wide-ass ape of a man he called his right hand and said, "Finish him off. I've gotta cool down."

Angelo nodded, and Dorian headed to the Mercedes.

In the car's light, he checked his hands and face, his suit and shoes. His short, deep brown hair was still combed into place. His face was still clean, eyes eager and devious. It wasn't as bad as he'd thought. Maybe he could've gone a little easier on the guy, but heat of the moment and all got the better of him.

Damn, that dude had pissed him off, more than most of the assholes he'd had to beat into submission before. Maybe Dorian was more pissed about the fact he hadn't wanted to be there in the first place than he was about blood on his suit and the swelling in his hand. Didn't matter. Shit was over now. He'd get a line or two in him, then rail some tight-assed twenty-year-old in the back of the nightclub as he rode out his high. Maybe then the guy in the field and the busted hand wouldn't be a bother anymore.

Another mark on the scoreboard, nothing more.

He shrugged, slapped the visor mirror closed, then thrust the shifter of his Mercedes into drive as he stomped his foot down on the gas. He hauled ass out of the swamps and back toward Slidell, zipping through backstreets, then onto the main thoroughfare. The Mercedes couldn't have been much more than a blur as he pushed the limits of the law's allowed speed. Cops wouldn't screw with him. They knew his car and knew his plate. He took good care of them, and most of them turned their heads for him. It worked best for everyone that way, because nine times out of ten, Dorian was doing the citizens of southern Louisiana a service by ridding the streets of troublemakers.

All things considered, he didn't consider himself *that* brand of criminal. Sure Dorian wasn't a saint by any stretch of the imagination, but he was different from the average asshole who just went out looking for trouble. He was merely a businessman protecting his assets. The people he "handled," they were lowlifes, bottom-feeders.

The valet at Dorian's favorite spot—Sin & Seduction, a nightclub on the outskirts of the French Quarter—stepped to the curb before Dorian even pulled to a complete stop. A red pitchfork flashed beside the front door. Red velvet ropes kept the ordinary, nameless, faceless partygoers from the classier clientele. A line of those poor, pathetic souls snaked around the corner. If nothing else, there was a high dose of satisfaction in having enough clout to bypass *that* disaster.

"Mr. Grant," the valet said with a smile and a nod.

Dorian nodded back, tossed him the keys, then snuck around to the side of the two-story building and straight to the steps that led up to the VIP entrance. He bypassed the crowd as the bouncer grinned and lifted the velvet rope for him.

Inside the club, it was the same old story: assholes to elbows, barely enough room to move or enough quiet to think. That's what he liked about the place. He could sit back, toss down some high-dollar whiskey, and forget everything that had happened in a day of his life. He didn't have to hear the screams of the people he'd beaten the hell out of, or had Angelo beat the hell out of. In the club, with the noise and lights, the sweaty bodies and booze and drugs, he didn't have to think about the names his father had called him until the day the asshole died. There wasn't room for the memory of his mom dying before he ever really had a chance to truly appreciate her. There wasn't room for shit, except his high and the lucky little dancer who would have the privilege of playing with his cock that night.

He leaned back against the leather of his VIP booth, held up two fingers, and before he could even loosen his tie, a half-naked waiter brought the bottle of Johnny Walker Blue and a shot glass to his table.

"Thanks," he mumbled.

"No problem, Mr. G," the waiter said with a wink and a grin.

Dorian lifted a twenty from his pocket, ran the edge of the crisp bill down the firm line of the kid's abdomen, then tucked it in the front of the waiter's neatly pressed slacks. He gave the kid's crotch a little pat. Dorian said, "That's for you. Keep me full tonight and I'll keep the money comin'. Feel me?"

"Yes, sir, Mr. Grant." The kid shot Dorian one hell of a promising smile before sauntering away.

Dorian shook his head and relaxed against the booth. Waiters could be amusing and all, but what he really wanted was a dancer. Those boys always had the best moves. They were always the best lays.

2

IT WAS a normal night at the club, for the most part, anyway. Normal, save for the fact Jansen—AKA "Sweet Heat"—had finally gotten his spot on the main stage. After working at Sin & Seduction for close to a year, in the back where no one ever saw him and no one really cared to, he finally had his chance to shine, to show off for the masses and work the pole as people shouted his name. It was his chance to dance beneath a spotlight that rained splendid rainbow-colored glory over a body he'd worked long and hard to keep as close to perfect as a human being could get.

Holy shit! This is really happening!

It still felt like a dream. When his boss had come to him and offered him the audition spot, everything in the world stopped moving. He'd barely been able to breathe. It was the answer to everything: a fix for being a nobody with no money, no car, no future, and a shitload of unreachable dreams. It was his chance to make real changes in his life.

Giving nothing more than a curt nod, he'd accepted the audition with only a day or so to prepare himself, and now, he wondered if he'd made a mistake.

Everything was riding on this dance… this one chance.

He could already feel the rush. He could do it. He could be a shining star, even if his only claim to fame ended up being in the local gay scene.

Now, Sin & Seduction wasn't a gay club, not officially, though it might as well have been. The men who went to that place usually went looking for a hot, young piece of ass… more often than not, they wanted a male. At any given time, the bathroom stalls would be filled with patrons giving each other head or a quick hand job. The dancers had a special place, down in the club's basement, to take the well-paying customer for a quick rendezvous. None of that was official, of course. As laid-back as life in The Big Easy seemed to be, there were still rules to follow, and whoring wasn't legal, not by a damn sight.

The women, with their skimpy dresses and heels they could barely walk in, were another story. They'd fuck, well… pretty much anything with two legs. They might try to hit on a man, might even get lucky, but those who didn't find a man to slam them into a toe-curling homerun, they'd look elsewhere for a good time, even if it was another woman who wanted to offer them that particular brand of "good times."

But Jansen, he was "strictly dickly" as the straight chicks always said. He'd known what turned him on from the moment he had his first hard-on, and trust, it wasn't the Victoria's Secret catalogues his mom had always gotten in the mail. No, he had a thing for the men's underwear section of the Sears catalogue. He would tuck them away for a special occasion before his mom ever got wind of their arrival, then whip them out for a little fun when the parents left him home alone.

Ah, the good old days of being a kid, when everything was easy and life was handed to him. Although his life had been far from easy. His mom had a thing for drunken losers who liked to slap kids around. She never saved a damn dime for him to go to school, never seemed to care if he made something of himself or not, and that lack of parental guidance landed him in nightclubs, dancing and stripping to scrape together enough money to pay his bills and still eat every now and again.

Maybe now something would finally change for him. Having the spot on the main stage at Sin & Seduction meant money, more money than Jansen had seen in a long damn time. Chances were, some VIP would see him and invite him back to a private table, then pay him a shit-ton of money for a naughty little dance, and maybe, if he was really good, they'd invite him for a night in the hot tub. Being a dancer in the back meant he bought his own beers and partied with coworkers after the club shut down.

No one wanted to be that brand of loser. And losers like that didn't make bank.

The backstage area was stocked with costumes to fulfill every libidinous fantasy known to man, and some fantasies that most sane people would've never dreamed of. Those corny mirrors, framed with huge white bulbs that showed off every single unflattering blemish the naked eye couldn't normally see, lined the walls. Jansen's rich chocolate-colored hair looked boring in those cruel lights. His skin looked sickly. But that crazed, about-to-hurl, panicked look in his deep brown eyes, the lights had nothing to do with.

His best friend reached around his body—a more than friendly hug—running his thumb beneath the hem of Jansen's white tank top. With a soft voice, Jason spoke against Jansen's ear, lips just barely fluttering over his flesh. "Don't look so worried, honey. It's only a dance."

"Says you." Jansen turned in Jason's arms, now facing the only person in this whole God-forsaken world who understood him and looked after him. "I need this. I need them to love me."

"They will. Now stop frowning." Jason smoothed his thumbs across Jansen's brow. "You're barely in your twenties, and already you have wrinkles."

"I'm twenty-five, and I've lived the life of a forty-year-old already, Jason. Frown lines are to be expected."

"Whatever. You still need to calm down, or you'll make yourself sick before that hot little bod of yours ever makes it onto the stage."

"I swear, I'm trying."

Jason curled his fingers around the thin bands of Jansen's G-string and settled it into place so it highlighted the curve of his friend's perfect ass. With eager hands, he followed the bands around to the front and gave Jansen's "business" a little tug to plump the bulge between his thighs. The first thing the crowd would notice would be the size, no matter if his rather impressive bulge—according to Jason—was covered by loose pants or not. No, Jansen wasn't small in that area, not by any stretch, but Jason knew every trick the stage lights and the right attire could play on curious eyes.

After Jason settled the matter of Jansen's "business," he reached back and grabbed the tear-away black slacks Jansen had picked for his number tonight. "You'll be fine, baby. You're one of the hottest boys here," he said.

"Thanks."

Sweet Heat stepped to the edge of the room. He stood just behind the backstage curtain, shifting back and forth on his feet, wringing his hands and sweating like a whore in church. If he hurled in the middle of his routine....

"Here," Jason said, interrupting Jansen's ridiculous little internal breakdown. The glow of stage lights caught Jason's auburn hair in a way that made his head look like a flowing stream of fire. Jason looked down, bright green eyes narrowing at his open palm. Jansen's stare followed.

"What is that?"

"Ecstasy. Figured it would loosen you up a bit."

"Thanks," Jansen said as he swiped the little yellow pill and popped it in his mouth. He swallowed it back without needing a chaser, then looked out over the crowd. So many dark silhouettes: a sea, really. The place was packed tonight, and the thought of all those eyes watching his every move made his stomach churn again.

Some of those men would consider having their way with him, doing things to his body he hadn't allowed since that night—just over a year ago—when he'd woken up in the hospital in the worst pain he'd ever felt in his life. Jansen would thank every god and then some that he didn't remember what had been done to him. He would gladly kiss the feet of those gods for finally ridding him of the nightmares of being taken against his will in the dark, dirty parking lot behind that sleazy Slidell nightclub.

The music for his routine cranked up, the bass rumbling against his chest, the highs piercing his eardrums. His gut tightened more. His stomach started doing backflips.

Jason reached for the fedora on the table beside them, dropped it into place on Jansen's head, then patted his shoulder. "Knock 'em dead, tiger."

Jansen's heart raced as he waited for that one verse in the song he'd chosen to be his cue to take the stage. Oh God, if he screwed this up, it would be over. He would be relegated to a back stage, and no one would give two shits about him. He would be living off ramen noodles and wearing secondhand clothes for God only knew how long, and forget the idea of getting a new car. He could barely afford to pay the rent as it was. Everything was riding on this one dance. Everything.

"I can't do this," he said as he shifted back and forth on the balls of his feet. "I can't. I can't."

"Calm down, baby," Jason said.

"I'm trying."

"Don't worry, the X will kick in and you'll be fine, I swear."

Then he heard his cue, and Jansen started for the stage.

The lights were too bright and the music too loud. He thought he would die right in the middle of the stage, but then a euphoric feeling came over him. The pounding of his pulse wasn't from being nervous but more from the high he'd been praying for. The tingling in his skin and the twitching in his cock made a devious grin curl his plump pink lips.

"Holy shit," he gasped. Perfect timing.

Sauntering into the flashing lights felt more like dancing through a rainbow. Feeling the bass pulsing, mingling with the mids and highs of club music, felt like walking into a night of mind-blowing sex. Every sensation in his body came alive at once. If he didn't know any better, he would've sworn he had just walked onto the set of *Willy Wonka and the Chocolate Factory.*

He twirled and gyrated out onto the catwalk, tossed the fedora back, then ripped his white tank top away. The fabric burned his skin in a magical way, and he hissed, but he didn't miss a beat. If anything, the sudden thrill, the sensation of having clothing ripped from his body, made his dance just a bit more provocative.

As soon as the tank top was gone, the lights above shone down on his chest. Red and blue and green glistened in his sweat and showed off his muscles. A hundred—no, definitely more than a hundred—blackened, empty faces stared up at him, all screaming and yelling. "Sweet Heat!" That was a lame stage name and he knew it, but that's what he got for asking his drunken best friend for help.

He wrapped his hands around the pole, dipped down and ground against its silvery surface, then came back up and kept dancing to the end of the catwalk. With a smooth slither and a confident swagger, he sauntered down toward the crowd. Rolling his hips to the right, then to the left, he was certain they could see just how well-endowed he was. He ripped the black pants away, then dropped down to his knees at the edge of the stage, and the crowd rushed toward him, reaching out to stuff money in his G-string as he ground his groin against their greedy palms. They all wanted to get a feel of what Sweet Heat was packing beyond the thin gold fabric of his G-string.

Catcalls and loud music pounded his senses. This was heaven for Jansen, now that his high had kicked in. He'd found his groove and could dance all over that stage as long as the bass of the music and the cries of the crowd held strong. He knew from the response, he'd be back up there again soon. He knew the boss would let him have the limelight because he'd draw in business, and a packed house meant fat wallets for the men in charge. "Sweet Heat" would definitely be a star.

3

DORIAN sat back in his private booth, watching people come and go, watching each nondescript, average, ordinary fucking dancer take the stage, shake his ass for a bit, then leave. Such a bore. The women were okay. A few were hot. Whatever. He preferred watching the men, but even they lacked something tonight. Maybe he just didn't want to be there either. Maybe he should've gone back to the very comfy, slightly over-the-top mansion he had tucked back in the middle of nowhere. He could've spent a little one-on-one time with the hot tub, but then he'd have too much time to think about the asshole whose blood soiled his five-thousand-dollar suit. He slammed back another shot, and another, and another.

Johnny Walker Blue, at over two hundred dollars a bottle, was one of his personal favorites when booze ended up being the drug of choice for the night. *What the hell,* Dorian thought. He would lay his head back against the leather seat of his well-bought VIP booth and drown his miseries in a nice Scottish blended whiskey. He could even close his eyes and try to forget everything, try to relax.

But then this new guy sauntered onto the stage.

"Fuck me," he gasped.

Leaning forward, Dorian steepled his arms, pressed his elbows against the tabletop, and locked his fists under his chin. Curious brown eyes completely focused on the kid, he watched every nervous step the dancer took. Gorgeous, no doubt about that, but the kid completely lacked any confidence. Regardless, he'd piqued Dorian's curiosity.

Chocolate brown sprigs of hair peeked out from a stupid black fedora that also covered the top of the dancer's face. Dorian couldn't see his eyes, but the perfect point of his chin and plump, pouty lips gave away his good looks. The thin, muscled forearms and the ripples beneath his shirt were enough that Dorian's cock jumped with interest. A little more than *just* his curiosity had been piqued.

Oh yeah, he thought as he watched the dancer's lean, muscled body grind against the center-stage pole. The kid rolled his hips, and the only thought that crossed Dorian's mind was, if he could move like that on stage, he'd be fucking amazing in the sack.

Then the dancer ripped off his shirt, and that was all she wrote for Dorian's steely composure. Red, blue, and green lights glistened in the sweat that clung to the perfectly carved curves of the dancer's chest. Dorian imagined running his tongue over every crease, dragging those sexy, pierced nipples into his mouth with his teeth. He could almost feel that promising bulge between the dancer's thighs against his palm.

He took a long, hard pull from the bottle of JW Blue, then reached down and grabbed a handful of his stiffening cock as he shifted against the dark leather seat. He kept watching the object of his lust shake his shit for the masses while he imagined himself riding that kid until they were both too far gone to even move.

Now, Dorian Grant had never been a desperate man. Never had to fight to get laid, and he never really got excited over it either, but this fucking kid…. Jesus, Mary, and Joseph, the way his body reacted, and without even seeing what the dancer *really* had to offer. Oh yeah, he would be getting a private dance before the night ended. If everything worked out, he might even take the guy back to his place and do him *just* right.

He watched Sweet Heat dip down to his knees. Boy, the kid had worked the crowd over but good, could've had those desperate people eating out of the palm of his hand if he wanted. Hell, Dorian would almost give in to his every wanton desire, but that's not how the big man rolled. *Oh, hell no!* That beautiful boy would do anything and everything Dorian desired by the time he got done with him. Dorian would be the one in control. He just didn't play that submissive shit. He was an alpha male, and alphas bowed to no one… including hot-ass dancers with the kind of bodies wet dreams were made of.

As he gripped his crotch a little harder, a moan rumbled up through his throat. He didn't do commitments, but this kid stood a damn good chance of a repeat performance, even though the first act hadn't yet begun. His name could very easily get etched in a little black book and stashed away for future reference.

Dorian took another shot of whiskey, then another, and with a two-finger wave in the air, he called the bouncer over. "I want that fuckin' kid," he yelled over the music. "I want him up here as soon as his dance ends."

The bouncer nodded, got on his walkie-talkie, and called down to the stage. Pretty soon, Sweet Heat would have his sweet heat wrapped around Dorian's dick, and if the big man had his way, he would ride that firm ass well into the morning hours.

4

THE music started winding down. The MC called out another name, but the crowd didn't want Jansen to leave the stage. "Sweet Heat!" they all cried out in a symphony of desperate sound. They wanted to see him rubbing his ass up and down that pole some more. They all wanted to shove their hands down his skimpy G-string while they copped a feel of the well-endowed package rocking between his thighs.

Jansen had a more than pleasant, egotistical smile plastered all over his face. *Score!* He did it! He actually pulled off some pretty hot grinding and won the hearts of every drunken soul in the house. They nearly stampeded to get to the stage. He couldn't believe it.

Holy shit!

His best friend met him backstage with his arms crossed over his chest and an envious smirk spread across his face. Jason shook his head. Between two fingers, he held out a light green slip of paper. "You've got a new fan, Mr. Superstar."

Jansen ripped the page from Jason's fingers and read out loud. "Mr. Grant would like to see you in his VIP booth on the second floor."

It might've been sad to someone who didn't understand, but this was a way of life for dancers like him. This was a huge break for people who didn't have a chance at making it big otherwise. He'd been waiting for a year to get one of those little green slips of paper that meant he'd made it to the big time, as far as New Orleans nightlife was concerned, and someone wanted him. That little slip of paper meant he'd begun ascending to the top, and maybe, just maybe, he could start living like a human being again.

But there was much more to it than that. Jansen had been born to perform. He loved dancing. It was his life. He'd had every dance lesson he could afford, sunk every hard-earned penny into it. His mom and her drunken husbands had never spent a damn dime on him or his education. Everything he had, he earned with his own blood, sweat, and tears, and now all that hard work promised to pay off. The proof was in the fact that someone enjoyed his show enough and wanted him enough to send down for him.

Grabbing Jason's face, he pulled him forward and laid a hard kiss on his lips, grinned, and said, "Don't wait up for me." Then he peeled out of there and tore up the stairs to the second floor in nothing but a gold thong, with a heavy dose of excitement coursing through his veins.

"You be careful, you fool," Jason yelled out to the fading image of his best friend disappearing in a blaze of golden-thonged glory.

Jansen hightailed it up to Mr. Grant's booth. He hit the top floor landing panting. The ecstasy had already done a number on him. His skin tingled. Pupils dilated to hell. He wanted to touch anything and everything he could. He wanted to be touched by anyone and everyone. He needed to be stimulated, needed... to be fucked.

Not good.

The guy in the black-on-black Armani suit had a bottle of Johnny Walker Blue Label turned up to the sky. He reeked of money and power and things Jansen had never experienced in his life.

He'd hit the jackpot.

"Mr. Grant?"

The big man leaned forward, looked down Jansen's body, spotted the bulge between his legs, then let his eyes wander back up. In a firm, commanding, more than manly voice, Mr. Grant said, "Come here."

Jansen's body stiffened. A jolt of something dangerous and intoxicating shot through him, and he felt a little tingle of thrill ripple down his spine. Absently, he moved closer to the booth. As soon as he was within an arm's length, Mr. Grant reached out and hooked his fingers around the tiny golden band of Jansen's thong. He pulled Jansen forward, so close his crotch was inches from the man's face.

"Dance for me, boy." The words left Mr. Grant's mouth in a drunken growl.

Sounds from the club below roared up toward the private booth on the balcony overlooking the joint. Bass pulsed. Lights flashed blue and red and green. Sweat glistened on Jansen's body. He straddled the stranger's legs, pressed his barely covered, thick length against Mr. Grant's groin. He could feel the hard press of the stranger's shaft even with Armani slacks between them. Jansen gyrated, ground harder against his thighs.

Mr. Grant's head rolled back as he gripped Jansen's hips so hard the sudden stabbing pain of fingertips biting into muscle made Jansen hiss. He shook it off, fought to keep this… thing with Grant going strong. Jansen pressed his lips to Grant's throat, kissing his flesh, sucking his neck. The stranger wrapped his hand around the back of Jansen's neck and pulled him down until his ear met Grant's mouth.

Grant said, "I'm gonna fuck ya tonight."

Honestly, Jansen didn't know what had come over him. Wait. That was a lie. It had to be the ecstasy. He hadn't meant to entice the man, not like that. He thought he'd give Grant a dance, maybe a hand job at the most, then Mr. Grant would send Jansen on his way. But the dynamic had changed, and as soon as Jansen felt the erection pressing against his thigh, something else had taken over. The X he'd taken before hitting the stage controlled his every movement and his innocent little dance had become a salacious, sex-laden innuendo.

Whatever. Didn't matter. That is, until Mr. Grant said he was going to fuck him tonight; then he lost his confidence. He felt like he had the morning he woke up in the hospital with an ache in his body that radiated up from his ass and exploded in his head. Jansen was afraid the guy would try to take him with force, make him do things he didn't think he could do again.

He looked up at Mr. Grant, smirked, and said, "Not tonight, but for the right amount of money, I'll blow you right now."

Well, Dorian didn't want a fucking blowjob under the table at a nightclub. He wanted to snort a few lines off the curve of the dancer's fine ass, then drill him hard from behind. Maybe do it again in the hot tub or the shower. He'd fuck him backward and forward, then do it all over again.

Wrenching the kid up by the hair, Dorian glared into his intriguing brown eyes and said, "Are ya a whore? Ya fuck men for money on a nasty nightclub floor?"

Sweet Heat didn't speak, didn't shake his head. He just looked at Dorian with a heavy dose of fear in his eyes.

The only time men looked at Dorian like that was when he or Angelo was about to beat their heads in. He didn't know how to take it. Coming on strong in sexual situations had always worked for him, and this little shit just threw a wrench in his plans.

"Get up!" Dorian yelled over the music. "We're goin' back to my place."

"No, I… I can't," Jansen stuttered. "I, um… I have to work."

Dorian tilted his head back and called one of the bouncers over to his private booth. "Pretty boy's shift is endin' now," he said, and the bouncer nodded. "Have the valet get my car. We're leavin'."

"I… I can't go with you."

"Why not?"

"I just… I can't."

Dorian leaned in, one hand slipping between Sweet Heat's thighs, fingertips lightly stroking his hardened shaft. His lips gently grazed the moistened flesh of the kid's neck as he whispered, "Ya wanna come home with me." A fact, not a question. "I'm gonna make ya feel things you'll never wanna forget. I'll treat that body like a crown fuckin' jewel, kid."

The husky, lust-laden sound of Dorian's rich voice and the brush of lips against Sweet Heat's flesh made the kid shudder. The feel of the kid's fear and the excitement in his groin turned Dorian on even more. Sweet Heat nodded slowly. "Please don't hurt me," he breathed.

"Oh, hurtin' ya is the last thing I had in mind."

One ragged breath, then another. Sweet Heat lowered his head. "I'll go."

So beautiful. So submissive. It took a load of willpower to keep from devouring the kid right there. No, Dorian would take care of him, do him right, make him cry out to whatever god he believed in.

The bouncer had fetched Jansen's clothes. Mr. Grant wouldn't even let him out of his sight long enough to change. Maybe he thought

Jansen would run, and maybe he would've… if he hadn't been high and horny. This guy promised to take care of at least one of those problems.

Jansen's hands shook as he slid into his jeans. He could barely pull the zipper up, could barely snap the button into place. He pulled a black Sin & Seduction shirt over his head, then strapped on his Converse knockoffs. When he looked up again, Mr. Grant was reaching in his coat pocket. He pulled out a black, silky piece of fabric and said, "Cover your eyes."

5

DORIAN had always kept an air of mystery about him. He took precautions for everyone's safety. No fucking way would this kid *ever* know what kind of car he drove or where he lived. The blindfold was meant to protect both their asses. He damn sure didn't want some strange guy he'd picked up in a bar following him home one night, just in case the kid was already a little south of Loony Town. That kind of shit was hard to pick up on when drugs and alcohol distorted everyone's reality.

The dancer's eyes widened. If fear were tangible, his would've been a brick wall between them. "I can't," Sweet Heat whimpered, shaking his head as he tried to back away.

"I'm not going to hurt ya, kid," Dorian said, reaching out to grab his wrist. "Ya want your sweet little ass to stay safe, this is your best bet. Now tie the fuckin' blindfold on before I change my mind."

"Please don't hurt me."

"I ain't gonna hurt ya. How many times do I have to tell ya that? Look around. Everyone up here knows you're goin' with me. Ya think it would be a wise idea for me to hurt ya?" Dorian leaned in and held the cloth in front of the dancer's face. "Sorry, kid, but this is to protect us both, okay?"

Sweet Heat nodded slowly.

Dorian watched the dancer's fingers shake as he wrapped the cloth around his head. He should've told the kid never mind, but he didn't. There was something curious about him. Not innocent, but not like the rode-hard assholes Dorian was used to. No, there was something else there; something like the most treasured gem under the stars, like climbing to the peak of Mount Everest just to brag about conquering the mountain. Dorian had to have him. If nothing more than a taste, just to be able to say he'd had Sweet Heat in his bed or shower or hot tub.

He guided the dancer down the steps slowly, carefully. They headed out of the club down to the black sedan waiting at the back door. Dorian slipped the valet two bills, then they took off without anyone else being the wiser.

All Jansen could hear was soft music and the thrumming of tires. All he could feel was the cool night air against his face. All he could see was the pitch black of the cloth Mr. Grant had made him tie around his eyes. His heart pounded in his ears. His pulse raced in his chest. He'd screwed up again, done something so stupid he'd probably land in the morgue this time.

It didn't make sense for him to follow Mr. Grant's orders, but he had. Anyone who knew Jansen's past would've called him crazy for going home with a strange man, but there was something about Mr. Grant, like an air of power that wouldn't be denied. But there was also the mystery and the seduction. Jansen ached to know that kind of power, to feel it conquering him. The need to have that man controlling his body almost overwhelmed the fear, which made Mr. Grant even more dangerous than he might have been otherwise.

"Please don't kill me, okay?" Jansen managed to choke out. "I don't have shit. I don't do shit. And I don't know shit."

A low, guttural sound erupted from Mr. Grant's body and Jansen came unglued. He started to shake even harder, panting each desperate breath. He couldn't breathe, and the confined space of the car felt like it was closing in on him.

"I ain't gonna kill ya, kid. Relax," Mr. Grant said. "Like I told ya before, I want your body, not your life."

The engine roared a little louder, as if Grant had pushed the accelerator as far to the floor as he could, as if he were eager to get Jansen back to this mysterious home he'd spoken of. The sound and feel of the newfound speed made Jansen's muscles tighten and his pulse thump a little faster.

"Ya need to loosen up," Grant said with a laugh that held little threat. "When we get to my place, I'll give ya hit of X. Getcha head *just* right."

But another hit of X didn't really matter at this point.

Taking a deep breath, Jansen rubbed his sweaty palms against his jeans. "Look, I have to tell you something. You have to be gentle if you're going to... if you plan to fuck me tonight. I, um... I had something bad done to me, and they, um... they had to do a lot of surgery to make me right again. I mean, can you please just take it easy on me? You'll be my first since...."

Dorian tilted his head, frowning over the steering wheel as New Orleans skyline flew by. No wonder the kid looked so fragile. He was.

Frustration had already killed Dorian's erection, but he knew once he had Sweet Heat naked and pressed to the bed, it would be all hands on deck again. His sailor would be ready to salute. And somehow, Dorian had to remember to take it easy on the kid. Dorian Grant might've been a monster in some eyes, but he never... *never* set out to hurt the innocent, and that's exactly what this kid was: innocent.

The black Mercedes pulled into a driveway that led deep into the trees, circled around a fountain, and spilt back out onto the main drive. He put the car in park, then went around to the dancer's door. Taking his hand, Dorian led him inside the mansion, through the foyer, and up the stairs to his bedroom.

"Open your mouth," Dorian demanded as they stepped into the room.

Sweet Heat parted his plump, kissable lips.

Dorian slowly, playfully slipped a hit of X onto the kid's tongue. "Now swallow," he whispered as he reached behind the dancer's head to untie the black silk blindfold. It fell away from Sweet Heat's face, fluttering down to land on the tan Berber carpet at their feet.

It took a moment for Jansen's eyes to react to the change in light. His pupils narrowed, bracing for the sudden presence of soft light surrounding him after the nothingness of being hidden behind dark silk. The walls in this room were light-colored, tan or maybe off-white. An empty king-sized bed with a tall black leather headboard and dressed in crimson linens sat to his left. It was flanked on both sides by dark wooden nightstands and matching lamps with the same crimson shades. A dark wooden dresser with a huge mirror sat to his right. But in front of him stood the figure of a god, with a chest that da Vinci would've been proud of.

Mr. Grant's upper body was solid. Jansen could tell without even touching him. And despite the raised line of jagged scar over his sternum, the sight of Grant was completely enticing. The tattoos only added to the art of the stranger's form. Jansen imagined himself tracing the lines of the flower, then the bird, with the tip of his tongue. He absently licked his lips while he imagined the taste of Grant's body as he pressed kisses over every bare inch.

A rosy shade of red flushed the dancer's cheeks. Dorian let a soft laugh slip past his lips as he reached down and unzipped his own pants. Black Armani slacks pooled at his feet, left him standing there in nothing but black briefs. His deep brown eyes set on the dancer as he hooked his fingers on the waistband of his underwear. He slowly pulled them down his thighs, exposing the dark patch of hairs surrounding the semi-flaccid cock between his legs.

"You want it?" Dorian said in a seductive voice, gaze slowly traveling downward.

Jansen nodded.

"Make it hard again. Do me right, and I'll treat ya to a night of fuckin' heaven."

Dropping to his knees, Jansen's big brown stare drank in Mr. Grant's length, every beautiful inch of it. He wrapped his hand around the mysterious man's growing erection and opened his mouth. The hall light shone in from behind them, haloing Mr. Grant in a golden glow. It only made him appear more godlike, larger than life.

A moan rumbled up through Mr. Grant's chest as Jansen circled his tongue around the head of the guy's cock. Back and forth, back and forth, he brushed his tongue across that thick shaft. Jansen took as much as he could and let it tickle the back of his throat. Grant started to roll his hips. Jansen bobbed his head faster and faster.

Damn, that dancer had one talented fucking mouth and apparently one deep-ass throat. Dorian wasn't small by any means—had gagged many men in his time—but this kid was taking it all like a champ. Dorian fisted his hand in the dancer's hair as he drove harder and faster into Sweet Heat's mouth. The firm tip of the kid's tongue ran over the length of his shaft, around the ridge, and over the head. Pulse throbbing, Dorian felt the nice, aching pressure of an orgasm building in his sac. He was about to lose his load straight down Sweet Heat's throat.

"I hope you like to swallow, dancer," Dorian rasped as his eyes rolled back in his head.

Jansen picked up the pace in the way of an unstated "yes." His lips tightened.

Dorian's thighs quivered. "Oh fuck! Oh fuck! God! Fuck!" and with that string of four-lettered praises for a job well done, his load poured down the dancer's throat like his body had sprung a leak of the *best* kind.

And with a ragged, coarse growl, Dorian said, "This ain't over yet, boy."

6

"SHOWER," Mr. Grant said in a hoarse, winded voice. "No fuckin' around."

He led Jansen to the bathroom and tossed him a towel. Jansen had to admit, this big, demanding guy scared him, but in the same breath, there was something absolutely exciting about him. Something so exciting it made his nerves twitch... in a good way.

"What's wrong?" Mr. Grant said from behind him just as a thick, strong hand grabbed a handful of Jansen's ass with enough force to make him take a few steps forward.

Jansen bit down on his lip as another wave of heat flushed his face. He wanted so badly to turn around and look right at Mr. Grant, but something in his gut warned him against it. "Nothing, I... I was just looking around."

Fuckin' liar, Dorian thought. Something was wrong. The kid was standing naked in the middle of the bathroom, stiff as a board, and all he was doing was "looking around"? Dorian pressed his naked body against his new friend's backside, reached around his waist and grabbed a handful of Sweet Heat's hard-on. The dancer rolled his head back against Dorian's shoulder.

"You don't want to shower with me?" Dorian purred against his cheek.

"W-why do we have to shower?" Sweet Heat asked.

"Well, kid, you've been dancin' all night, and I beat the shit out of someone. In this case, blood and sweat just ain't sexy."

"I, uh...."

"You, what?" Dorian brushed his lips over the side of Sweet Heat's neck as he stroked his palm over the dancer's cock.

He walked them closer to the shower and reached out a muscled arm, hand turning the knob. Cold water sprayed out of the showerhead. Some of the overspray hit their chests. Sweet Heat jumped, and that only pressed him harder against Dorian's body. The feel of it made Dorian purr, made his dick twitch and ache to be inside the dancer's amazin' fuckin' body.

Dorian brushed his rock hard cock against the luscious curves of the dancer's ass, teasing the split in those gorgeous mounds. He could dive right in, bend him over the vanity, and take him for the ride of his life.

"Mr. Grant," Sweet Heat said in a breathy voice, interrupting Dorian's fantasy.

Dorian felt the kid's body tensing. "Shhh…. Relax. I'll be easy."

The water warmed, and Dorian eased them into the shower, never letting go of the dancer's erection. He relished the feel of it hardening and pulsing against his palm. There was a certain amount of satisfaction in knowing he had control of someone like that. He walked Sweet Heat to the wall, pressed his chest against the tiles.

Dorian trailed hard kisses up and down the dancer's neck as he reached down with his free hand so his fingers could stroke the valley of two beautifully perfect cheeks. Fuck, that kid had one hell of an ass on him: firm and rounded just enough that Dorian's hand covered one cheek perfectly. He slid a finger inside, pulled it out, then slowly pressed it inside Sweet Heat's warm opening again.

The dancer turned his head until his cheek rested against the cool, moist wall of tiles. As soon as Dorian penetrated Sweet Heat's body with his thick finger, he felt more than heard the kid gasp and hold in the breath as if he were afraid to let it go. Sweet Heat closed his big brown eyes and exhaled slowly, muscles unclenching as Dorian gently eased his finger in and out, in and out again. Dorian kept kissing the dancer's back, silently praying the kid would relax enough for them both to enjoy this.

Dorian slid another finger inside, and the dancer clenched again. A hiss slipped through his ground teeth. "Relax, baby. I ain't gonna hurt ya. I promise," Dorian said as he continued to press soft kisses to Sweet Heat's shoulder.

The kid was lucky. Normally, Dorian didn't go easy, but something about that beautiful, delicate man made him want to be gentle. Maybe it had been the fear he saw in the dancer's soft brown eyes when Dorian had told him he was going to fuck him. Maybe it was the pieces of his story. Dorian didn't know, but he knew he didn't want to scare Sweet Heat off. If for no other reason, he knew he would want another go at the kid.

As his fingers worked to loosen the dancer's body, Dorian had begun to stoke himself until the first bead of cum leaked from the head of his erection. He drew it down his shaft, then stroked a little faster, until his cock was hard and ready, and there wasn't a chance of doing any more damage to the kid's body. He eased the tip inside, then waited for the hiss of pain to push through Sweet Heat's lips, but the hiss never came.

"You all right?" Dorian asked.

The dancer nodded.

Dorian pushed in a little further. The kid wasn't as tight as the rest of the twentysomething-aged boys he'd been with. He could only assume it was because of what had been done to him. That looseness let Dorian keep going, giving him one inch after another.

Jansen couldn't believe this big brute of a man was being so gentle, couldn't believe it didn't hurt, but it didn't. Mr. Grant took his time, eased him into the first sex he'd had in over a year, and it was nothing short of heavenly. Jansen could finally relax and enjoy sex again. The relief was incredible.

"Oh God," he rasped.

Grant picked up speed, diving in a little harder and deeper with each thrust as hot water rained down around them. He locked his mouth down on Jansen's shoulder, teeth nipping at the skin, toying with moist flesh and pressing against firm muscle.

In and out. In and out. A little harder, a little faster with each thrust. Grant's cock stroked the nub inside Jansen's body. If Grant kept going like that, Jansen would lose his load all over the shower. The pulling and pulsing in his jewels meant seconds before that blessed, mind-numbing, toe-curling explosion of heated bliss, and honestly, he wasn't ready for their little tryst to end.

Then suddenly, Sweet Heat's head ripped back and he growled into the air. Dorian felt the warmth of the dancer's cum running through his fingers, felt his ass clench and his legs quiver. The throbbing in Dorian's cock turned volatile. He gripped the kid's hips, dove deep inside him, in and out, in and out, until every drop was gone from his body.

With a shared hiss, Dorian pulled out of that divine, heated tightness. He rasped, "Hope it was good for you." By the look on the kid's face, it was good for him. Very good.

Sweet Heat's face pressed against the tiles, lips slightly parted while his lashes fluttered against his cheeks. He took short, stabbing breaths as Dorian moved around the shower like nothing had happened.

Standing under the spray with his now-flaccid cock in his soapy hand, Dorian said, "Get cleaned up. Your clothes will be on the bed. Maria'll send the car to take you home. Make sure ya cover ya fuckin' eyes before ya walk outside my doors. Don't want my guard doin' it for ya. He'll give ya a thousand dollars when he drops ya off."

"Y-yes, Mr. Grant," Sweet Heat panted against the tiles. "Will I see you again?"

After waiting and not hearing another word or even a breath from Mr. Grant, Jansen rallied the composure to turn around, but the mystery man had already left. He was gone without a trace, like he'd been a product of Jansen's overactive imagination. Despite knowing what he would get himself into before he ever left the club, it still sort of hurt Jansen's feelings. He'd never been treated quite like that before, like a cheap whore.

"Shrug it off," he whispered. "What did you think would happen?"

Clean clothes waited on the edge of the bed, just as Mr. Grant had promised. Jansen gave his body a little hug. He suddenly felt dirty for what he'd done. It was stupid, feeling that way. Dancers did the same shit all the time. Some of them even ended up with a hell of a lot better lives than they had before. Either they fucked enough rich men to buy their own happiness, or the rich men took them in as live-in lovers. What was the harm in what he'd done? Really?

Who was he kidding? None of that made him feel any better. The money was great. It would pay all of his bills for a month, but that didn't make him feel any less used. He just wanted to dance. Jansen just wanted to be seen and loved by his audience, not treated like a whore.

He threw his clothes over his body, took one last look around the room, inhaled the scent of sex and Armani Gio one last time. "So much for being special," he mumbled as he closed the door on one amazing night.

The bright moon still hung in the night sky. It spilled a soft hint of light into the dark foyer of Mr. Grant's mansion. He'd been there for almost an hour, and it had only felt like minutes, but it may have been the best minutes of Jansen's adult life. He wanted to see Mr. Grant again. What he'd done, the dominant strength and utter pleasure, Jansen knew he wouldn't forget it. He knew he would eventually start to crave it.

"You ready, kid?" A deep, rich voice called from behind him.

Jansen spun on his heels and stared up at a colossal man with dark, scary eyes and a long black ponytail. The dude was so huge he could barely cross his arms over his chest. Jansen nodded slowly.

"Don't forget the blindfold," the guy said, holding out the black silk scarf.

Jansen took the piece of fabric and fastened it around his head. It was double-checked, and when the mammoth man was satisfied, he shoved ten one-hundred-dollar bills into Jansen's hand. They headed out to Mr. Grant's car: the chariot that would carry Jansen away from his knight in tarnished armor.

The surly guy with the tree-trunk arms said to someone Jansen could only assume was the driver, "Get this kid back to his place. Report back to Mr. Grant when he's home safely. I'm out for the night." He stood back up, grabbed Jansen's arm, sat him down in the car, then slammed the door behind him.

7

DORIAN had left the bedroom for his office. He really didn't want to be there when the kid finally hauled his ass out of the shower. Dorian didn't do well with attachments, and already Sweet Heat had acted like he didn't want to leave. Not that Dorian would've kicked his ass out the door anyway, and even that was sort of a problem.

The window to his office overlooked the wrap-around driveway. He waited and watched for the headlights to swing around before he'd go back to his room. He wasn't into those awkward, post-sex moments where a good-bye was inevitable, but not exactly wanted.

As soon as he saw the bright red glow of the Mercedes's taillights, he padded back down to his bedroom and slammed the door behind him. He slid out of the black satin robe he'd covered his body with, then climbed into his bed. Thank God they hadn't fucked there. Maria would've lost it. She'd just cleaned those sheets, and he knew better than to screw with his housekeeper when it came to linens. That woman was crazier than him and Angelo combined.

When Dorian finally climbed into his bed, sleek red Egyptian cotton caressed the hard curves of his naked, tattooed body. He'd started coming down from the high of the drugs and the low of the booze, the adrenaline rush of beating someone to a pulp and the euphoria of the toe-curling sex he'd just had. Dorian stared up at the ceiling. Tonight wasn't much different than any other night of his life. Fight. Get lit. Fuck. Sleep... if he was lucky. But for whatever reason, tonight things felt different.

As he lay there, letting his mind trample over the peace a night in his bed had to offer, he couldn't stop thinking about the dancer. That one had been different in ways Dorian didn't quite understand and couldn't explain, even to himself. He knew he wouldn't easily forget that kid. He knew he'd have to go back for him eventually. But would Sweet Heat see him again after what he'd done, after the way he treated him? Of course he would, because Dorian could give him anything and everything he'd ever dreamt of, and then some. Dorian wasn't looking for love, but he had enough money he could buy it for the night.

He reached over to the nightstand, grabbed a stogie, and fired the damn thing up. He'd replaced the tobacco with pot. On the streets, they called that a blunt. He needed to feel numb. He needed to forget the guy whose head he'd beaten in, and he needed to forget the kid from the nightclub. Remembering Sweet Heat, thinking about him and wanting him, would put a wrinkle in Dorian's life he didn't need right now, but the more he tried to push the dancer out of his head, the more the kid clung to the surface of his thoughts.

He rubbed his rough hand up and down his chest, over his flaccid cock, and he hissed. The flesh was still too tender to touch. Or maybe the nerves were still raw, and wanting to feel the dancer's warm body again made matters worse. His cock twitched, his sac giving a little tug. He'd end up hard again if he kept thinking about Sweet Heat, and the blowjob, and the shower, and the way the kid's body moved when he danced.

"God help me. That boy'll be the death of me."

Dorian pictured the dancer back on stage, the way his hips rolled like fluid, and the way the muscles curled beneath all that beautiful tan skin. He could see all the hands reaching up to Sweet Heat, revering him like he was some kind of god. They all wanted to touch him, fondle him, get a little feel of the kid's goods. And the more he thought about it, the more he hated the idea of a hundred strange men watching *his* dancer shake his shit on stage. Dorian hated the idea of all those hands feeling and groping something he'd been so intimate with.

"Fuck me," he groaned. Was he seriously getting jealous? *Nah, couldn't be.*

Stabbing out the blunt, Dorian watched the glowing orange tip fizzle out into nothing more than a few wasted ashes. He rolled over in the bed and killed the lamp on his nightstand, then buried his face in the pillows. What sort of nightmares would plague him tonight? Would he see a bloodied face, or would he see the dancer's beautiful, lust-filled eyes?

"Shit," he hissed. He was so screwed. A one-night stand wasn't supposed to have this kind of impact, especially not on someone as hard, and empty, and unwilling as Dorian Grant.

That settled it; Sweet Heat was off limits until Dorian got his head screwed back on again. He would handle the affairs of his business and his cock the same way he always had. Fuck 'em, then hit the ground running. No looking back.

The idea was great in theory, but in practice, it would probably be much more complicated than a few silently promised words. In fact, he knew it would be. He already wondered if Angelo had taken the kid home, if he was safe, if the dancer thought about him at all. Dorian couldn't wait to run back to Sin & Seduction for another private dance. And because of those rampant thoughts, he couldn't manage enough peace for the first inkling of sleep.

Cursing, Dorian climbed out of the bed. He snatched a pair of black silk sleep pants from the footboard. He stared in the mirror, at the tattoos on his chest and arms. They told a story of a life that had been sullied from birth. Sure, he'd been born into money, but money had its own problems, dirty problems.

The ruby encased in rose petals, permanently painted over his heart, had been put there for his mother. That was his first tattoo, his memorial for the woman who'd given him life. Ruby, whose bright red lips curled into a smile every time she saw him. Twenty-three years had passed since her death, yet he still expected to see her standing in the kitchen when he ran down the stairs. He still expected to feel her warm, loving hugs when he needed someone to just be there to hold him and comfort him.

The swallows over his right pec were the newest on his chest: his good omens to help him find his way. Surely, the life he lived right now wasn't the life he would always live. Yeah, it was a necessity, but that didn't mean he liked it. Dorian did what he had to do to survive. Maybe one day it would get better.

A long scar of raised, mutilated pink flesh drew a line down the center of his chest, separating his past from the future he prayed for. That scar was his present: the bad shit he did, the violent man he'd become. He could almost feel the blade tearing through his skin again.

And the prick who'd dug the knife into his chest, that guy had been "a friend."

That's why Dorian Grant didn't have friends. He had employees and acquaintances. He didn't give a shit about anyone, and no one gave a shit about him. Life worked that way.

Well, it had worked that way until a hot little number from a club happened upon his lap.

Sweet Heat was definitely off limits for a while. Hell, he might even stay away from Sin & Seduction. That place had been bad juju here lately.

8

MR. GRANT'S driver dropped Jansen in front of his shitty apartment in Gretna, far from the ritzy outskirts where Grant lived, down deep in the crude streets of New Orleans where all the somewhat normal people, who had somewhat normal jobs and lived somewhat normal lives, belonged.

Jansen got out of the car with no promise of seeing his strange new friend ever again. The sleek black Mercedes pulled away in a rush, kicking up gravel and broken cobblestone behind it. He watched the car disappear from sight, half regretting that he'd ever gone home with Mr. Grant in the first place, half wishing he'd been asked to stay.

How pathetic! Dude had treated him like a whore, and now he pined for someone who didn't want him? Okay, maybe "pined" was the wrong word, but that wasn't the point. He'd actually enjoyed the sex. Was that a crime? No! He was young, and Mr. Grant had shown him a good time. So yeah, he wanted to do it again.

Jansen climbed the rusted metal steps to his second-floor apartment, pried back the metal screen door, and fought with his keys to get inside before the Gulf Coast winds knocked him on his ass.

He plopped down on a couch that had seen better days—like back in the seventies—and stared at a dark wall that had never been decorated, despite Jason having lived there for years before Jansen came along.

The night had been a long one. He should've been tired. He should've been on the verge of dead to the world, but his mind wouldn't stop its incessant rambling. So he stared and wondered if anything would ever change.

The longer he sat there in silence, the more he thought about Mr. Grant and their night together. Again, Grant was the first man Jansen had been with in a long time, the first man he let fuck him since that tragic night in the parking lot of a rundown Slidell nightclub. With Grant, he'd been just as scared as he had been that night, but that man, that brute, had actually taken care of him.

Absently, he reached down and started to rub his dick. Thinking about Grant—the sex they'd had—made Jansen hard again. The way Mr. Grant stood over him, staring down at him as he knelt down in front of that beautiful, tattooed man and the way Jansen just started blowing him in the middle of the room was something he didn't normally do, or at least, he never had before. And it was probably the hottest thing he'd ever done.

Then the shower. *Holy shit, the shower!* Grant had felt so amazing inside of him, stroking an orgasm right out of his body. *So fucking hot.* And with that thought, Jansen was completely rock hard again.

Before he really realized what he was doing enough to stop, or maybe at least go to his own room, he had his zipper down and his hand wrapped around his erection. He could only pray Jason didn't come home in the middle of that shit. Not that it would matter. Jason wouldn't care, but still. He wouldn't want Jason to walk in on him stroking one out.

He lay back against the couch, eyes closed as he relived Mr. Grant being inside of him, driving hard into his body, lips and teeth toying with his flesh while hot water rained down around them. Jansen could feel Grant's hot breath against his skin, smell his cologne, and taste his cock on the back of his tongue. The man had set his body on fire, made him enjoy having sex again. It was amazing, miraculous, and if he ever had the chance, he would probably thank Grant for giving that back to him.

Jansen's hand rode up and down, stroking his hard-on from base to head. That wonderful, promising throbbing started in his legs and pulsed straight into his groin. He stroked faster as the memory of Grant's voice, barking demands, filled his head. No one had ever done anything like that to him.

He stroked faster, felt the soft flesh of his palm riding over the delicate flesh of his erection. His heart started to race as he imagined Mr. Grant commanding "come for me" in his ear.

"Yes, Mr. Grant," Jansen rasped as his back arched and his legs spread a little wider. Jansen wanted to please him. He wanted Grant to enjoy watching him as he got off for him. Faster and faster, he fisted his hardened cock, pulled back and forth. His sac tightened. Faster. Faster. "God! Ah!"

Jansen came hard, damn hard. The shit exploded all over his hand and clothes. All he could do was sit there and pant with his eyes clenched and his heart pounding in his ears. He wished he could see the pleasure on Grant's face. He wished he could kneel down and have his beautiful new friend be proud of him.

"Ah, hell!"

He was losing his mind. What? He wanted that stranger's approval? Did Jansen want his love, or was it just his attention? Did he want to believe Grant would find him again? Or did he just need to face the reality that he would never see that stunning, dominant man again?

9

"YOUR friend is home, Mr. Grant," the driver said through a crack in the office door. Dorian nodded. It was nothing more than an acknowledgment and a silent dismissal. He couldn't think about the dancer right now.

Hours passed. He tossed and turned in his bed, fought with the sheets and fought with his brain's little tirades. Early morning became late afternoon. Afternoon became night. He paced his room, paced the halls, went to his office, then back to his bedroom. At some point, he even made his way down to the kitchen for some of Maria's gourmet best. Nothing helped, and without those long missed hours of R&R, Dorian's temper was now on full alert.

Since nothing else seemed to help, he thought he'd get a little work done, but word from Angelo had spun him off into a whole new level of pissed off. Apparently, the asshole whose head he'd had to beat in last night had a business partner who thought Dorian wouldn't come for him too, and Dorian intended to show him just how *dead* wrong he was.

Angelo had his wide-ass body sprawled across the black leather couch in Dorian's office. He'd just smoked a damn joint and looked like he was about ready to pass out. Dorian had done a few lines and was ready to go find that asshole and beat his head in.

"We really need to get our schedules straight," Dorian said without looking up from the financial statements on his computer screen.

Wide-ass quirked his brow and mumbled something that sounded like, "What?"

"I'm ready to handle business, and you look like you want to eat the couch."

Angelo gave his boss a lazy-eyed laugh as he slowly turned his head. "I'm all good. Let's do this."

"Yeah. Right."

Wrenching his head from side to side, Dorian cracked his neck as he stood up from his desk. If he did handle this "business" today, he'd want to see the dancer tonight, and that was a problem. Dorian couldn't let that kid fog his mind. Lack of sleep was doing a fine job on its own.

"I want to get this guy and take him to the warehouse."

That made Angelo sit up on the couch. The leather creaked under his massive weight. A wide smile stretched across the behemoth's face as he cracked his knuckles.

"I want his ass dead too," Dorian added. "And if there are any more of them, we'll beat the shit out of them as a lesson. Nobody fucks with me."

Angelo nodded.

Dorian fished the cell phone from his pocket, pacing as he raked his fingers through his short brown hair. The housekeeper, Maria, came in just as the newest asshole on Dorian's shit list answered the phone. Dorian said a stiff, "Hey," watching as Maria gathered the wrinkled, bloody Armani suit jacket from the back of the chair. He kept his stare trained on her, waiting for her to leave the room.

"I need to see you," Dorian said to the guy on the phone. If that stupid SOB had been standing there, Dorian would've smelled fear rolling off his body. "Yeah, ya know what the fuck this is about. Meet me at the warehouse, and you'd better be there. If I have to come lookin' for ya, you're a dead man."

He hung up the phone, slipped the thing back into his pocket, and nodded at Angelo. "Let's do this."

"Can we stop at McDonald's first?"

Dorian gave him a droll stare that seemed to last forever. "You're fuckin' kiddin' me, right? Like you need another Big Mac." He wrapped his hand around the back of Angelo's thick neck and gave him a hard shove. "No, we ain't stoppin' at fuckin' McDonald's first. I don't see how ya eat that shit, anyway. C'mon, let's handle this business. I'd like to try to sleep at some point."

"Shouldn't have stayed up fuckin' all night," Angelo mumbled under his breath as he followed behind Dorian.

"I heard that shit."

They climbed into Dorian's black sedan, then rolled down to the warehouse district, not far from Sin & Seduction, the nightclub where the kid from last night worked. As they passed the converted warehouse, with its red flashing pitchfork and the line of people dying to get inside, he wondered if Sweet Heat was there, grinding his sweet ass against the pole again, waiting for people to stuff money in his thong. The thought only served to piss Dorian off even more. God help the asshole he was about to pay a visit to.

Angelo parked behind an old, darkened warehouse and grabbed the Slugger from the backseat before climbing out of the car to meet Dorian at the trunk. The place looked abandoned, and that's how they liked it. That's why they picked that spot to confront troublemakers before they decided if a visit to the swamp was needed. Sometimes people got lucky and walked away with their lives. Sometimes they became gator food.

The man they'd come to visit met Dorian in the parking lot, hands clamped together like he'd been praying for his life long before Dorian and his goon ever showed up. In a shaky voice, he said, "I swear, Mr. Grant. I ain't cookin' no books. What Charlie did with the matters of your business, I don't know nothin' 'bout. I ain't have nothin' to do with it."

"Not out here," Dorian said as he wrapped his hand around the back of the guy's neck and pulled him into the warehouse.

First, Dorian swung around and nailed him right in his eye socket. The guy stumbled backward, then Angelo gave him a shove from behind and his knees hit the ground hard. He knelt down in front of Dorian and begged, hands locked together, praying to God to spare his life. It was a damn shame, watching him cry like a woman. It was so pathetic, Dorian almost wanted to let him go... *almost*.

Angelo cracked the dude across the back with the Louisville Slugger. He fell forward and his face planted against the concrete floor. He cried out louder, begging them both not to kill him. After all, he had a wife and a new baby.

"Fuck me!"

Now, Dorian *wasn't* a monster, but family didn't mean shit to him. What good was having a father that wasn't around, or better yet, one who was a criminal?

So, he had two options. He could let the guy go, and maybe the moron wouldn't try to scam him again. Or he could kill him, make a lesson out of his ass, just in case someone else decided to get brave and scam a few hundred dollars off the top.

Right after Angelo popped the dude in the mouth with the bat, hard enough to bust his lip but not do any real damage, Dorian gave him a nod, signaling for Angelo to back off. Then Dorian lifted his foot and gave the guy on the ground a swift kick. It connected with his ribs hard enough to make him spit blood onto the warehouse floor. He cried out like hell, like Dorian *would* kill him, maybe torture his ass into a slow death.

"Ya lucky. I'm feelin' generous." Dorian knelt down, fisted the guy's hair, and ripped his head back. The idiot's eye had swollen shut already. "You remember this shit the next time ya try to screw me over. I'm lettin' ya go now. You fuckin' take care of ya family, you act like ya have some sense and an honest bone in ya piece-of-shit body, and we won't have to face each other again. Clear?"

"Yes, sir! Yes, sir!" the man proclaimed as he gathered himself from the floor. He bowed and thanked both men, and bowed again as he backed away.

Dorian looked over at Angelo and said, "Let's go. I need a fuckin' shower." Angelo tossed the bat to the corner of the warehouse and started to follow him. "What the hell are you doin'? That asshole's blood is on that thing. Ya think you're gonna leave it here? Use your fuckin' head, man."

Angelo grabbed the Louisville Slugger as Dorian muttered curses, then followed him out to the car. After close to a half hour of driving, they finally pulled into the driveway of the mansion. Dorian sat there with his head back against the seat, eyes closed. He couldn't stop thinking about the dancer. He wanted to see him again. He wanted to be with him again. And here it had been more than a day since he'd been to bed.

Fuck it!

"Go home," Dorian said as he climbed out of the car. "I'll catch up with you later."

He went upstairs, showered and shaved, and changed into one of his less pompous Armani suits, all black with a cobalt blue dress shirt. He slathered on the cologne one of the ladies from the office had picked out for him and checked himself over. He looked like hell, eyes dark from no sleep. Screw it. He'd do a line or two, then he'd be ready to go all night.

He slipped a couple hits of X in his pocket, knowing Sweet Heat would want it. Then he went down to the sedan and started back toward the warehouse district, back toward the club.

10

JANSEN had worked the room and worked the crowd, wound his way through the sea of bodies, searching for the one man who'd consumed his world for the last twenty-four hours. He hadn't seen Mr. Grant all night. He looked everywhere, and the elusive stranger simply wasn't there. What did he think? Did he honestly believe Mr. Grant would come back tonight? He should've known better. He was no one, just another nameless, faceless fuck.

Ouch. That hurt.

He gave up. Soon, the MC would be calling his name anyway, and he had to be ready for the show. Jansen had to put on Sweet Heat's happy face, take himself to a place where Mr. Grant didn't matter and stardom was on the horizon. He had to get his head in the game.

Shoulders rounded, Jansen slumped down in a backstage chair and stared at himself in the mirror. Even his deep brown eyes looked sad and desperate. His lips refused to give up just a hint of a smile. God, he was screwed. He had to get it together.

Jason appeared behind him and patted his shoulder. "You're up, baby. Main stage again."

"Yeah, I know."

"What's wrong?"

Jansen shook his head. "Nothing. I was just… nothing."

"Doesn't look like nothing to me."

"It is. I'm fine, I swear."

Letting out a hard sigh, Sweet Heat grabbed his police hat and nightstick. The cop getup was his gimmick tonight. Costumes were a favorite with the patrons of Sin & Seduction, and for some fucked up reason, the law dogs really worked the crowd up. Jansen would dance to some corny cop song, swing his big stick as he pranced around the stage. If he got brave, he might even do something questionable and possibly lewd with the stick. Not that the stick or the costume or the song or the crowd mattered right now.

Jason narrowed his eyes as he watched his best friend absently move around the backstage area. He crossed his arms over his chest, tilted his head, and said, "You sure you're okay?"

"I'll be fine," Jansen said.

"If it's that man from—"

"I'm fine," Jansen interrupted, aggravation coloring what normally would've been an excited voice. "The show must go on, right?"

"You're absolutely right!" Jason patted Jansen's perfectly plump ass. "Get out there and knock 'em dead, baby."

With a tight-lipped grin, Sweet Heat pranced out onto the stage, swinging his big stick and shaking his ass. The crowd erupted, cheering and calling out his name. Jansen smiled like he didn't have a care in the world, but that was a lie. The whole charade was a lie. While he gyrated and danced and ground his body against the pole, he couldn't stop thinking of Mr. Grant.

Bass pounded. Sirens sounded. Fog filled the air. The faces in the crowd were nothing but a sea of black emptiness. Jansen's eyes narrowed on the second floor, to the VIP section he'd gone to the night before. He didn't see Mr. Grant's muscled form. The booth was empty. Disappointment hit him like a ton of bricks, but he didn't stop dancing. He didn't let on to the sudden heartbreaking devastation.

Hands groped him from ankle to crotch. So many hands, all begging for a moment against his flesh. They deposited money in his thong to thank him for the cheap thrill. Sweet Heat rolled his hips and dropped to his knees, thrusting his cock in all those anxious faces. The more lewd his dance became, the more they all clamored to shove money in his underwear.

He *was* just a cheap whore.

This was supposed to be about dancing and the spotlight. This wasn't supposed to be about cheap thrills, or was it? Christ, he wanted off that stage. The whole experience had been so much better with ecstasy.

Almost mechanically, he shifted his eyes up to the second floor. Mr. Grant's booth was still empty. *This so completely sucks*, he thought. But he couldn't let the crowd know. He had to keep up the fake smile and promising pretenses, had to hide his disappointment.

Knees pressing against the stage, Jansen rolled his head back and closed his eyes. He thrust his crotch forward in a long, slow, slithering movement that started in his head and ended in his thighs. The crowd erupted again. More hands fought for just one touch of Sweet Heat's flesh.

He'd given up on seeing Grant tonight. Jansen swore to himself he wouldn't look again. He swore he would get Mr. Grant out of his head, but then he looked up again and saw a darkened silhouette leaning forward, watching his every move.

A rush of excitement pounded through him. He couldn't wait for the song to end. He just knew the elusive Mr. Grant would send for him, and they would go back to his place, fuck all night, then... well, then he'd send Jansen away again.

Shit, I'm nothing more than a whore to him, and I'm happy to be that. How lame does that make me?

Jansen jumped to his feet, then sauntered back toward the pole. He kept his eyes locked on Mr. Grant's darkened form. This time he ground hard, dipping his torso forward so the lights shimmered along the line of his sweaty back and glistened against the mounds of his ass as his cheeks embraced the pole. His eyes never left his gorgeous stranger. The curve of his plump lips promised another night of fun if only Mr. Grant would send for him.

11

LIKE the night before, the valet stood at the edge of the curb, waiting for the sleek black Mercedes that seemed to come every Friday and Saturday night. As soon as Dorian pulled to a stop in front of the club, the man stepped out with his hands neatly tucked behind his back. He gave Mr. Grant a slight bow and a welcoming smile.

Dorian tossed his keys. The valet lurched forward to catch the jingling ring. Not a single word was spoken. Dorian didn't even bother giving the other man a second glance. He moved toward the VIP entrance with determination, like a man on a mission. The only thing on his mind was the dancer; seeing him again, being near him again, feeling his soft skin again.

So much for that vow of restraint.

Designer Italian boots pounded against the stairs as Dorian headed up to his private booth. The bouncer held open the glass door. He gave Mr. Grant a curt nod, but again, Dorian didn't give two shits about the staff or their forced greetings.

He hit the top landing, tearing his eyes toward the stage, like the lights and music had some sort of magical, magnetic pull. It was the dancer. That was the pull. That's why he'd gone back to the club despite needing a night off to sleep. He saw Sweet Heat, ripping away a button-down police shirt and tossing back a black uniform hat with a silly, fake gold badge. The getup made Dorian laugh.

A fucking cop, really?

As soon as the waiter saw Dorian sit down, he brought over the big man's regular bottle of booze. The half-naked kid with carrot-colored hair sat the JW Blue down on the table and turned to walk away. Dorian grabbed his wrist. He told the waiter to send Sweet Heat up as soon as his show finished. Of course, the request came with a folded hundred-dollar bill, and thus, the waiter was more than happy to oblige.

Dorian leaned back against the leather seat of his private booth, hidden in the darkness, and he watched. Lights glistened in the dancer's sweat as he rolled his hips and ground his cock against the pole. The sounds of the music, the sirens, and the screaming voices all faded away, and nothing existed except Sweet Heat's luscious body and moves that had the ability to make Dorian come unglued.

But something wasn't quite right.

Lips pressed tight, the dancer scoured the crowd. He looked for something or someone he couldn't see. Clearly, the idea that he couldn't find what he was looking for bothered him. Dorian saw it in the crease of his brow and the flare of his nostrils. It affected his show. The kid wasn't giving his all like he had the night before. His routine bored Dorian, but his body…. Well, his body excited the fuck out of him. Every time he saw the dancer roll his hips and thrust his business against the air for all those excited, wanting hands, Dorian's cock twitched. It throbbed and pulsed and ached to be touched.

Dorian leaned forward so he could get a better view. The sea of people in front of the stage all shoved their hands in the air, grasping for a quick touch or chance to shove singles inside the dancer's G-string. Sweet Heat's plump, perfect lips curled into a smile when he spotted Dorian, but that tantalizing smile quickly faded.

What the hell did *that* mean? Was he happy to see him or not?

"Fuck."

As Dorian leaned back, the music came to an end. He hoped the dancer would make his way up to the booth soon. He wanted nothing more than to have that deliciously teasing body pressed against his. He wanted to feel Sweet Heat move his hips and his thighs and his legs just like he had on stage.

He waited, not so patiently. Then he waited some more. It didn't look like the kid was going to show. Maybe Dorian had screwed up too bad to take it back. Then the beautiful dancer appeared at the opening of the booth. Dorian smelled Sweet Heat's body, his cologne and his bodywash, before he ever saw his face. The kid stood there staring without saying a word.

The dancer's gaze slowly moved down Dorian's body, down to the glass of liquor, down to the two little yellow pills sitting on the table, waiting and ready to launch them both into a frenzied, lust-filled high. Dorian pointed to the pills and said, "One for you. One for me."

Jaw clenched, Jansen thought about it for about a second, maybe two. He considered not taking one, but ecstasy had always been a weakness. Their eyes met in a heated stare, a silent power play. Who would give in first? The scary, dominant male or the submissive kid? The intensity in Mr. Grant's hard brown eyes made Jansen shudder. He would've knelt down right there and wrapped his mouth around Mr. Grant's cock, had he been told to.

Dorian nodded toward the drugs.

Jansen lowered his head.

The dominant man won.

Jansen swiped a pill, popped it into his mouth, and swallowed it down without a chaser. He climbed onto Mr. Grant's lap and straddled his legs, grabbed the other pill, and seductively placed it on the tip of his tongue. Their lips locked. Jansen forced his tongue into Mr. Grant's delicious mouth.

Mr. Grant sucked the pill off Jansen's tongue and kissed his way to an ecstasy high. He held Jansen's hips, pulling him so tight Jansen could feel every inch of Grant's cock growing against his thigh.

"I'm gonna fuck ya again," Mr. Grant said just before he gently raked his teeth across Jansen's bottom lip.

Jansen slipped his hand down between their bodies, palm riding over the mound of hardened muscle beneath Mr. Grant's dress slacks. Music and lights and smoke wafted up from the club's first floor. The euphoria of ecstasy took over. Jansen stroked Mr. Grant harder, faster. He wanted—no, needed that man's glorious erection inside of him, drilling into his body.

"I want you," he rasped against Mr. Grant's ear.

Slipping his hand around the gold G-string, Dorian pushed one finger inside Sweet Heat's warm, puckered opening. The dancer moaned, eyes rolling back. Dorian's head dipped down, lips caressing the kid's throat while his finger stroked his tight warmth.

Jansen winced and bit down on his bottom lip.

Slowly, Dorian eased another finger inside. He worked them in and out, loosening up the dancer's muscles, readying him for a seriously deep fucking. That gentle shit from last night was cool and all, but Dorian wanted more. He was high from the coke and high from the X, drunk from the whiskey, and still ready to fight the man from the warehouse. The contradiction was doing something weird to his head. He wanted to take Sweet Heat with a vengeance. He didn't want to be gentle or take it easy. He wanted to pound against him and drill inside him as deep as he could go.

"Let's go back to your place," the dancer panted as his fingers clung to Dorian's shoulder. "We'll screw as long as you want to."

Dorian rolled their bodies, and his hips landed between the dancer's thighs. He pressed his lips against Sweet Heat's bare chest and kissed over each pec, then down to his stomach and back up again. The kid moaned as Dorian bit down hard on his pierced nipple.

"Not my place. Here," Dorian breathed raggedly.

Dorian was a bastard, he knew he was, but Sweet Heat needed to know what kind of man he was dealing with. He needed to know Dorian wasn't the one who fell in love and settled down. He didn't take one man home and keep him close. Hell, he barely had the same guy more than once.

The gold of Sweet Heat's G-string bulged with promise. Dorian slipped his hand around and grabbed the dancer's cock, stroking as his chest pushed those sexy, muscled legs up in the air. He couldn't wait to fuck him, didn't want to drive back to his place. Besides, when this was over, he swore he was going to go home and try to sleep.

Dorian slammed his cock inside the dancer as he pushed Sweet Heat's legs back farther. He gripped the back of the booth, nails digging into the leather, rolling his hips with a fury he didn't have last night. Dorian drilled as hard as he could, pounding faster and deeper with each and every thrust. Sweet Heat tensed around him, but he didn't so much as whimper.

Jansen bit down on his bottom lip and tried to keep his breathing even. The mixture of pleasure and pain was intoxicating. It was almost too much to bear.

He moaned so loud it rumbled in his ears as he white-knuckled the back of the booth and buried his head against the leather. "You're hurting me," he cried out, though he knew Mr. Grant couldn't hear it over the music. Though, maybe he didn't want Grant to hear it. He knew if he was weak, that beautiful stranger wouldn't want him anymore. The man was all power and dominance and authority, and if Jansen acted like a pussy for even one split second, he knew Grant wouldn't come back.

As stupid as it sounded, he needed Mr. Grant to want him. No one had wanted him since the night that man in the parking lot destroyed him. That hurt. Honestly, despite what he kept telling himself, Jansen was a hopeless romantic. He wanted tenderness and love, but the men he'd met hadn't seemed to want that. They wanted primal, animalistic fucking, and that was something Jansen hadn't been able to give anyone… until Mr. Grant had walked into his life.

Jansen cried out in pain as Grant drilled into his body, but the sound was swallowed by the music. Each and every solid thrust made him want to retreat, to curl around himself and cry, but he wouldn't stop Mr. Grant. The man would fuck him up good. Maybe he would even end up in the hospital again. Who knew, but he wouldn't give in. He couldn't give in. Jansen would let Grant destroy him because that hopeless romantic in him thought it would make Grant love him.

Wet heat exploded inside of the dancer's tender ass; then Mr. Grant pulled out and zipped his pants like nothing had ever happened. Jansen started to sob, but he knew Grant would never notice. It was too dark, too loud, and the man who just fucked up his world obviously didn't give a shit about what he'd done. Jansen wiped the tears from his face and turned his head—cheek pressed against the back of the booth—so he could watch Mr. Grant walk away without a care in the world.

Grant pulled out his wallet, then tossed ten one-hundred-dollar bills on the seat. "Thanks, Sweet Heat," he said as he started for the door.

"It's Jansen," the dancer said around a whimper as he hugged the back of the booth. A sheen of sweat blossomed on his brow. "The name is Jansen."

Mr. Grant glared. "I don't care what your fuckin' name is," he growled. Then he tore out of the door and out of the club.

The words speared Jansen in the gut. So Grant didn't care, didn't give a shit about him or his name and probably wouldn't care if something happened to him. Jansen was so stupid, so ridiculous and hopeless. And for fuck's sake, he smelled Mr. Grant all over him.

Wincing, he lifted himself from the booth, then struggled to get down the steps. He had to get that smell off of him. He had to get away from anything and everything that reminded him of what he'd done and what he'd hoped for. He took one short breath, then another. His palms started to sweat, and his pulse raced. A fiery pain radiated up through his body. The room started to spin. His knees quivered, buckling under his weight.

Jason met him at the edge of the steps, eyes widening.

Panic set in. Jansen started hyperventilating. He felt Jason's arms around him.

Jason yelled out, "Call 9-1-1!"

"No!" Jansen cried. "I'll be okay. Just take me home."

Then the room turned dark and the sounds of the club faded away.

12

JANSEN'S ass burned like it had been ripped apart. The pain shot up his spine and tensed his shoulders. It exploded in his head and pounded in his chest. Closing his eyes again, he curled against the couch and the body beneath him. He squirmed and whimpered as a soft voice asked him to calm down.

A hand held his, but he still wasn't awake enough to put himself in a particular time or place. He assumed he was still at Sin & Seduction. The low hum of club music vibrated his chest and the walls around him. The air smelled like club air: all sweaty and filled with stale booze and smoke.

The music slowly began to die down. Jansen had yet to try any significant movement. He squirmed a little here and there, only because he couldn't seem to get comfortable, but standing or even forcing himself to sit up was completely out of the question.

"Jansen?" Jason's soft voice said from somewhere above him. He felt a hand brushing over his hair. "You awake, baby?"

"W-what h-happened," he choked out without opening his eyes.

"You blacked out," Jason said as he tightened his hand around Jansen's while he continued to brush his best friend's hair with his free hand. "I think you had a panic attack, babe."

"How long have I been out?"

"A few hours."

"What time is it?"

"Almost four in the morning."

"Will you please take me home, now?"

"Sure, I just need to check out with the bosses upstairs. Can you stay here while I deal with them?"

Nodding, Jansen curled himself back into a fetal ball on the couch. He listened as Jason's feet slapped against the backstage flooring and echoed against the cinderblock walls. Jansen thought maybe he could sleep it off a bit longer while Jason dealt with the people in charge, though sleep wasn't happening, not right now and probably not any time soon. He just couldn't stop thinking about Mr. Grant. And as the minutes passed, as the images of Grant paraded through his head, the more upset Jansen became.

He just wanted to get out of the club. He just wanted his own bed.

Jansen started to lift himself off the backstage couch when pain rippled through his body. He gave up, let himself fall back to the cushion. Last thing he remembered was being taken by Mr. Grant in the VIP booth after his second main stage dance. He remembered Grant giving him a hit of X, then Jansen had attacked him, or so he thought. In reality, Grant had been the one who attacked Jansen. Then Jansen remembered seeing his best friend, Jason. He'd said a few words, and that's where the memory ended.

"What are you doing?" Jason called from across the room. He charged toward Jansen and grabbed him by the waist to keep him steady.

"What else happened to me?" Jansen demanded, tears clinging to his lashes, fingers gripping Jason's forearms. "Tell me what happened."

"You were bleeding, honey." Jason pressed his cheek against the crown of Jansen's head. Jason held his best friend close to his heart. "I cleaned you up and dressed you, but…. Jansen, I think you should go to the hospital."

"Why?" Jansen cried. His heart broke into a million little pieces. "Why would he do that to me? He knew about me! I told him!" Mr. Grant was suddenly no better than the nameless, faceless asshole who had taken him in the parking lot. "Why would he hurt me like that?"

Tears filled Jason's eyes, too, but he fought them back. Jansen needed his strength right now. Jansen needed his support. "He's bad news, baby. You should've known that after the first night. You shouldn't have gone back up to him."

"But he wasn't like that, at first. I told him I had problems, that I needed him to be gentle. Jason, he was. He was careful not to hurt me. Then… then this?"

"Sweetie, you don't know that man. Sure, he's a regular at the club, but what do you really know about him? What does he do? Where does he live? Is he clean?"

Jansen cried harder. He didn't know. He didn't know anything about Mr. Grant, didn't even know his first fucking name. How the hell could he have let this happen again? Didn't he learn anything the first time around? Now he wouldn't be able to dance for weeks. He was so screwed.

"Honey, calm down," Jason said.

But he didn't want to calm down. He wanted to strangle the life right out of Grant's body and make him pay for the pain he'd caused.

"If you see him again," Jansen said through clenched teeth as he locked his eyes on Jason's, "tell him he's dead to me. Tell him I hate him. Tell him I can't work and won't be able to afford rent or food. Tell him how badly he fucking hurt me. And if he doesn't act like he cares, I want to know about it. I want to know that I am nothing more than a whore to him."

Truthfully, Jansen didn't want to know. He didn't want to think that Grant had used him to get a nut, then tossed him aside like yesterday's trash. He wanted to believe he was special, that Grant had seen something in him he hadn't seen in any of the other men. He wanted to believe Grant had come back to him because he enjoyed being near him.

How pathetic was that?

"Why don't I get you home?" Jason asked as he lifted Jansen from the couch.

Jansen nodded, holding his best friend tight as they made their way out to Jason's piece-of-shit car. He carefully climbed inside, sitting more to the side and curling against the back of the seat.

Jason frowned as he closed the door behind him. Jansen knew how badly Jason wanted to go off, how badly he wanted to curse Grant's existence. He could tell by the pinching of his best friend's lips, by the squaring of his shoulders, by the pissed off glare in his eyes. Right now, Jansen didn't need to hear those angry words. Right now, Jansen needed to rest and recuperate and try to forget about the asshole who hurt him. Jason climbed in the driver's seat, cranked the car, then pulled away.

Staring out the car window, Jansen watched the streets of New Orleans pass by, one by one. The sky was becoming lighter; the early morning sun began to push up on the horizon. He wondered if Grant lived down any one of those streets. He wondered if the stranger worried about him, if Grant even knew what he'd done. What would happen if they ever saw each other again? Would Jansen have the strength to tell him to go away? Or would he melt in the beautiful stranger's arms? Would Grant try to hurt him again?

Mr. Grant was a sadistic bastard, and maybe, just maybe, owning that would be enough to make Jansen realize he needed to steer clear. To save himself, his body and his soul, he had to be strong enough to tell the man no, to stay away despite his urges to be near him.

He could do it, right? After all, Grant didn't give a shit about him, right? No addiction had ever owned him or controlled him. *Just remember.* That's all Jansen had to do. If he could remind himself of the physical and emotional pain, he could make himself stay away.

The car hit a bump, and Jansen winced. He let out a ragged sigh as he shifted in the seat. His head started to pound again, chest aching. He raked his fingers through his hair, tightened his hold on the robe someone—probably Jason—had draped around his body before he'd woken up backstage. It smelled like *him.* Grant's cologne had soaked through the fabric. Was it *CK* or maybe… Jansen took another whiff, more like a deep breath. No, he wore some high-dollar shit Jansen had never smelled before. Whatever, it was the most amazing thing he ever breathed.

Closing his eyes, he leaned his cheek against the window. He couldn't stop thinking about Grant. Sure, he'd told himself he never wanted to see him again, but that had been far from true. What a joke, pretending he had some sort of willpower. He didn't. The fact he couldn't stop thinking about Grant proved that.

As his imagination relived that first night, the way he went down on Grant, then the way they screwed in the shower, his heart started to sink into his toes. The night had been utterly perfect—up until the point Grant had given him the thousand dollars and sent him away. Sexually speaking though, it was a stark contrast to what had been done to him last night. Grant had been careful not to destroy what the doctors had worked so hard to put back together. Grant had been a tender, caring, amazing lover as he eased himself in and out of Jansen's delicate body. He'd acted like a man who was capable of being good to someone.

Jansen felt himself start to stiffen. God, Jason was sitting right beside him, hopefully keeping his eyes on the road and not the boner suddenly rocking between Jansen's thighs. He quickly clamped his hand down on the growing bulge, and he shifted in the seat again.

"You okay?" Jason asked.

"Yeah, I'm fine. Just… can you go a little easier on the bumps?"

"Oh yeah, sorry." Jason looked over. Jansen could feel his gaze traveling southward. He pinched his legs a little tighter, curled into himself as much as he could. Jason said, "You sure you're okay? Having a little trouble down there?"

"Shut the fuck up."

Jason laughed. "You're thinking about him, aren't you?"

A sharp right turn pulled Jansen away from the window and made his ass roll against the seat. He winced. "Leave me alone, please."

"If you saw him right now, you'd be with him, wouldn't you? You'd fucking blow him right now, wouldn't you?"

"No. I don't know." With a hard sigh, Jansen looked over at Jason. "There's something about him. I have to believe he didn't do this to me on purpose. He was gentle the first time. I told him, well… kinda told him what happened at the nightclub in Slidell, and that he would be my first since… you know. And, Jason, he went easy on me. I don't know what the fuck happened. I don't know why he flipped like he did."

"Look, I've heard stories about him. He's not careful or caring. He's a fucking nut bag." Jason reached over and touched Jansen's leg.

"When I see him," he said, "I'm going to tell him you never want to see him again, just like you said. It's for your own good."

"You're right. I know you're right."

A sharp left and Jansen rolled again. At least they were in Gretna now and their apartment was less than a mile away. Jansen didn't think his tender ass could take another moment of Jason's driving.

A few more hard bumps, then Jason pulled into the driveway of their shitty second-floor apartment on the seedier side of New Orleans. He rushed to the passenger side to help Jansen out of the car. Together they took the steps one at a time. Jansen white-knuckled the rusted railing as he carefully planted one foot down before trying to take the next step. They clung to each other as Jason walked him back to his bedroom. Jansen face-planted on the bed. He didn't want to move again.

"You want the TV on?" Jason asked.

Jansen nodded against the pillow. The noise helped. It kept his mind away from the dark place with that dangerous man. But God, what he wouldn't give to be held by the very man who'd put him in that pain in the first place. There *had* to be more to Grant. All that tenderness had to have come from somewhere.

"Okay, sweetie," Jason said. "My shift at the deli starts in a few hours. I have to try to get some sleep before I go. Don't worry about anything. I'll deal with Grant, and I'll get some food to bring back for you when I get off work. Just stay in bed and get to feeling better, okay?"

Jansen nodded again.

Jason kissed the back of his head.

Jason killed the light, left Jansen alone in the dark with nothing but the TV to occupy his mind. Jansen tossed back a few of the Lortabs the hospital had given him the first time around, hoping like hell they would knock his ass out, and the man on his mind would go away. Of course, the Lortabs didn't exactly knock him out. They barely dulled the pain.

He stared at the TV, knowing there were images there, knowing there was a story being told, but missing the whole damn lot of it. God, he wished he had Grant's phone number. He wished he had a way to hear his voice. He wished he had a way to ask Grant if he had meant to hurt him so he could face reality and start getting over him.

But hell, every time he thought about the beautiful, dark and dangerous stranger who now seemed to consume his every waking moment, he got turned on… like, rock hard turned on. He imagined having Grant's wondrous cock in his mouth, letting his tongue run over and under, feeling every perfect imperfection, toying with the sensitive ridge of Grant's head while he cradled the man's sac in his hand. He imagined the moan that had rumbled up through his body and the way he'd called out a bitching stream of four-lettered curses when he came. Jansen could feel Grant's hand around his dick, stroking with the same rhythm as his thrusts.

Shit, he was hard again, high on tabs, and rocking a serious hard-on. *Way to go, Jan!*

Screw it. At least he was alone.

He slipped his hand inside his sweatpants, wrapped his fingers around his cock, and closed his eyes. The shirt he wore the first night, the one drenched in Grant's cologne, laid right beside his head. Jansen could smell him and feel him, and as long as he kept his eyes closed, Grant was there with him, working him over with that big hand of his, biting at his back as they fucked.

It didn't take long before the pressure built and his sac tightened, before his shaft began to throb harder and every muscle in his body tensed. As Jansen milked one hellacious load from his body, it was Grant's voice and Grant's body and Grant's cock that made him come all over his fist. It was the idea of a man who probably didn't exist outside the barbarian that made him cry out to God, and it was that imaginary man who would be with Jansen as he fell into a drug-induced sleep.

13

WHY the fuck did that damn dancer have to tell me his name?

Dorian had planned to walk out of Sin & Seduction without a care in the world and a content smile on his face, maybe even the remnants of a pretty hellacious buzz. Just a normal night in Dorian Grant's life. Yeah, well, Sweet Heat put the kibosh on those plans. Now that he knew the dancer's name, it opened up something inside of him he wasn't quite ready to deal with. He'd gotten really comfortable with not caring. It worked for him. Now, this "Jansen" kid had to come along and screw it all up.

Thanks, kid.

Sure, he could fuck the guy up, down, and sideways, throw cash at him, and pretend like nothing had ever happened, but now he knew the dancer's real name. *Never name them. That's how you get attached, just like fuckin' puppy dogs,* Dorian silently reminded himself. "Attached" just didn't work for him, not right now and probably not ever.

Okay, but let's be real for a second. Dorian had become "attached" well before he ever learned Jansen's name. Granted, it was like jonesing for a specific kind of high that only a certain type of drug could give him. He would be lying to himself if he said he didn't think about Jansen while they were apart. It would be a lie to say he didn't wonder about him and crave another taste of him. Just like being addicted, *not* being in love.

After leaving the club, Dorian went straight home, straight to his room without stopping to bark orders at his staff or eat any of the food Maria had prepared for him. He just wanted to be clean again, like hot water could wash away all the bullshit. It couldn't. He knew that, but the idea alone was comforting enough.

With a sigh, he slammed the bedroom door and went straight to the mirror. Dorian stared at himself, at the monster hidden behind the Armani suit, behind the tired eyes and tense shoulders. Even his reflection seemed to look down on him. It knew the demon staring back at it. It knew the violence Dorian was capable of.

He tossed his suit jacket on the bed, loosened his silk tie, then rubbed his hands over his face. Deep breaths. Slow, deep breaths. Never once had he questioned the life he'd been living. He didn't like it, but he dealt with it by pushing it out of his head. Never once had he cared enough about himself or anyone else to really take stock of the things he'd done. Recent developments sure as hell seemed to be changing that so fast it made his head spin.

Dorian stripped the rest of his clothes, leaving a small fortune in fabric behind him as he padded toward the bathroom door. He went to the shower, stood there, and let the hot water wash over his naked body. The muscles slowly started to relax.

As he scrubbed shampoo through the back of his hair, he had a second to look down at the light-colored tiles of the shower floor. A swirling trail of pink circled around the drain. He didn't think much of it at first, figured it was the blood that had dried on his fists after beating the shit out of Mr. Family Man at the warehouse. He wasn't sorry for that. The guy had gotten what he deserved. But when Dorian looked down at his hands, they were spotless, completely clean.

So, where the fuck did the blood come from?

He searched his body but couldn't find it. Not a single drop on his chest or neck. He would've seen it in the mirror before getting in the shower, had it been on his face. "What the fuck?"

Then he looked down at his legs, and there it was, dried traces of crimson on the insides of his thighs and his crotch. It wasn't horror movie blood or anything gruesome. Just a subtle film of dark red clinging to his skin, a faint swirl of pink running over the tiles, but he knew where it had come from and why it was there.

"Fuck me!" he gasped. It was Jansen's blood. That look on the kid's face hadn't been pleasure. He'd been in pain.

Dorian's back slid against the tiles. He ass-planted on the floor of the shower, stared down at the faint traces of blood on his inner thighs, and he hated himself for what he'd done. The one thing the kid had asked for, and Dorian hadn't given it to him. All the warm water in the world wouldn't wash that away. It wouldn't wash away the sickened feeling in the pit of his gut. It wouldn't wash away the guilt.

"Dammit."

He sat in the bottom of the shower, staring down at the tiles until his hands shriveled and the hot water turned frigid—much like his heart. The traces of pink had long since bled away. Maria called his name from the bedroom. She said she would take his suit to the cleaners, if he so wished. He didn't say a word, only stared at the remnants of a crime he hadn't meant to commit.

That night, Dorian went to bed wondering what the hell he'd done to Jansen, how badly he'd hurt him. Christ, Jansen had seemed fine when Dorian left the club. Pissed, but otherwise, Jansen was okay. Yeah, Dorian might have been a bastard for not kissing him or taking him home to cuddle, but they didn't have that kind of arrangement. They fucked. He paid. They parted ways. That's all they were to each other, right?

Then why in the hell did Dorian feel so guilty? Why did he feel the need to find Jansen, to make sure he was okay?

For all his macho bullshit, the thought that he might've hurt Jansen killed him. Dorian realized then, the dancer had just become *that* wrinkle in his life. Jansen had become the distraction he didn't need, the distraction that could get him killed or cost him everything. He either had to man up and own what was going on in his head, or he had to forget about the kid altogether.

"Why couldn't you be like the others? Why the fuck did you have to make me care?"

14

LATE morning came all too soon—or rather, three in the afternoon, according to Dorian's phone. Sun spilled in through the dark curtains covering the windows of his corner bedroom. He didn't want to get out of bed, could've stayed there for two more days, but the light just wouldn't let him. It insisted on waking him up so his mind could relive the bullshit he'd been through, the way he treated Jansen, and the blood he found on his groin earlier. And to make matters worse, he really wanted to go see Jansen. He really did want to know if the kid was okay or if Dorian had done serious damage.

With a sigh, he grabbed his phone and held it in one hand as he tapped the screen with his pointer finger, silently arguing over calling the club or calling.... Shit! He didn't have a number for the kid. *Just fucking perfect.*

Okay. Alright. No need to flip out. Maybe he could drive to Gretna, to the place where his driver had taken the dancer after their first night together. What the hell would he say, though? "Sorry, I was an ass and I hurt you? Forgive me?"

Maybe he should just give Jansen a few days, let him have time to recuperate.

Dorian let out an aggravated growl as he pitched his phone to the center of his bed. If he were to put himself in Jansen's shoes, he'd never want to talk to himself again. He would have lain in his bed, marinating in his anger while he rehearsed the major ass-chewing he would give himself.

Was it even possible to make amends now?

"Just let it go, Dorian," he mumbled to himself, scrubbing his hands over his face.

He snatched his robe from the foot of the bed, then headed down to the back of the house, back to the lush gardens and, most importantly, the hot tub where he could—hopefully—relax away the tension and bullshit he'd been dealing with lately.

Thankfully, the house was empty, because he didn't have his package completely covered until he hit the bottom step in the living room. His employees had seen a lot in their years, so when he was in his right mind, he did his best to spare them. He pushed through the French doors, out into the late afternoon sunlight, dropped his robe, then climbed on in.

Warm water bubbled up around him as he sank down into the hot tub. A hard, relaxed sigh rumbled up through his body. He spread his arms and leaned against the tub's wall. Just a few hours. If he could stay there—without interruption—for a few hours, life might be good again.

Staring up at the bright blue sky, he took stock of his life and the crap he'd done, how he'd hurt so many people and never really had any *true* remorse for any of it. For the first time in a long damn time, he felt bad about the shit he'd done. It was all Jansen's fault, this newfound guilt, and it seriously had the potential to put a major kink in the way he'd been doing business.

A shadow loomed over him. He knew it was his Angelo by the way the sun suddenly disappeared. No one—truly *no one*—was as wide as Angelo.

"What do ya want?" Dorian barked.

Angelo knelt down beside his head. "Thought you was sleepin' in, boss."

"I did. Now, what the fuck do ya want?" Angelo's mammoth fist appeared in front of Dorian's face, fingers slowly uncurling to show off the pills he'd brought for his boss. Yellow, small, ecstasy—one of Dorian's favorite drugs—nestled in the wrinkled surface of Angelo's big-ass palm. Dorian looked back up at him, eyes narrowed, head slightly tilted. "What the hell do I want with that shit?" he barked, but they both knew good and damn well what Dorian would do with "that shit."

"You ain't goin' out tonight?" Angelo asked, pulling his hand back.

"I don't know. Not really in the mood."

"Boss, I know this ain't my business, but whatever has ya twisted, ya need to forget about—"

"You're right," Dorian interrupted. "It isn't your fuckin' business. Gimme that." He grabbed Angelo's wrist and snatched the X from his hand. He popped one pill and laid his head back, waiting for it to kick in. But he knew no matter how high he got, he wouldn't be able to stop thinking about Jansen, and he had to get that kid out of his head. It was best for both of them. Obviously, Dorian didn't know how to be what Jansen needed. Obviously, Dorian was bad news for the kid.

Best just to forget.

"Do me a favor," Dorian said over his shoulder to the big guy looming over him. A smile curled his lips as euphoria started tingling in his nerves. "Go to the club and get... someone. I don't give a fuck who. Just bring someone back. And not that Sweet Heat kid."

Now, Dorian knew how bad that looked, but the idiot had a point. Jansen was a wrinkle in the fabric Dorian didn't need. If another guy's mouth or ass or whatever helped him forget about the sexy dancer, then, fuck it, he'd be forgotten... maybe.

It had to have been at least an hour before Wide-ass came back. The kid he had with him couldn't have been any older than twenty. Long golden-blond hair framed his innocent face. Blue eyes searched the back patio of the mansion. Dorian saw a gleam in his eyes, like he'd hit it big and Grant was his meal ticket out of Sin & Seduction. Dorian had news for him. He didn't roll that way.

He looked over at Angelo and told him to get lost. "Take the night off. Go fuck your wife or something." Wide-ass laughed. "Then get yourself a Big Mac. I don't care. Just go."

When Angelo finally left, Dorian stepped out of the water, cock swinging in the wind. He scrubbed his fingers through his soaked hair as he approached the kid. He said, "Strip, golden boy."

The kid didn't hesitate. He shimmied out of his jeans and ripped his T-shirt over his shoulders faster than Dorian could take another breath. He was hot. Wasn't Jansen, but he'd do in a pinch. Maybe after the night ended, he wouldn't think about Jansen again.

He fisted his fingers in Golden Boy's hair, pulled the kid down until his knees hit the rough concrete of the patio. "Open your mouth." Golden Boy did. Dorian thrust his flaccid dick between two plump, parted lips and said, "Get me hard."

Soft hands cupped his jewels just as the dancer's mouth started riding up and down his shaft. Dorian tightened his fingers in the kid's hair. The vibration of Golden Boy's moans tickled Dorian's cock. He wasn't as talented as Jansen in that respect, but what did Dorian care as long as he got off?

"I said get me fucking hard. What part of that didn't you understand?"

He shoved Golden Boy's head down hard until the kid's lips surrounded the base and kissed Dorian's deep brown patch of coarse, curly hair. Golden Boy buried his nose, taking Dorian to the hilt, throat tightening like he wanted to gag.

As sick as it was, Dorian couldn't help but laugh. He threw his head back and belted out a low, throaty chuckle that echoed beneath the patio cover. The sound made the guy attached to his dick shudder, but Golden Boy didn't dare stop. He lapped back and forth across Dorian's cock, teased the ridge and tickled the head before letting his lips ride back down the shaft.

"That's it. Keep going," Dorian said. His voice held a lot of authority, as if he needed to instruct the kid on exactly how he wanted to be handled. If that had been Jansen, no instruction would've been needed. Fuck, there he went again, thinking about the dancer. Dorian's sac tightened in the guy's hand, erection growing harder, throbbing against the kid's tongue.

Okay, so Golden Boy got him hard. Big fucking deal. Dorian was high on X and thinking about being with Jansen while some strange kid blew him next to the hot tub. Who wouldn't get hard?

"Come on," he said as he wrenched Golden Boy up from his knees. "Hot tub, now."

Golden Boy grinned as he sauntered over to the hot tub like he was the best shit on the block. Dorian wanted to pop him in the back of the head, let him know he wasn't shit compared to Jansen. Hell, he wasn't shit compared to half the guys Dorian had been with.

"Want me here?" the kid asked as he leaned against the steps with his ass stuck in the air.

"Yeah, right fuckin' there."

Dorian climbed down into the hot tub, stood behind him, and took a minute to check out his ass. It was okay, almost as cute as Jansen's.

Fuck me!

He had to stop. The point of this was to forget about Jansen, not to compare every toy he played with to the man he apparently cared too much about. And that little epiphany just pissed Dorian off even more.

He gripped the kid's hips with tightened fists, pressed the head of his cock to Golden Boy's ass. It wasn't going to be as easy as it was with Jansen. It wasn't going to be as enjoyable. Sex with this kid would take too much effort, would be too... average. He was nothing like Jansen. *Nothing.*

Reaching into the wooden box beside the hot tub, Dorian fished for a condom and the bottle of lube. Yeah, he kept the shit out there. That hot tub had seen more action than a porno, and it was one of his favorite places to do the deed.

He ripped the foil square open with his teeth while he jerked and tugged at his cock to keep it hard. Golden Boy purred and rolled his hips, pushing his ass a little farther out of the water, like he knew Dorian was watching him and somehow the sight of that tight ass was supposed to keep Dorian hard long enough to roll that uncomfortable, piece-of-shit rubber down his business. It pinched in all the wrong places, and had Dorian not been so eager to fuck the kid and get it over with, if he wasn't so eager to forget about Jansen, he might've sent Golden Boy home, then rubbed one out himself.

But he couldn't do that, not now. Not after the show he'd put on. He had a reputation to keep, one that didn't involve bloody baseball bats and trips to the swamp. Admittedly, he loved being known as one of the hottest lays in New Orleans. Having his head all twisted up over some dancer wasn't going to change that. Not if he could help it. He raised the kid's ass farther out of the water, gelled two fingers, then slipped them right on in.

"Relax," he barked. Golden Boy moaned. "If this shit's doing that much to you, you ain't gonna be able to handle my cock, boy."

"I can handle it. I can handle it," Golden Boy rasped.

"Yeah. Okay."

Dorian coated his dick but good, lubed it like they were kids on a slip n' slide. He gripped the dancer's hips again and eased on in. Dorian felt him clench and barked for him to relax again. The kid was getting on his nerves already, but that wouldn't stop him from getting off before sending him packing.

Reaching around, Dorian wrapped his hand around Golden Boy's dick and started to stroke. Each glide of his hand was met with a thrust of his cock, and the more Dorian jerked the kid off, the more he relaxed and the faster Dorian drilled into his body. He was pounding good and hard, and Golden Boy wasn't so much as whimpering anymore. In fact, he moaned and cried out, "Oh God! Oh God!" He was about to come, and Dorian wasn't even close. This shit just wasn't working. He wasn't Jansen, and nothing would change that.

"Fuck!" Dorian growled, wrenching hard on the kid's hair. Golden Boy's spine bowed. He cried out. Dorian slammed harder. In and out. In and out. His cock nailed the kid hard, stroking his "G-spot" while he jerked faster and faster with his hand.

Finally, his jewels started to tighten, thighs tingling. His heart started to race, and he came hard. Then he felt the warmth of the kid's spilled load on his hand.

He pulled out, sat back down in the water, and let it wash that shit from his hand. Golden Boy started toward him, lips parted like he wanted a kiss.

"Whoa." Dorian pressed his palm to the air. "What the fuck are you doin'?"

"I thought...."

"Ya 'thought' shit. Getcha clothes on. My driver's comin' to take ya home. He'll pay ya five hundred dollars when he drops ya off."

"That's it?"

"Well, fuck, yeah. What did ya think would happen? Ya think you'd come here and we'd fall in love then you'd move in with me or some shit? Ya got the wrong one, kid."

Golden Boy pouted, climbed out of the hot tub, and gathered his clothes as he made his way toward the back door. He looked back once and Dorian smirked.

Nah, he'd never compare to Jansen.

15

DORIAN climbed out of the hot tub and stood there for a long moment, dripping and spent. He'd been such a bastard to that poor kid, but that had always been Dorian's way. Nothing needed to change now, even if he had suddenly developed a conscience. His feelings, his moral compass, only pointed in one direction, and that blond-haired, doe-eyed kid wasn't the one.

As sure as Dorian stood there, he knew Golden Boy would want a repeat performance. Dorian wouldn't even entertain the idea. Hell, he didn't really enjoy the first time 'round, but he suspected that had been more Jansen's fault than his or the kid's. He just couldn't seem to get Sweet Heat out of his head, no matter how hard he tried.

"Boss?" Angelo called from the French doors. Dorian swung around, flaccid cock whipping in the wind. Angelo shook his head and averted his eyes. "Ya need to make an appearance at the sportin' goods store in Marrero. Ricky called and said some neighborhood thugs went up in there actin' a fool. Said they made a mess outta the displays. Stole some shit too."

"You can't handle that alone?" Dorian sniped, reaching for a towel to cover his package so Wide-ass would quit acting so damn twitchy. "Ain't that what I hired *you* for?"

"No offense, boss, but I think ya need to show up. Let the neighborhood know you're all eyes and ears, and ain't shit gonna get past ya."

"Right. Of course." Dorian gave him a droll look, then shook his head. He took a deep breath as he tightened the towel around his waist, then padded past Angelo. "Let me throw on some clothes, then we'll roll out. Get the sedan ready."

Angelo headed straight for the garage, Dorian up to his bedroom. He wouldn't bother washing the remnants of bad sex from his body, not that the hot tub had left much anyway. Really, he just wanted to get this shit over with so he could come back home and relax, maybe drink some scotch or something.

He slipped into a pair of faded designer jeans, strapped on his Italian leather boots, then pulled a black semi-casual shirt over his head. A platinum cross hanging from a platinum chain gleamed against the dark of his clothes. For some stupid reason, he didn't go anywhere without the damn thing, even though he hadn't acknowledged God since the day his ma had died. Seriously, what kind of God could see the justice in taking away the only good thing in a young boy's life? What kind of God would leave that boy in the hands of a sorry bastard like his father?

Dorian raked his fingers through his short brown hair. It didn't have to be perfect, not for what he was about to do. A couple squirts of Armani Gio knocked out the smell of chlorine and sex. Maybe when he got back he would climb in the shower, then chill for the rest of the night. Maybe.

Reaching into the top drawer of his dresser, he searched for his gun. Dorian Grant never handled business without it, even if he didn't need to use it. It intimidated the shit out of people and normally made dealing with the idiots a lot easier. They never wanted to argue when they saw the hand-cannon strapped to Dorian's side.

He found it, his handgun—a Walther .45—and fastened it to his belt as he stared at himself in the mirror. He didn't plan on going down into the parish to kill anyone, but that shiny piece of well-manufactured steel would be on his hip just in case shit got out of hand.

He gave himself one last glance, making sure he had all his shit together before tearing down the stairs to meet Angelo and the sedan in front of the mansion. With a less-than-sunny disposition curling his hard features, he rocked one scary mug. If those thugs were smart, they'd say, "Yes, sir, Mr. Grant," then carry on about their business, but Dorian doubted he would get off that easy today. It just didn't feel like that kind of luck was in the air.

"Let's do this," he said to Angelo as he climbed into the passenger side of the car.

The drive to Marrero took less than thirty minutes, pretty damn quick, all things considered. It was the middle of the day in New

Orleans. Construction cut the Huey P down a lane, and unfortunately, people around those parts didn't play well in construction.

Angelo pulled up just outside the entrance to the sporting goods store. It wasn't much; an old metal building with rust stains running down the front. Graffiti gave it the only real color it had. Loose gravel and broken glass made the driveway dangerous to everything that touched it. The neighborhood was so shitty Dorian had to have bars installed on the front windows after some punk kids tried to set the place on fire by throwing Molotov cocktails through the huge panes of glass in the front. Thankfully, those little wannabe criminals didn't make their homemade bombs right, and the fire fizzled out before any real damage was done.

Angelo climbed his big ass out of the car, stalked around to the back, and leaned against the tail end with his huge tree-trunk arms crossed over his broad chest. It didn't take a close look to see the pistol strapped to the side of his waist, not that anyone with any brains would want to get close enough to look in the first place.

Dorian climbed out of the passenger side and started for the door when he heard voices on the side of the building. Kids in their late teens or maybe early twenties, cursing and going on about the stupid, petty crimes they'd pulled. They laughed and bragged, cursed and laughed again.

Whistling softly at Angelo, Dorian gave a slight nod just to let the meathead know what was going down. He rounded the corner and found four guys, all dressed in gray hoodies, standing in a circle. Smoke rose up from the center. Dorian took a deep breath. Pot.

He laughed.

All four heads rose at the same time. The cloud of smoke billowed out from the huddle. One of the older-looking boys smirked. A gold tooth gleamed from behind his cocked lip. He kicked his hat to the side and narrowed his glazed green eyes on Dorian. "What the fuck you want, old man?" he slurred as stepped out of the circle of smaller bodies.

"You the ones messin' 'round in my store here?" Dorian thumbed toward the rusted wall beside him.

The leader—or whatever the hell he wanted to call himself— laughed, wiping the edges of his mouth as he took a few steps forward.

He had a cocky swagger about him, one that begged to be knocked down a notch or four. "This your store, huh?" Dorian nodded. "Hm… guess that means you da fairy everyone been talkin' 'bout."

Dorian's brow arched, head tilted slightly. "What'd ya call me, boy?"

"I gotcha 'boy'," the guy said, grabbing his crotch. He gave it a solid tug as he sucked his gold tooth. His nose flared and his lip curled. "Fuckin' fairy."

"That's what I thought ya said."

Faster than the kid could blink his eyes, Dorian cocked his fist in the air and came across his face with a hard right hook. Three carats of solid diamonds slashed through the thug's cheek. He stumbled back, and Dorian hooked him again, this time right in the abdomen, this time much, much harder. The hit knocked the kid flat on his ass.

The thug squirmed, holding his gut as his "homies" backed away. He yelled curses at the three of them, called them a bunch of pansies. "I swear to God, y'all better kick that old man's ass or I'm gonna fuck up every last one of ya!"

Dipshit's friends charged toward Dorian, and that's when Mr. Walther came out of its holster. With his finger close enough to the trigger to be threatening, Dorian pointed the barrel at the crowd, and the three boys stopped dead in their tracks.

"Now, what did ya think you were gonna do?" he teased.

No one responded.

"I didn't think so."

The older boy rose to his knees. He glared at Dorian like he wanted to kill him. Maybe he did, but this wasn't going to be the day. Today, Dorian Grant might've been bold enough to put a bullet in a few kneecaps just to prove a point.

"You kids gonna run back home to ya mommies and leave my shit alone, right?"

None of them spoke. None of them moved. No one even dared to bat an eye at the man with the pistol in his hand. They would probably come back, probably vandalize his place again, but Dorian wasn't in the habit of killing punk kids, and he honestly didn't want to start now.

"Go!" he growled, and whatever time the kids had been frozen in snapped back to the present. They took off, hightailing it down the street like they stole something. Dorian rounded the corner and found Angelo leaning against his Mercedes, shoulders convulsing as if he was trying hard not to belt out an earth-shattering laugh.

"You all right there, Chuckles?" Dorian asked, clapping his hand on Angelo's back.

Over three hundred pounds of fat and muscle began to shake harder. Angelo came unglued, doubled over with laughter. "You shoulda…. They were…." He took a few deep breaths, trying like hell to compose himself. "I swear to God, one of 'em shit his pants. Man, I ain't never seen a group a punks so scared before."

"Yeah, well, doesn't mean they won't come back. That one asshole in the ball cap called me a fairy. Do I look like a fuckin' fairy? Do I have wings sproutin' out my back or some shit?"

Angelo laughed harder.

"You're useless, ya know that? Look, you stay out here and laugh. I'm gonna go inside and check out the situation. They come back, beat the hell outta 'em. Ya think ya can handle that, Chuckles?"

"Yeah, boss. Gotcha."

Shaking his head, Dorian left Angelo at the car to keep watch.

Inside the store, Ricky pushed a broom around the old, kind-of-white, kind-of-gray linoleum, trying to clean up the mess the quad of thugs made. A few shelves had been knocked over. A display of mouth guards had been destroyed. Basketballs and baseballs and footballs and whatever kind of balls rolled around between the aisles.

Dorian shook his head again. Had those thugs been grown men, his wrath would've been a hell of a lot worse. They probably wouldn't have walked away without having the shit kicked out of them and maybe even a few broken bones.

Clara, the cashier, sat behind the counter, rocking back and forth with her hands over her face. Poor thing was really too old to be working, especially in this part of town, but the system had failed her, and the life of poverty she grew up in didn't give her the means to retire. He went behind the counter, and when he laid his hand on her back she screamed.

"It's just me, Clara. You okay?"

"Yes, Mr. Grant." She nodded slowly, tears streaming down her face. "Just scared."

"I know. Look, I'm gonna take ya home. You get some rest, okay?"

"I can't go home, Mr. Grant. I need the hours."

"Don't you worry about the hours." He looked out at the mess and the kid pushing the broom. That's when he noticed the busted neon sign. He silently cursed those bastards and swore he'd get 'em good if they came around again. "Ricky? You got this? I'm gonna take Clara home."

"Yes, sir, Mr. Grant. I tried to tell her to go, but she wouldn't."

"Please, Mr. Grant," Clara begged. "I need the money."

Dorian helped her up from the stool. He blocked the view so Ricky couldn't see him reaching in his pocket. He pulled five hundred dollars out of his wallet and put it in her hand. It would be better used to help an old woman than buying drugs and a lay for the night anyway.

He closed her fingers around the bills and held her hand as he looked her in her scared brown eyes. "I want you to take a few days off, at least until I can get better security here. Ya hear me?"

"Yes, sir," she said in a wavering voice as she looked down at their locked hands.

"Good. I'm takin' ya home now. You're gonna get some rest, right?"

"Yes, sir."

He looked back out at the kid, who hadn't stopped watching, and said, "We're leaving. You lock up and make sure the cameras are running, ya hear?"

"Sure thing, Mr. Grant," Ricky said.

Dorian wrapped his arm around Clara's shoulders and walked her out of the shop. He opened the back door of the Mercedes, waited for her to climb inside, then closed the door behind her. "We're takin' her home," he said to Angelo.

The big guy nodded, hurrying around to the driver's side.

16

AFTER taking Clara home, Angelo and Dorian returned to the mansion. No more than a few words had been spoken the entire hour they'd been in the car together. Angelo knew his boss well enough to know what kind of mood shit like the incident with the thugs put him in, and it wasn't a mood that involved small talk and light-humored banter. He could see in the deep set of Dorian's hard brown eyes that all that crap had gotten to him. Dorian didn't like being a thug, but it was a life he'd been shoved into at a young age, and there didn't seem to be much he could do about it now.

"So, you goin' out tonight, boss?" Angelo said as he pitched the key ring over the car and into Dorian's hands.

"I don't know. The idea of sittin' 'round here all night kinda makes me twitchy."

"Ya could sleep, ya know?"

"Yeah. Sleep. That'll happen," Dorian snorted as he made his way toward the front door. Angelo kept a safe distance behind him and sure the hell didn't open his big mouth. The smallest thing would set his boss off, and the last thing anyone wanted was to see Dorian Grant on one of his tears.

Angelo watched from the far side of the foyer as his boss took the stairs two at a time. He'd never say it out loud, only because it would piss the big man off, but he worried about Dorian. Something wasn't clicking right upstairs. Dorian's head wasn't in a good place, and it hadn't been in a while.

Sitting down on the edge of his bed, Dorian stared into the dresser mirror on the far wall of his bedroom. His tired eyes made him look worn way beyond his years. Those hard dark eyes were empty, soulless. Maybe the drugs were finally doing a number on him, not that he cared. He wouldn't stop. If it took him to an early grave, then what-the-fuck-ever.

He honestly hated the man staring back at him, hated him more than the guy he'd had a hand in killing a few days ago. What he did to people, it was wrong, but he wouldn't stop. Just like he wouldn't stop slowly killing himself with dope.

"Mmm... coke," he purred as he rolled a little brown cylinder between his fingers. He eyed the granules of white powder inside it. Enough of this shit and his heart would probably stop, or karma would truly be lady justice and make him survive but turn him into a goddamn vegetable or something.

Dorian pushed up from the bed, then padded over to the dresser, and dumped the powder out onto a mirror he'd laid out just for that purpose. He took one of the fifteen or so credit cards out of his wallet and divided the shit into five lines. He stared down at those five white lines as he licked the powder from the edge of his credit card before tucking it away.

Taking a rolled twenty-dollar bill to the first line, he snorted back the line and let the high course through his veins, slam into his brain, and knock away part of the morbid thoughts he'd been having. His skin began to tingle. He wrenched his neck from side to side, popping out the kinks.

So far so good, maybe now he could get dressed and muster up the balls to tell Jansen he was sorry for what he'd done and he'd really love it if the kid would come home with him tonight. Not for sex, but just a little intimacy, if that's what Jansen wanted.

Jaw clenching, body twitching, he could feel the high making its way through his system. "That's it." It felt good, too good, and yet he still couldn't stop thinking about how bad he'd screwed up what could've been a perfect life.

He didn't deserve half the shit he had. He didn't deserve someone like Jansen. That kid would probably make him a happy man. He'd probably give up his lifestyle, settle down like some of that "great American dream" bullshit. Would probably be happy having sex with only Jansen for the rest of his life. God help him, the idea didn't sound half bad.

"No. No. No fucking way," he said as he stood from the bed and started to pace again. He couldn't do it. He couldn't walk away from any of it. Because he couldn't walk away from the money, he couldn't walk away from the violence. And without the drugs, he couldn't deal with the violence. The drugs kept him numb, made him forget the shit he did and the shit he'd been through. It was a vicious cycle with no way to break free.

He stripped out of the shirt he'd been wearing and tossed it across the room. It smelled like pot and sweat and the remnants of fighting with those stupid fucking thugs. He stared in the mirror again. His body looked good for a man on the high side of thirty, even despite the scar down the middle of his chest. That only made him look hard, scary. The tattoos helped. He had muscle, nice muscle, but the tattoos took at least five years off. The dark circles under his eyes added ten.

With that same rolled twenty dollar bill, he snorted two more lines and felt his heart start to pound harder. His eyes dilated. Muscles flexed.

Grinning at his own fucked-up reflection, Dorian pulled a black button-down over his shoulders. He fastened all but the top two buttons. His platinum chain gleamed under the soft light of his bedroom. His hands were shaking, almost too bad to button the shirt, but somehow he managed. And the moment he was satisfied with what he saw, he leaned back down and snorted the last of the coke. He was so high he could barely stand still.

Wringing his hands, he paced the room like a caged animal, though freedom was only a few feet away. If he wanted to leave, he could. He could run away and never come back if that's what he chose to do.

Yeah, leave. Run. Get the fuck out of here. Yeah. He nodded a little too convulsively. At least he agreed with himself. At least he was in a right-enough frame of mind to know he had to leave for a bit, maybe get some good old Cajun-scented New Orleans night air.

Dorian leaned down to pick up one of his designer Italian boots, and as he righted himself, he accidentally looked in the mirror again. Jansen was definitely too good for him. Dorian Grant was a hazard, scarred and broken and fucked up, and that kid deserved someone who could love him and take care of him. What did Dorian know about love anyway? The last person who ever loved him died before he was old enough to understand why.

Cocking his hand back, he glared at himself for a long moment. He saw the rage and self-hatred in his eyes, saw the asshole he was burned into the very fiber of his being. He couldn't change any of it, didn't want to and wouldn't try. Not even for Jansen, because trying to be something he wasn't would be a sick fucking lie, and the kid deserved better than that.

He threw the boot at the mirror, at the grim reflection of one seriously hated man. The damn thing shattered into a million tiny pieces, but at least he didn't have to look at himself anymore. At least the soulless eyes of a drug-addicted murderer didn't stare back at him.

"Fuck." Now he had to clean that shit out of the boot so he didn't cut his foot all to hell.

He dusted the shards away and, of course, cut his finger in the process, because nothing in this world could be easy. Then he slipped his foot into the boot, snatched the keys to his dad's—no, *his*—fully restored '69 convertible Camaro, and tore out of the house like a man running from the devil himself.

Tonight, he just wanted to feel alive again, wanted to feel heaven against his face. He wanted to own the earth and the moon and the stars. He wanted speed and muscle, and... he wanted to find *his* dancer.

He had to do this. He had to find Jansen. He planned to go looking for him and hoped to God Jansen would see him. He needed to see him. Dorian was starting to like that new wrinkle in his life. And this time, if Jansen gave him a chance, he wouldn't send him away with a wad of cash like some filthy whore. He would invite the guy to spend the night, maybe have Maria make breakfast for them in the morning. He would do Jansen a solid, go down on him and not stop until he came... a few times. Dorian wouldn't try to fuck him. After what he'd seen on his hands and thighs, Dorian knew he'd fucked up and he'd hurt Jansen.

Now he just wanted to make it better.

As he tore down the hall toward the garage, he blazed past Maria. "Can you clean that shit up in my room? Broke the fucking mirror. Thanks."

She mumbled something in Spanish, probably spells of the Santeria. He'd probably get himself killed tonight, but he didn't care. He would go out with a bang if he did. And he'd make damn sure to find his sexy dancer first.

A '69 convertible Camaro, rolling ninety down the Huey P could be considered attempted suicide, but whatever. Let's not go there. He wanted to feel heaven, remember?

The salty, Cajun-scented air of the Big Easy pounded against his face. New Orleans was actually a shithole, but he wouldn't live anywhere else. There was more sin, more chaos and social vagrancy to be found there than anywhere in the world. Those were his kind of people.

He was so high, every inch of his body had turned numb; all of it… except that thing that wouldn't stop beating inside of his chest. He'd tried to kill it, tried to stop it with drugs, tried to kill it with a fast life and dangerous ways, but nothing ever worked. Now it had a reason to keep beating. Dorian's heart needed Jansen. He knew it to be as real as every polluted breath he breathed.

Pulling to a stop in front of Sin & Seduction, he stared up at the flickering neon sign, and for the first time in his life, he wasn't sure about anything other than the need to be near the dancer. He might even grovel, and that shit was something he swore he would never do, but for Jansen… anything was possible. And don't call it fucking love, because Dorian didn't do "love." He was a lustful, sinful bastard. That's the life he'd always lived. That's the life he liked.

The valet stood by the car and cleared his throat. Dorian hadn't even realized he'd been standing there. He turned his head to face the guy, and he caught trails off everything. Swear to God, the world moved in slow motion. The lights of the club slowly faded to the line of the hundreds of eager people waiting to get inside, to shitty New Orleans streets, to the buildings around them, to the valet who still had his hand out waiting for his keys. Every color and shape blurred into the next.

Dorian laughed hysterically, pitched his keys to the valet's hand and pulled a *Dukes of Hazzard* move, climbing over the car door, but he wasn't that damn smooth. He stumbled forward and caught his balance before he had a chance to fall flat on his face. Again he laughed like a maniac.

Heading toward the front door like every other human being who wanted a chance to see the inside of the club, he felt a hand wrap around his forearm. "Mr. Grant," the bouncer said, "VIP entrance is that way." He pointed toward the side entrance Dorian had used a thousand times before.

Dorian turned his head, and he frowned, scrubbed his hand over his once neatly brushed hair and laughed. "Yeah, it is, isn't it?"

He stumbled over to the VIP entrance, jogged up the steps and through the door. He went to his regular booth and plopped down in the seat.

Lights flickered. Bass pounded. Some sad-ass cover of an eighties pop song blared over the house speakers. Some shitty knock-off dancer rubbed his gold-covered cock up and down the pole. The idiots down front went crazy, stuffing bills in the dude's G-string. Pathetic. They wouldn't know talent if it ground against their laps.

It was early enough Dorian wouldn't have missed Jansen's dance. He could be patient. He could wait and watch for him. Then he would indulge in whatever hot number Sweet Heat pulled off tonight, and once it was all said and done, he would send a note down for him to come to the VIP booth. Stellar fucking plan, but hours passed and Jansen never made it to the stage. Dorian started to get pissed.

Why wasn't he dancing? What the hell?

Five glasses of Johnny Walker Blue mixed with the contradicting high of coke and low of booze was screwing with his head. Couple that with the anger and anxiety battling for control of his body, and Dorian was a mess. He looked at the bouncer and said, "I wanna know where the fuck Jansen... ah... Sweet Heat is. I wanna know why the fuck he isn't dancing. Send someone up who can explain that shit to me."

He sat back and waited, and waited, and waited. Finally, a guy with long red hair and bright green eyes appeared beside him. He was so nondescript, so boring, Dorian didn't notice him until he called his name. "What?" Dorian barked.

"I'm Jason," he said, "Jansen's roommate."

Well, that made Dorian perk up a bit. "Why the fuck ain't he dancing? Where is he?"

"Well," Jason crossed his arms and pursed his lips, "maybe because he's doped up on pain pills because of what you did to him."

Dorian's heart started pounding so hard he thought it would rip out of his chest. He sat forward, leaned his arms against the table and gave this "roommate" a hard glare. "Where the fuck is he?"

Jason's brow quirked. "He's at home, resting, trying to recover from the shit you did."

"I want to see him," Dorian demanded as he shoved himself up from the booth.

"He doesn't want to see you."

Dorian's heart sunk in his chest. That hurt. *He* was actually hurt. "What do ya mean?"

"Exactly what I said. He doesn't want to have anything to do with you."

The world around them disappeared. The urge to kill slammed into Dorian's being. His hands locked around the guy's throat. They tumbled to the ground, Dorian straddling Jason's waist as his clenched fingers tried to squeeze the life out of the dancer's roommate.

"Tell me where the fuck he is," Dorian bit out.

Jason's face started turning red. He bucked and struggled and writhed. Then Dorian felt huge hands wrap around both his arms and wrench him back. Jason coughed and struggled to breathe as he pushed up from the floor. Eyes widening, he backed away. He bent over, clamping his hands over his knees. "You're. Fucking. Insane," Jason somehow growled between each ragged breath.

Maybe Dorian was insane, but that didn't help him find Jansen. That didn't get him what he wanted. The killer in him woke up, and it smelled fresh victim. He imagined beating the guy down, breaking limbs until he gave up everything Dorian wanted.

Shaking his head, he tried to get the killer to hide where he belonged… in the back of his mind and the pit of his soul, where all the bad shit in his life lived. Even in his doped out, drunken state of mind, he knew killing the roomie wouldn't win Jansen over.

Dorian pulled away from the bouncers. "Get the fuck off me!" He glared at the guy bent over and leaning against the wall, and Dorian pointed his finger in Jason's face. "You tell him I need to see him. You tell him I want to see him. And so help me God, if the message doesn't make it back to him, consider yourself a motherfuckin' dead man. Feel me?"

Jason rubbed the red marks Dorian had left on his throat as he nodded.

Dorian gave the bouncer a hard shove, then disappeared through the VIP door. He snatched his keys from the valet. He rounded the corner, stomping around toward the back of the building and down into the deep, dark depths of the valet lot. He stumbled forward, approaching his car. That's when he heard the footsteps behind him.

"Hey," a familiar but indistinguishable voice called out.

Dorian spun on his heels, and that's when a fist connected with his jaw. He didn't even have enough time to figure out who the hell had just cleaned his clock before he hit the ground.

17

JANSEN hadn't moved from the bed much. The Lortabs had done a fine job of keeping him doped up pretty heavily, which was a good thing since he'd been in a righteous amount of pain, both physically and emotionally. The burn had started to fade, but the broken inside held on strong.

The day had come and gone in waves of consciousness. He had thoughts and dreams of Mr. Grant, most of which he tried to push away. He knew good and damn well that man was no good for him. Jansen knew he deserved better, but he didn't want better. He wanted Grant.

Damn, he didn't even know the man's first name, and he couldn't stop pining over him. How lame did that make him? And for God's sake, they had sex, nothing more, no stimulating conversation, no "let me get to know you better."

The front door slammed, and Jansen jumped. He rose up from the bed with a hard wince. Jason growled out his name as he barged through the bedroom door. "That man you've mixed yourself up with is bad news, Jansen. I swear to God, he's got a screw loose!"

With a sigh, Jansen blinked as he relaxed against the bed. It took a second for the pain to go away, for his muscles to let go and let the shock of someone slamming through his door fade away. "Jesus, give me a freaking heart attack, why don't you?"

Jason didn't say a word, though Jansen could hear every ragged, exaggerated breath he took. That sounded like one pissed off roomie to him. He looked up from the pillow, and when he saw the red marks all over Jason's neck, his eyes widened. "What the hell happened to you?"

Wincing again, Jansen leaned forward and started to stand until Jason stopped him. "Your friend tried to kill me," his roomie said.

"He didn't."

"Yes, the fuck, he did!"

"Why?"

"Because, apparently, he didn't care for the idea of not seeing you again." Jason sat down on the edge of the bed, rubbing his neck as he glowered. "He said he wants to see you, and by the way, he said if I didn't pass the message on to you, he'd kill me. Thanks."

"I'm sorry, Jason. I didn't mean to get you involved."

Jansen eased back on the bed and tried to relax. A heady mix of contradicting emotions made his head spin and his heart ache. Part of him was excited that Grant wanted to see him again, while the other part was too terrified to even think about it.

"How are you feeling?" Jason asked with a renewed calm in his voice.

"Better." Jansen burrowed in the covers, rubbing the dope-induced sleep from his eyes. "Is it sad that I want to see him, that I miss him?"

Jason shook his head. "Whatever floats your boat, baby. Just, please do me a favor." Jason touched Jansen's leg, and he leaned down to kiss Jansen's forehead. "Be careful, okay? That guy is scary as hell and I... I don't want to have to be the one to identify your body, okay?"

Jansen nodded.

Closing his eyes, Jansen pulled his Grant-scented shirt against his chest and hugged it tight. He buried his nose in the fabric. Visions of that night with Grant danced in his head, from the moment Jansen had dropped to his knees and filled his mouth with that glorious cock to the grand finale in the shower. That man was a god, and the dancer's body ached to feel a little more of his plentiful bounty.

Jansen couldn't do this anymore. The shit had been torturing him for far too long already. He couldn't sit back and wait another second, couldn't just lie in the bed and wish Grant would come to him. He couldn't lose another moment of sleep and damn sure wouldn't sacrifice his sanity for this mess.

Rolling out of the bed, he hissed as his ass hit the edge. One slow, deep breath, Jansen inhaled and exhaled. The physical pain slowly faded, though it still lingered, reminding him to take care. He planted his feet on the Berber carpet and held the edge of the bed with his clenched fists. *Shake it off, Jansen. You need to do this,* he thought as he shoved himself up from the mattress.

He pulled a sweatshirt over his tank top, then padded into the living room. Jason lay on the couch, staring absently at the TV. Jansen looked over at him and said, "I'm taking the car. I'll be back in an hour or so, I swear."

"Where are you going?"

"To the club, see what I can find out about Grant. Maybe someone knows how to get in touch with him."

"You're crazy."

"Maybe, but I need to see him. I need to know why he hurt me and if he plans on doing it again. I need to know that I'm not just a whore to him, and if I am, I need to move on. Whatever the case may be, I need to know so I can move on or... or something."

"I understand, but if you're not back in an hour, I'm coming looking for you."

"Fine," Jansen said as he swiped the keys from the coffee table.

After carefully winding in and out of traffic, easing over every bump and pothole, he pulled the car around to the back parking lot of Sin & Seduction, where all the staff parked. It was dark. Not bad, but dark enough it made him a bit twitchy. Street lamps cast copper-colored light over rigid brick walls. The contrasting darkness threw shadows on the surrounding buildings. Alley rats and God only knew what else scratched at the ground and in the dumpsters. The place was creepy, even more so because he'd been attacked in a situation just like this. Normally, it didn't bother him. Normally, he had Jason with him, and their laughter or talking or whatever took away from just how eerily dangerous this place was, but tonight, he'd gone alone.

Moving still hurt enough to make him more than uncomfortable, but if he was careful, it wasn't completely intolerable. Honestly, he didn't know what the hell he was doing there. He should've stayed in bed. After all, Jansen knew he wouldn't find anything here. Mr. Grant wasn't the type of man who left his information lying around for lovesick nightclub workers to find. Grant was a mystery. He would always be a mystery. Even if Jansen became more than a whore to him, he was the kind of man who would hide everything, if not for shame, then for some proclaimed feeling of safety or some bullshit like that.

Jansen started across the valet parking lot, heading for the back door. He couldn't stop thinking about the mysterious Mr. Grant. About how gentle he'd been that first night, how he'd treated him. He had to care in some small way. Men didn't treat whores with that kind of tenderness. They just didn't.

"Jesus Christ, I'm losing my mind," Jansen whispered. "And now I'm talking to myself."

As he reached for the door, he heard a faint moan coming from between the cars, a brushing against the concrete. He instantly stilled, keeping as quiet as he could. Maybe it was nothing more than an overactive imagination. Maybe it was something he didn't need to witness happening in the darkness. Then he heard the moan again and the sound of a shoe scraping the ground. Jansen panicked. His heart started pounding hard. Sweat beaded on his brow. The moan got louder and Jansen lunged for the back door. He couldn't lock his fist around the doorknob fast enough. He couldn't get inside.

"Help me! Help me!" He banged on the door as he screamed. "Let me in!"

One of the giant bouncers pounded through the door. He gripped Jansen's shoulders and gave him a quick tug to pull him into the club. "You all right, kid?"

"No," Jansen cried. "No, I'm not. I freaked. I heard moaning and...."

The moaning started again. The bouncer tucked him behind his huge body. "Who's there?" he called out. Another moan. "Stay back, kid."

Jansen did.

He watched the bouncer walk the aisles of cars, waving his flashlight back and forth. Jansen's pulse pounded harder in his ears.

Every muscle in his body tightened. Then he heard the big man bark out a "Fuck!" The bouncer's head whipped back, eyes wide. He said "Call an ambulance" just as he dove to the ground.

Jansen went back into the club, straight to the bar. He reached across, yanked the phone from the back-bar and dialed 9-1-1. When the operator picked up, he yelled, "Send an ambulance to Sin & Seduction, valet parking garage!"

He didn't wait for questions he didn't have the answers to, didn't wait for anything. Jansen slammed the phone back down and ran out to where he'd seen the bouncer disappear.

"They're coming," Jansen called out as he rounded the row of cars.

All he saw was designer leather boots, but not just any boots. He had only seen those boots on one person. Jansen's hands had been on those boots the night he knelt down in front of Grant the very first time they'd been together. He charged to a dead stop, heart responding with the same shock. A gasp tore through the air as Jansen's eyes widened and his gut clenched.

"Grant!" he cried out, voice shaky with fear. His feet finally found life again, and he rushed toward the rounded mass of bouncer hovering over his lover. "Grant!"

The bouncer threw out one of his huge arms and stopped Jansen midstep. He put his massive body between the dancer and the man Jansen hadn't stopped thinking about since they met. "Let me go!" he cried. "Let me see him!"

"You don't want to see him, kid."

"Yes, I do! Let go of me!"

Jansen wrenched himself away from the big guy, and that's when he saw Grant lying on his back, with his head turned to the side, covered in blood. "No," he gasped as he fell to his knees beside the lump of body. A breath hitched in his throat.

Grant's eyes fluttered. Dried blood mingled with new blood. His body shivered. His face was bruised, lips busted, eyes swollen. It looked like his nose had been broken. And his hoarse groans sang a sad song of infinite pain.

Jansen reached out and touched his hand. Grant moaned louder.

Everything around him faded away. Jansen only saw Grant, saw his blood and his gnarled fingers. "Baby, hang on. The ambulance is coming," he whispered. Grant's eyes met his. He was still in there, maybe hanging by a thread, but he was still there. "Just a few more minutes, I swear. Don't let go, okay?"

Sirens wailed in the background. The bouncer yanked Jansen back. "No!" he screamed. "I can't leave him alone! Let me go!" And somehow, he managed to pull away from a guy easily twice his size. He fell to his knees in such a way he was sure Grant could still see him. His lover's eyes could barely open, but Jansen didn't want him to think he'd been left alone. "I'll stay with you. Just please hang on for me, okay?"

The paramedics came. Grant groaned as they hefted him up onto the gurney. One of them looked over at Jansen and the bouncer and said, "Do either of you know this man?"

"I do," Jansen blurted before he had time to think things through.

"Come with us."

They put Grant inside the ambulance. Jansen huddled in the corner, hugging his body and crying like a baby. He was so scared. Grant looked so bad. He couldn't lose him, not yet. "Please don't let him die," Jansen mumbled incoherently through his tears as the paramedic did his thing. "Please, God, don't let him die."

18

STANDING in the corner of a tight hospital room, with drab white walls that suffocated the air and machines that spelled out the possibility of doom with every stupid little chirp and beep, Jansen watched the doctors and nurses worry over Mr. Grant. They had his body in some sort of contraption to keep him immobile. Casts set his arms and legs. Even half dead, the man had put up a fight. Hearing his curses and cries had made Jansen cringe. God, he could barely stand to look at him, all that pain and brutality painted all over his flesh. It tore away the fabric that held the dancer's world together.

The doctors and nurses poked and prodded, checked this and that. They attached tubes to his arms, poked needles here and there. They spoke a language Jansen only kind of understood but didn't comprehend at the moment. He heard their voices but couldn't bring himself to listen to the words. Something about broken bones and punctured lungs… "Lucky if he'll be able to walk again."

Jansen's heart sank. Mr. Grant wasn't a man who would take that sort of news well. Even though he knew little about his elusive lover, he could feel the strength and power in that man, and being crippled would probably break his soul.

He hugged himself a little harder, backed away from the bed, and stared down at Grant with fear and sadness in his eyes. Though watching the whole scene hurt the very core of his being, Jansen stayed, and he wouldn't leave his side unless Grant made him.

One by one, the doctors and nurse left the room. A few of the nurses patted Jansen on the shoulder and asked him if he needed anything before they left. He could only manage to shake his head. If he tried to speak, he knew tears would begin to fall again, and once they started, they wouldn't stop.

The room was silent again, save for the sounds of the monitors and Grant's struggled, watery breaths, save for the occasional groan and moan as consciousness found its way into Grant's world again. Grant slowly turned his head, lazy eyes fighting to stay open. He looked at Jansen and smiled, though his lips were swollen and busted. The side of his face was bruised. A split in his flesh ran from the edge of his jaw to the top of his cheek.

Jansen wanted so badly to paint kisses all over his lips and his battered face. Jansen wanted to tell Grant how thankful he was that he'd woken and that Grant would survive this, but Jansen couldn't bring himself to move an inch. The man still scared the hell out of him, despite the casts and injuries, despite the tubes and contraptions.

He finally forced himself to take a step forward. "Mr. Grant, I...."

"Dorian," the man in the hospital bed said, and his voice sounded so alien: gravelly and hoarse. "My name is Dorian. You can call me Dorian."

Jansen watched as Dorian looked around the room, though the man's body didn't move an inch. It was obvious Dorian was slowly becoming aware of his surroundings. His gaze darted back and forth, from the door to the machines, to Jansen then the casts. Jansen took a deep breath as Dorian relaxed against the bed.

"Hospital, huh?" Dorian asked softly.

Jansen nodded.

Dorian wiggled his fingers around the cast. "Come here."

Swallowing back the fear and sadness and the pain he felt for Mr. Grant, Jansen slowly stepped forward, but only approached the bed because he was afraid to touch him. "I... I didn't want you to be alone when you woke up." Something inside him pushed him to brush his hand over Dorian's head. He could feel tears welling in his eyes and burning his throat.

"I won't stay unless...." Jansen took a deep breath, let it ease through his pressed lips. "Unless you want me to."

"No, don't leave."

Closing his eyes, Dorian struggled to breathe. Damn, every fucking inch of his body ached, but he was too high to be bothered with it. He knew he couldn't move, though he didn't really know what had happened. To make matters worse, he could already feel the need for revenge brewing beneath the surface of his skin. "I need a favor. I need ya to get my phone and call the first number on speed dial. When the guy answers, tell him I need to talk to him."

Dorian watched the dancer dig through his bloodied clothes. He couldn't help noticing his fingers trembling and the tears falling down his cheeks. He felt like such an ass for dragging that innocent kid into his shit, but it wasn't exactly his fault. He didn't ask Jansen to go looking for him.

"What's wrong, Jansen?"

"Everything. Nothing. I don't know." Jansen found the phone, clenched it in his hand as he turned back to face Dorian. "Who am I calling? What are you going to do?"

Dorian said, "I know who did this. I'm calling my head of security so he can handle it."

"By 'handle', do I even want to know what you mean?"

Dorian shook his head as best as he could.

"Can we... just forget about that for a minute? You just woke up in the hospital, after being beaten within an inch of your life. Can we let it go for right now, please?"

"No. That fucker knows he signed a death warrant, and he'll run. I gotta do this now." And by God, if Angelo saw Dorian's number and didn't answer, there would be hell to pay.

"Fine," Jansen bit out as he pressed the first button on the speed dial. A thick, bassy voice that sounded like it had been birthed in the middle of the bayou said, "Boss?"

"No." Jansen swallowed, then said, "Mr. Grant needs to speak to you."

The dancer held the phone to Dorian's ear. Pain tore through Dorian's chest. He stared straight up at Jansen as he coughed. In a rasping, weak voice, he said, "Hospital. I'm in the fuckin' hospital." He coughed again. He couldn't look at Jansen anymore. The dancer looked so upset, so disappointed. That disappointment was like a spear to Dorian's heart. The last time he'd felt anything close to that was from his mom. "The guy we let go. The family man, he did this to me. Handle it. Handle it fuckin' now! Screw his family!"

Dorian looked back up at Jansen. The sadness in his eyes killed the big man's soul, but he had to handle this the way *he* handled things. Dorian had to teach those assholes a lesson. No one... *no fucking one* attacked him and lived.

What Dorian did, it wasn't Jansen's business, and part of Jansen truly understood that, maybe even wanted to accept it. None of this mess had anything to do with Jansen, but he was stuck there, holding the phone while Dorian Grant barked out orders to his personal security guard. Who the hell needed 'round the clock security anyway? The bad guys! He was starting to see what Jason had warned him about. Grant was dangerous, dangerous in a mafia sort of way, the sort of way that could easily land him in an early grave surrounded by mourning loved ones.

Did Jansen really want to get mixed up with that?

Dorian gave him a nod, and Jansen ended the call. He set the phone aside, then backed away from the bed, hugging his body tightly. He kept a comfortable distance from Dorian. His stomach had been doing backflips since the moment he'd spotted the man bleeding on the pavement, and the wracked nerves had just gotten worse as the hours had passed.

Looking over at Dorian, all helpless and broken, Jansen only wanted to care for him and nurse him back to health. He wanted to be by his side and support him. *God help him*, he thought he even wanted to love him. But damn, if Jansen crossed him, would Dorian "handle" him too? Would he wake up with a gun in his face, or would he be beaten to death for doing something Mr. Grant didn't like?

"Talk to me," Dorian said. "What's wrong?"

"Mr. Grant... Dorian, I... I don't even know you. I was told you're dangerous, that getting mixed up with you was a mistake, a mistake that could eventually cost me my life."

Dorian knew exactly what the fuck he was and what he'd done in his life. He didn't need some kid reciting a list to him, but hearing Jansen say it hurt like nothing he'd ever felt before. He might as well have been staring in that busted mirror again. He might as well have been staring at a reflection he hated, one he wanted to see dead more than alive.

"They're right," Dorian finally said. "I am dangerous."

He watched Jansen sink down in the chair like every bit of his life and will had been sucked out of him. The heartbreak of truth shone in the kid's eyes.

In a low, broken voice, Jansen asked, "Am I a whore to you?"

Fuck me!

Dorian didn't know how to answer that. Truth be told, at first, Jansen was nothing but a whore to him. At first, the dancer was a good lay and nothing more. Now, with him sitting there, with Dorian's blood on his hands because he'd tried to save him, with Jansen seeing the hardass all beaten and broken, Dorian didn't think he was. But admitting that to Jansen would take this whole... thing they were doing to a level he wasn't sure he was ready for.

"Don't answer that," Jansen mumbled. "I don't think I can deal with the truth right now."

Jansen shifted in the chair. He didn't even know why he stayed. Obviously, he was nothing to Dorian. He should've left right then. Jansen should've stayed in bed regaining his strength and letting his body heal after what that monster had done to him.

God, I'm such a glutton. What, having my ass ripped to hell and back wasn't enough pain for me. I have to sit here and let this man I don't know break my heart too?

Jansen got up, gathered his sweatshirt, and started for the door.

Dorian's hoarse, concerned voice called out, "Where ya goin'?"

Without turning around, Jansen said, "Home. I need to rest."

"Come back, please. Don't go yet, okay?" Slowly, Jansen turned around. His big brown stare trained on the floor. He was being so submissive, like he had to obey Dorian's orders so Grant didn't get pissed off at him. "Look at me," Dorian said. Jansen did. "Will ya touch my hand, please?"

Jansen's eyes narrowed, like Dorian had confused him. He approached carefully, slowly. Not that Grant could do anything. He was a busted mess, for God's sake, but that didn't make him lower his inhibitions. He sure the hell wouldn't throw caution to the wind for some stupid desire. He also couldn't fight the pure need that had been building for that man since the moment he'd laid eyes on him.

Jansen finally reached the bed. He let his gentle fingers brush over Dorian's hand.

That gentle touch felt good, better than anything Dorian had felt in a very long time, like someone actually cared, and not because he paid them to. "I don't see ya as a whore," Dorian said as he looked Jansen in the eyes. "I'm not good with feelings and shit. I'm not good with lettin' people get close to me. So, if that's what ya want from me, ya gotta be patient. Ya gotta be understandin', okay?"

19

KNUCKLES rapped against Dorian's hospital room door. Angelo peeked his dark, beady eyes in through the window. Dorian looked down at Jansen, whose head was face down in his folded arms at the side of the bed right next to Dorian's hip. Poor guy was crashed. The kid had stayed with him all night, taking care of him, talking to him, making him laugh. Seemed like Jansen was quickly smoothing out that wrinkle he'd made in Dorian's life.

Dorian wiggled his fingers, brushed the tips of Jansen's messy brown hair. "Jansen," he whispered in that hoarse, alien voice that would obviously be his for a little while longer. "Jay," he said again. This time Jansen started to turn his head, and a subtle grumble left his perfect, pouty lips. He looked up. "I need a minute alone with Angelo, baby. Can ya…."

Jansen looked over at the door, then back to Dorian. He took a deep breath and nodded slowly, giving Dorian a disappointed, uneasy look. "I'll um… I'll find some coffee or something."

Dorian gave him a tight-lipped smile.

Jansen stood and kissed his forehead before leaving him alone to discuss "business" with the mammoth at the door. He and Angelo exchanged tense glances in passing. With a sigh, Dorian settled his head against the pillow and waited for the click of the doorknob.

Watching his dancer leave, every step the kid took, Dorian suddenly felt a bizarre emptiness, a loneliness. And when Jansen stopped at the door to give him one last, hurt look, the tough-ass bastard nearly crumbled. He just couldn't let Jansen stay for this. It was better for everyone if the kid didn't know the gory details of what had been done to the asshole who'd put Dorian in that bed.

"So, what the fuck, Angelo?"

"Business is handled, boss," Angelo said as he sat down beside the bed. He narrowed his eyes, looked Dorian over, then finally met his glare. "Good damn thing I didn't see this shit before. I might have tortured his ass a little more. You hangin' in there?"

"What did you do to him?"

"Took him to Louisville. He kissed wood… a lot of it."

"And?"

"And, he ain't breathin' no more, boss. Fed his ass to the gators."

"C'mon, Angelo. What else?"

"No offense, Dorian, but let it go. The fucker is dead, but um… he didn't do this alone. He had his damn dumbass cousin helpin' him. Cousin bailed. Fucker ain't in NOLA no more, I promise. We think he headed down to the Glades. No big, though. I got family. We'll handle him good."

"Good," Dorian said in a flat voice. There was a long moment of uncomfortable silence between the two of them before he finally said, "Go to the mansion. Tell Maria what's goin' on. With the hospital and shit, I mean."

"She already knows, boss."

"I'm gonna need a room downstairs for a bit."

"She's already on it."

"Good." And that's why Dorian loved the staff he had. "I want arrangements made for Jansen to stay." Angelo's eyes widened. He opened his mouth to say something. Dorian beat him to it. "Not a fuckin' word. I figured I'm gonna be bedbound for a while. I don't wanna be alone." He left out the bit about the fucked up things his mind conjured when he was left alone. Angelo didn't need to know he was *that* brand of crazy.

"Alright, boss. You want it handled, I'm on it."

"Good, now go. Pay a visit to my businesses, do a little PR for me. Anyone who knows about this, needs to know this shit don't mean I'm goin' light on nobody."

"Got it, boss," Angelo said as he headed for the door.

Dorian was alone again, staring up at the nasty white ceiling tiles of the hospital room. Alone was never good for him. His head thought up all kinds of bullshit. This time, it conjured his ma. He hadn't seen her in almost twenty years. Her ghost brushed its hand over his head, nothing but love in her eyes. Did she know about the shit he'd done in his life? Was she ashamed of him? The ghost leaned down and kissed his forehead, whispered words he couldn't hear. Dorian closed his eyes and swallowed the new emptiness. His heart suddenly ached with a need to have his ma back in his life. He needed her more now than he ever did before.

Then he heard the door close. When Dorian opened his eyes, he saw Jansen standing there, sipping a cup of coffee. The sight of him made the hardass smile. "Hey."

"Hey. You okay?"

Dorian nodded, wiggled his fingers around the cast. That had become his sign to tell Jansen he wanted him close by. The dancer sat down beside him and brushed his fingertips over the little bit of Dorian's exposed hand. "I would've brought you a cup of coffee, but I… I didn't know if you even liked it."

"It's okay. I'm good." Dorian turned his head so he could see Jansen's face. Their eyes met. His jaw clenched. Dorian wanted to tell him to stay at the mansion, but if Jansen turned him down, Dorian didn't think he would handle that kind of rejection too well right now. "Ya didn't have to stay all night. I mean, ya can't be comfortable."

Jansen laughed. "I'm okay. Don't worry about me. Is everything okay here? I mean, with Angelo and all?"

Dorian nodded. "Everything's fine."

"I need to call my roommate before he flips out. I still have his car, and he needs to come get it. I won't have a way to leave, but I… I don't have anywhere I need to be. So, as long as I'm not bothering you, I guess…. I guess I can stay. That is, if you want me to."

"Jansen, I want ya to stay. I don't mean just here in the hospital. I want ya to come back to the mansion and stay with me for a little while. I'm gonna be hard to deal with, not that I mean to be, but I know me, and I know I'm not gonna be easy to be around for awhile. But if ya think ya can handle it, I'd like ya to be there."

Jansen could feel his lips pulling into a smile. Dorian had just asked him to stay with him, not necessarily live with him, but stay by his side for a little while. That, Jansen could do without question. That, he would be thrilled to do.

"Yeah. Sure, whatever you need me to do," he said, trying to stifle his excitement. He continued to absently stroke Dorian's hand as he watched his lover's eyes flutter open then closed, open then closed again. Dorian's stubborn ass was fighting to stay awake. Why, Jansen didn't know. He said, "Dorian, why don't you sleep? I'll be here when you wake up, I swear."

"I don't want to sleep. Every time I close my eyes, I see my ma." Dorian looked away, back at the ceiling tiles. Obviously, he didn't want Jansen to see whatever emotions might be hidden in the depths of his dark eyes, though Jansen didn't understand why.

"What happened to her?" Jansen asked in a soft voice as he laced his fingers with Dorian's as best as he could with the cast in the way.

"The cause of her death was never officially ruled a homicide, but I know my dad was behind it. I *know* he was. Honestly, I think Ma was going to try to leave him and take me with her. And Pops handled it the way he handled anyone who crossed him. I think Pops had her killed."

"Damn," Jansen breathed. "That's horrible. I'm... I'm sorry, Dorian."

With a hard wince, Dorian tried to shrug it off. He tried to play cold, like he didn't really care anymore, but Jansen could see right through that rough exterior of his. The dancer could see how badly losing his mom had hurt him.

Jansen reached up and stroked the backs of his fingers over Dorian's cheek. Dorian turned to look at him. If Jansen didn't know any better, he would've sworn he saw the beginnings of tears in the big man's cold brown eyes.

"Don't sleep then," Jansen whispered. "Do whatever makes Dorian Grant happy."

"Right now, this—" Dorian wiggled his fingers against Jansen's palm. "—this makes Dorian Grant happy."

20

STANDING in the smoker's lounge, or rather the big black stain on the face of a fairly highbrow hospital, Jansen bummed one cigarette after another. It wasn't that he was a smoker—hence the bumming. He kicked that habit a long time ago, but this situation with Dorian made his inner addict want to break out, and his inner addict wanted nicotine… badly!

The smoker's lounge was hidden on the back of the hospital where the good little nonsmokers wouldn't see them or have to smell that toxic cloud of filth. A few metal benches formed a square around a giant concrete ashtray filled with sand. Trees lined all four sides, a natural canopy to contain the pollution.

Jansen took another long drag, then another. The four or so people around him followed suit. He paced back and forth, hugging his sweatshirt tight around his body as he white-knuckled his phone. His stomach knotted like it needed him to expel the little food he'd eaten yesterday…. Or was it the day before yesterday?

Frazzled nerves had definitely gotten the best of him. Between each drag of his cigarette, he chewed down his nails. There was just too much… stuff rolling around in his head. Really, moving in with a big, scary mafioso type who he barely knew, who had hurt him in a pretty serious way? He'd lost his mind.

Jansen sank down on the bench, crossed his legs a little tighter than normal, curled his arms around his chest, and took another hard pull from the cancer stick. He hated those things now, but damn, what a relief for his frazzled nerves.

In Dorian's defense, though, he seemed sincerely sorry, and surprisingly, he'd been letting Jansen know things about his life, opening up to him. And, God, the man had been so hurt. Jansen stood and started walking his little circle again. But no matter how much he wanted to, he couldn't forget about the blindfold and the fulltime security guard who looked like he could take on a small army alone, or maybe the way they "handled business."

With a sigh, he sank down on the bench again. The guy beside him gave him a brow-crinkled stare. "What?" Jansen barked, though he knew the up-down routine he'd been pulling probably worked everyone's nerves. The man only shrugged and handed him another smoke. Closing his eyes, Jansen let out a breath as he lowered his head. "Thanks."

He popped the cig between his lips, and the man held a flame to the tip. Jansen's cheeks hollowed as he took a long, hard pull. The cherry glowed bright orange. Jansen mumbled an embarrassed, "Thank you," and the man gave a nod.

Jansen scrolled through the contacts on his phone until he found Jason's number. Jansen needed to call, needed to tell his roomie he wouldn't be back for a while. Hell, he might not even go back to work for a while, but he didn't want to assume anything. He didn't want to assume Dorian would take care of his expenses and most importantly, the bills. So beyond the time he intended to take off to recover and recoup, Jansen planned on being at work. "Planned" being the operative word. He kind of got the feeling plans didn't matter when Dorian Grant had something else in mind.

Jansen pressed the send button, then held the phone to his ear as he puffed the smoke down to nothing. He started pacing again, waiting to hear the sound of his best friend's voice. Or maybe it was the inevitable ass-chewing his overly dramatic BFF was surely saving for him.

"Hello," Jason said.

"Hey."

"Where the fuck are you?"

"At the hospital. Dorian... um, Mr. Grant, was hurt pretty bad. I found him in the valet lot at Sin."

"Is he okay?"

"He will be." Jansen took a deep breath. He ran his fingers through his hair as he paced away from the other smokers. "Look, he wants me to stay with him for a little while. I guess, just until he gets back on his feet."

"But you're keeping your room, right?"

"Yeah. I'll keep it, and I'll pay the rent. So, don't worry, okay?"

"I'm not. Well, I'm worried about you. Don't get too wrapped up in this guy, Jansen. I know his type. He'll kick you to the curb when he gets tired of you or you piss him off good enough."

"I'll be okay. Don't worry." Jansen snuffed out the third cigarette he'd smoked in less than fifteen minutes. "I'll be fine." Would he be okay? Truly? "See you at work. Hopefully, I'll be back in a few days."

"Fine," Jason said. "But I'll worry if I don't hear from you."

"I know, babe. I'll check in, I swear."

"You'd better."

"Yes, Daddy," Jansen teased.

"Goodbye," Jason said, and Jansen knew his bestie was probably rolling his eyes.

He hung up the phone and slipped it back into his pocket. His gaze wandered up to the window to Dorian's room. What had he gotten himself into? After the night in the hospital room, the talking and sharing, the laughs and the comfortable silence, things didn't feel so awkward or scary. He honestly never thought Dorian would expect him to stay at the mansion. That was a more than pleasant surprise. If Jansen were to be honest with himself, he would go ahead and admit he wanted to be there, that he had strong feelings for the beautiful, mysterious man from the VIP booth.

Sometimes honesty could be a hard pill to swallow, especially when the truth came from the self.

Returning to Dorian's room, he found his big scary lover sleeping like a baby. The tough guy looked so sweet and harmless lying in the bed with his eyes gently closed. He looked like a broken angel, and maybe that was Jansen's heart talking, but that's how he wanted to see Dorian: *his* broken angel. He brushed his hand over Dorian's head, then leaned down and kissed his forehead.

"Whatever happens, Dorian, wherever this goes or whatever becomes of us, please God, don't hurt me. Don't hurt me physically or emotionally. Honestly, I don't think I could take it."

21

RELEASE day! Finally! Rubber wheels squeaked against the linoleum as a nurse pushed Dorian's wheelchair down a bright, florescent-lit hallway toward the hospital's front entrance. Jansen hugged his sweatshirt around his torso as he followed behind the parade.

His body ached from sleeping in a hard vinyl chair for far too many days. His stomach growled because he'd refused hospital food as often as he could. Not that it mattered; the smell of disinfectant in the air was enough to kill the most desperate appetite.

A week had passed, and he'd only left Dorian's side long enough to go home and shower, go to the cafeteria, or steal the occasional smoke. Things were still strange at best. He didn't know where he stood with Dorian, not really. One minute they were laughing and smiling. Then something would set Dorian off. His emotions had turned into one of those wild and twisty roller coasters with all the loop-d-loops and thrills some human stomachs just couldn't handle. Though it had done a number on his guts, he'd gladly ridden that ride, because Dorian meant a lot to him, but….

Dorian grumbled Jansen's name as he wiggled his fingers around his cast.

"I'm right behind you," Jansen said softly.

"I want you beside me."

"Baby, I'll be beside you. I just can't right now." With the nurses fawning over him, it would've been impossible to squeeze in anyway. "Let's just get you home, okay?"

A sleek black sedan met them at the doors. Angelo stood beside the driver, arms crossed over his chest. He gave Jansen a cold, calculating stare as he reached down to help his boss out of the wheelchair.

It took three people to get Dorian into the car. His legs and arms were still in casts: legs to the thighs, arms to just above the elbow. His skin had begun to yellow from the fading bruises. The cuts had left dark red gashes over his cheek and lip. Hopefully they would heal. Dorian seemed to be more pissed about that than anything else. Regardless, he looked and sounded absolutely miserable. Every groan or moan that fell from his plump, kissable lips made Jansen's stomach turn and his body cringe.

Angelo climbed into the front seat. Jansen stood watching. The driver held the back door open, waiting for him to climb inside, but for some stupid reason Jansen couldn't seem to move another inch. It was like he was waiting for something seriously horrible to happen. Like Dorian biting his head off and telling him to get lost, or worse yet, having Angelo "handle" him because he had become a pain in Dorian's ass.

Dorian peeked his head out. "You coming?" he asked as his fingertips tapped against the leather-covered spot beside him.

Jansen took a deep breath and nodded slowly. His heart was in it. His heart wanted to be beside that man for a long time, but he couldn't make his mind stop screaming for him to run the other way. If this ended badly....

No. No, it wouldn't end badly. It couldn't end badly.

"Yeah, I'm coming," Jansen said as he handed the driver his bag.

Once he was in the car, the driver shut the door, and they pulled away from the sterile, looming brick façade of the prison where Dorian had spent too many of his days. The car headed through the bustling streets of New Orleans, under viaducts and over bridges, heading to the mysterious place Jansen had been taken to the first night he'd met Mr. Grant. Only this time, he would get to enjoy the scenery without having to peek around a blindfold.

Dorian looked over and wiggled his fingers.

Butterflies fluttered in Jansen's stomach.

"What's wrong?" Dorian asked.

Jansen shrugged. He didn't know what to say. Insecurity, maybe? He didn't know. He sighed, faked a smile, and said, "Nothing, I'm fine."

Leaning over, Jansen went to kiss his cheek, a subtle reassurance for them both that everything was and always would be just fine despite the bullshit, but Dorian turned his head. Their lips met. Jansen closed his eyes and let the kiss consume him.

Dorian's mouth embraced his in such a way Jansen thought he would lose himself completely. And God help him, Dorian's kiss felt so absolutely amazing, so perfect when everything about them was so damn far from anything resembling perfection, but the contrast was welcome and beautiful. It was dangerous and safe at the same time. It was exciting, and Jansen craved it all.

Dorian licked across the seam of his lips, and Jansen opened his mouth so Dorian could slip his tongue inside. It all seemed like a metaphor for the beginning of this new... thing between the two of them. Jansen let him in, and Dorian actually acted like he wanted to be there. He wondered if that meant the mysterious Mr. Grant would let him in too. Would Jansen ever truly know Dorian Grant, or would he be a patient plaything to keep the man company while he regained what he'd lost in the attack?

Pulling away from the kiss was cruel and dreamlike. Jansen opened his eyes slowly, and they met the weight of Dorian's deep brown stare. There seemed to be a new shine in his eyes, or maybe it was Jansen's imagination. He didn't know what to say to him after that. He slowly stroked the exposed ends of Dorian's fingers, tips brushing his soft skin.

Then Dorian said, "Thanks for not abandoning me."

As ironic as it was, that's all Jansen really needed to hear. He didn't expect him to say that, didn't expect much of anything from his obscure, secretive friend, but what Dorian had given him in that one little statement was the best gift he could've given.

22

AFTER the insanity of being back in his own home had worn down and the worrisome busybodies had Dorian settled into his own bed—which had been moved to a bedroom downstairs, one Dorian had never been in before—he began to weigh things: Jansen, the shit he'd done to get in this mess, how it could affect the dancer, the worry and nervousness he'd seen from him, how weak he was now. Dorian hadn't said much in those hours, only stared absently at the wall while Jansen sat stiff as a board beside him.

"You ever gonna tell me what's wrong?" Dorian kept his voice low, even, and almost distant.

Rolling onto his side, Jansen stared at him in silence. Even in the dark of his bedroom with casts keeping his limbs from moving, Dorian was still utterly gorgeous. He didn't look fragile or destroyed, though Jansen knew him well enough to know that was going through his head.

"I...." He didn't know what to say, honestly. He was with Dorian—who for all intents and purposes, was pretty much everything Jansen had ever wanted in a man. He was smart and attractive and kind enough, and, God, the man was amazing in the sack, but he.... "I don't know. I guess.... Dorian, what are we doing? What I mean is, are we together? Are you just keeping me around so you'll have someone to take care of you and keep you company?"

Jansen watched Dorian's bare chest inflate as he took a deep breath. Muscles flexed against his tanned, tattooed flesh. Dorian rolled his head against his pillow.

"What do you want us to be, Jansen? I asked you to be patient with me. I don't know how to do any of this relationship shit. I've been alone all my life, and frankly, I don't have a problem being alone for the rest of it."

Okay, that kind of hurt. Maybe it shouldn't have, but it did. Maybe Jansen should've known better than to expect anything from *Mr. Grant.* Yeah, sure, he'd been warned, but God, Dorian had kept him around. He'd asked Jansen not to leave, asked him to stay in his home.

"I don't want to be anything you don't want me to be," Jansen said as he rolled away. Dorian called his name, but Jansen couldn't bring himself to look at him. Dorian called his name again. Jansen turned his head slightly. "You don't owe me any explanations. Just let it go. Forget I said anything."

"No, you're upset, and I didn't mean that—" Dorian sighed. "—as bad as it obviously sounded." *Fuck!* Dorian wanted to reach over and touch Jansen, maybe even hold him. It was the first time he'd ever looked at a man and didn't immediately want to fuck him, then send him away. "That patience I asked for," he finally said. "I know it's going to be hard to understand and accept, but if we're...." What were they going to be? Where was this thing going? "Give me time, okay? I have a lot of shit goin' on in my head, and none of it makes any fuckin' sense to me. I'm givin' ya the best I have. Can ya just give me a little patience?"

That was probably the sincerest Jansen had ever heard him. He reached down, stroked Dorian's fingers, and nodded. Without looking up at his lover's gorgeous, pained face, Jansen said, "I can try. I just...."

He finally made himself look up. He wanted Dorian to see the concern and fear in his eyes, to truly understand why he'd been such a freak about all of this. "Whatever happens, don't abandon me. If you decide this isn't what you want, that I'm not what you want, tell me sooner rather than later. Don't put it off because it might hurt. If I start caring about you more than I do now and you kick me to the curb, it'll hurt more than I am ready for."

That one request told Dorian more about his beautiful, delicate dancer than any story he'd ever shared. This was a genuine person, with genuine feelings and a heart as big as the heavens.

He suddenly wanted to know more about Jansen, wanted to ask where his mom and dad were, if he had any siblings, what had happened to the other lovers he'd had. Dorian had his own abandonment issues, none of which he'd shared with anyone, but maybe… just maybe, this one would be the one he finally opened up to. For God's sake, the kid had seen him at his worst and still came home with him, still wanted to be in the bed with him and care for him, even after all the shitty things Dorian had done to him.

Fuck.

In that moment, Dorian realized just how much he cared about Jansen: really, *really* fucking cared. He could feel it in his need to make sure no one—including himself—ever hurt the kid or even gave him one second of grief. "I can give ya that," Dorian said, and to his ears, it sounded like a solemn vow, a promise nothing in this world would ever make him break.

23

ANOTHER few weeks passed. Jansen was surprised by how well Dorian had been taking everything, what with not being able to walk or use his arms, and needing someone take care of him so completely. He'd been grumpy and hard to deal with at times, but for the most part, Dorian Grant was a surprisingly good patient. At least Dorian had the meds. He could dope up and zone out, and life in la-la land stayed cheerful... for the most part.

Things—relationship-wise—remained tense between them. They were still in that awkward place where neither really knew how to act around the other or knew the right things to say. Jansen just wanted to help Dorian without making him feel helpless. He wanted to care for him without making him feel weak.

"Dorian?" he whispered, peeking his head through the crack in the bedroom door. Jansen had been in the downstairs weight room, trying to keep himself from turning into a flabby lump. Eventually he wanted to go back to work, and no one liked a chunky dancer. "You okay, babe? Need anything?"

Dorian grumbled something Jansen didn't understand. Dorian kept his glassy eyes set on the TV, which happened to be turned off. The light on a nightstand table cast a golden glow over his hard, worn features. It intensified the raised pink flesh of his scars, both old and new. His dark brown hair was a knotted, greasy mess, and his unwashed skin had a soft sheen to it.

Crimson silk sheets wove around his broken body. The white casts were so stark against all that deep red. Dorian's head had been burrowed in a mound of pillows. He looked like a man who'd given up on becoming a functioning human being again, which Jansen could certainly understand if not sympathize with, but he still hated seeing him like that.

He stepped farther into the room and took a deep breath of stale, tense air. In a low, careful voice he asked Dorian what he'd said.

"I fuckin' stink," Dorian barked out, voice coarse and grating. "I can smell myself deterioratin' in this fuckin' bed. I want a fuckin' shower, and I want out of these goddamn casts!"

"I know, babe, but you have to wait. Your bones have to heal." Jansen sat down on the edge of the bed. It dipped from the weight of his body, and Dorian winced as he tilted toward him. Jansen stroked the tops of his fingers over his lover's bare chest. He felt the muscles in Dorian's stomach flex like he wanted to pull away but couldn't. "Why don't you let me give you a sponge bath? Might make you feel better."

"I don't wanna fuckin' sponge bath! I want out of this bed!" Dorian tried to lean forward, and when the pain forced him back he growled out a terse, "Fuck!"

"Dorian, stop it." Jansen helped him back into his normal, semi-comfortable spot. He understood what Dorian was going through. It hadn't been too long ago that he'd been the invalid relegated to spending his days in bed. "You have to let someone do things like that for you without them having to fight you over it. At the rate you're going, you won't have anyone who will want to take care of you. Everyone's afraid you'll bite their heads off."

"They should be afraid!"

"No, they shouldn't. I shouldn't. Now, I'm *going* to grab a cloth, some soap and water. Then, I *am* coming back here, and I'm going to clean you up. You're not going to bitch, are you?"

Dorian glared.

An icy chill shot down the center of Jansen's spine. Dorian still scared him. Standing up for himself like that scared him. Maybe it shouldn't have, but it did. He knew if he had any sense at all, he would run for the hills and never look back, but he just couldn't. Something about Dorian pulled at him like a magnet, and he couldn't fight it.

Jansen came back to the bed with a large bowl of warm water, soap, and a washcloth. He lathered his palms, then started to clean Dorian's beautiful, battered body: gently rubbing his hands over his lover's tattooed chest; over his colorful, muscled arms; over his thick, sculptured legs. He washed the sweaty, filthy sheen from Dorian's aggravated face. Then he dipped both hands in the bowl of soapy water before running his fingers through Dorian's hair.

"Is this okay?" Jansen asked.

"Sure. I guess."

"I'm sorry, Dorian. I wish I could change this for you."

"Yeah? Well you can't, can you?"

Clenching his teeth, Jansen took a deep breath. He let Dorian's attitude roll off his back, let it go because he knew the man was in pain. He could deal with the short, snarky responses because it wasn't exactly abuse, merely aggravation. But he had to keep reminding himself of that, and those silent reminders seemed to make everything *kind of* okay.

With the moistened cloth, Jansen wiped away the soap. A thick drop of water rolled down Dorian's chest, over the muscles and sinews, over the beautiful expanse of his sculptured abs and down the "V" that led to a treasure beneath the silken sheets. It took everything Jansen had in him not to follow that shimmering line with the tip of his tongue. He wrung the rag, then ran it over his lover's body again. This time he dipped down between Dorian's thighs.

Dorian watched him, watched everything he did as if the whole thing disgusted him. It wasn't Jansen or his need to take care of the cripple. It wasn't the soft, sensual touches. The situation disgusted him. The fact that he could only lie there while someone else did everything for him made him sick. He hated being so helpless.

Jansen hooked his hands around the waist of Dorian's boxers. He carefully pulled them down his thighs and over the casts. Dorian would probably hate him worse for this, for leaving him hanging in the wind, but he had to clean the man up. He lathered the soap between his palms again, then worked it over Dorian's shaft and around his balls. It was meant to be innocent, meant to be nothing more than cleaning. But then he heard Dorian moan, and Jansen saw his back arch and his eyes close.

Dorian bit his lower lip as he groaned.

The slow, firm stroking had turned the poor man on. Jansen felt Dorian's cock getting hard against his palm. He didn't realize he was doing it, but that accidental hand job had turned an angry Mr. Grant into a happy, purring kitten. "I'm sorry, babe. I didn't…."

"Don't stop. Please, fuckin' God, don't stop."

24

JANSEN'S hands were so soft and gentle, nothing like Dorian was used to. He'd always played with the boys who liked to party on the wild side. Dorian Grant never hid his sadistic side—not in the eyes of the public or behind the dark walls of his bedroom. The rough stuff turned him on. He liked the kink. But with Jansen, things were so very different. Jansen seemed to want and need so much more, or maybe something far from his safety net entirely. Jansen obviously needed something meaningful.

The delicate surface of the dancer's flesh tickled every nerve in Dorian's hardened shaft. Chills shot up and down his spine. The soap made it slick. Jansen's hand rode up and down, and up and down again. Dorian's thighs quivered. Pressure began to build low in his body. He arched his back, thrusting his cock into Jansen's grip. Fingers tightened. Dorian's erection throbbed and pulsed and ached within the dancer's tender touch. He cried out, "God, don't stop. Don't fuckin' stop, baby."

Eyes closed, Dorian spread his legs as wide as he could with the weight of the heavy white plaster casts holding them down. Warm water ran down the base of his cock, his sac, between his thighs, and down his ass. It wasn't a lot of water, but fuck, the sensation was incredible, so incredible he didn't mind the moist sheets pressing against the curve of his cheeks. The warm water washed away the soap while Jansen gripped and stroked and worked his lover's cock into a full erection. No complaints from Dorian. No damn way.

Lowering his body, Jansen squeezed his shoulders between Dorian's legs and wrapped his mouth around that long, thick, beautiful erection. He took every inch, let his lips press around the base and slowly ride up to the tip, tongue swirling and curling over all that soft, sensitive skin, weaving back and forth over the thick vein, and circling over the ridge. His fingers worked gentle waves over Dorian's sac as he flicked his tongue over the slit, lapping away the first spills of Dorian's rousing pleasure.

Jansen just wanted to make his battered lover feel good again. He wanted him to be utterly content and relaxed and….

Fuck, he cared so much. How the hell did this happen? How the hell did he get so wrapped up like he had, with a man like Dorian?

"Jansen," he heard his lover gasp. "Jansen, stop."

Jansen's head shot up, eyes wide. "You okay?"

"Yeah, I'm okay…." More than okay, actually. Dorian smiled and gave a little nod. His Adam's apple bobbed in his throat. "I want to fuck you." He licked his lips. "I know. I know. I'm in casts and all, but if you get on…."

"I can't. Dorian, I can't." Jansen's heart started beating faster, hands shaking. He would swear he was getting ready for a panic attack. "I can't."

"Hey, calm down." What Dorian would've given just to touch him, to reach up and caress Jansen's worried face and kiss his soft lips. He wished he could reassure him, and not through a few lame-ass words. Dorian wanted to hold him. Damn it all to hell, he wanted to hold him against his body and wrap his arms around that beautiful dancer and swear everything would be okay, that he'd never let anyone hurt him ever again. "I won't do it. If you're afraid of… of me, I won't do it."

"It's not you, not really. I just don't think I'm ready for *that* again."

Maybe it was Jansen's imagination, but he swore he saw disappointment on Dorian's face. He didn't know where that disappointment came from. The reason he couldn't have sex was Dorian's fault in the first place. He'd hurt him. Something violent had come over him, and he'd hurt Jansen in a way neither his body nor his brain had been ready for. But for some ungodly reason, Jansen still trusted him, to the point he would put his life in Dorian's hands.

Jansen stood from the bed, then started to pace a small circle as his hand rubbed back and forth across his brow. Could he do it? Could he let Dorian have sex with him, knowing how delicate he was back there? Could he let that beautiful, sadistic man drive that fucking enormous cock in his ass, knowing he could do more damage?

"You have to be extremely gentle, Dorian. You can't treat me like a whore."

Though he deserved it, that honestly hurt Dorian's feelings. Sure, Jansen had a good damn reason to worry. He had a right to ask him to go easy, but damn it, Dorian thought he'd made it clear that he didn't see Jansen as a whore, not anymore.

"Jansen, don't, okay? I told ya, you're more than that to me. I don't wanna hurt ya. And goddammit, if anyone tried to hurt ya, I'd fuckin' kill them."

Dorian wiggled his fingers around the huge white cast that had been keeping his arm completely immobile, and he hoped like hell Jansen noticed. He hoped like hell the dancer would come to the bed and let him show him how much he wanted to take care of him, even if he was physically incapable of it at the moment.

Watching the change of emotion in Jansen's eyes made Dorian's heart stop and start again, made him almost afraid to breathe. He saw what he swore to be fear, and then Jansen's gaze softened, resembling something like acceptance, maybe even understanding. It was hard to explain how Dorian saw all of that in his eyes. Maybe it was the unfurling of his brow or the way his lips curled at the corners, but whatever it was, he knew Jansen had slowly started to give in.

If it felt more like making love, and Dorian kept his promise to be gentle, Jansen could let him have his body again. He hooked his fingers over the waistband of his sweatpants, and he pulled them down until they pooled at his ankles. His dick had gotten hard the moment he'd had Dorian in his mouth, and the promise of tender sex with the man he'd become so attached to only made the shit harder.

He approached the bed, knelt down at the foot, and let the soft silk sheets brush against his skin. Reaching across Dorian's body, he dug in the nightstand drawer until he found the bottle of lube Jansen had strategically put there just in case the need somehow arose.

"You're in control, baby." Dorian shifted his eyes back and forth between the casts. "Not much I can do like this."

Jansen squeezed a thick line of lube onto his palm, wrapped his hand around Dorian's cock, and with a nice, firm grip, he slathered it all over his lover's hardened shaft. He straddled Dorian's waist, then eased down on his dick, letting the head slip inside his body. He waited for the wave of pain to come before he eased off.

Dorian hissed.

Jansen hissed.

Dorian closed his eyes, and Jansen raised his body, then let himself slip back down slowly. This time, he took more of Dorian's many thick, hardened inches. There was no pain this time. Jansen didn't clench in fear. He was fully relaxed and wanted nothing more than to ride that glorious cock until they both came screaming.

25

THEY'D been lying in bed, Jansen's head on Dorian's chest with the dancer's arms around his waist. They were both staring at the TV, neither saying a word. A lot of weird feelings had been uncovered in those days and weeks and months after leaving the hospital, feelings Dorian wasn't exactly sure how to handle. Jansen aimlessly drew circles around Dorian's stomach with the tips of his fingers, calming, peaceful touches from one man to his lover.

Then someone had to knock on the damn door. Angelo said, "We gotta problem, boss."

"Fuck," Dorian muttered. "Of course we do." He turned his chest a little to get Jansen to raise his head. He didn't want Angelo seeing him—Mr. Hardcore Sadist—cuddled with anyone. Might take some of his "bite" away. "Well, come in, dumbass."

Jansen eased off the bed, thinking he'd give them some space to talk, but where the hell would he go? The bathroom? Screw it. He could hang out in the bathroom to avoid whatever conversation Angelo needed to have with his boss. He didn't want to hear the "problem" Angelo wanted to tell Dorian about, anyway.

"I'm gonna take a shower," Jansen said as he thumbed toward the door.

"This'll be quick, baby," Dorian said. "You don't have to go anywhere. I'll run his ass off."

"I feel icky. I really need a shower."

Dorian watched Jansen's naked body as he headed for the bathroom. Damn, he looked good: all muscles and tanned skin. He loved the way the dancer's perfect calves rolled and flexed as he walked. He said, "You don't have to go," just as the bedroom door opened.

Jansen palmed his crotch as his wide-eyed stare darted toward the door.

Dorian had no choice but to lay there with his shit all hanging out for Angelo to see. The ape turned his head and covered his eyes. Heat flooded Jansen's face as he rushed over to cover his lover's body with a blanket.

Dorian managed a "Thanks" before Jansen ducked into the bathroom. "It's safe now," Dorian said to Angelo. Wide-ass turned back around. "So, what's the fuckin' problem?"

Jansen had planned to hide in the shower, maybe let the water drown out the conversation in the bedroom, but curiosity killed him. He had to know what was going on, had to hear. He knew he would be disappointed with Dorian and probably disgusted, but he had to know. It was an obsessive-compulsive thing. He couldn't help it, and he found himself pressing his ear to the door.

At first, he couldn't hear much, just Angelo mumbling about business. Words, streams of jumbled noises in the sound of two angry, bassy voices, that's all he could hear. Well, if that wasn't disappointing. Then he heard one hell of a pissed off, "What the fuck?" from Dorian.

Jansen's back snapped bolt straight, ripping his head away from the door. As angry as Dorian sounded, Jansen had a feeling someone was going to meet their end in a not-so-pretty way.

"I swear before God, if I didn't have these casts on, I'd kill that motherfucker myself," Dorian growled.

The more Angelo told Dorian about Mr. Family Man, the more pissed off Dorian became and the more he wanted to bust out of those casts despite the docs telling him he wasn't ready. Apparently, the man he'd let go—the one with the wife and new baby—who had later come back and beat the dog shit out of him with his cousin—he had a brother who had connections.

Angelo said there was a hit on Dorian's head, good goddamn money too. "No worries, boss. We know this brother. We know where to find him."

"So why the fuck is he still breathin'? Kill the motherfucker."

Jansen stumbled away from the door, sank down on the toilet, and sulked. He scrubbed trembling hands over his face. His heart started to beat a little harder. Had he seriously just heard Dorian order a kill? Was Dorian really going to make Angelo murder someone? Jesus, would Angelo really do that? It all seemed pretty out-there, but not so far-fetched Jansen didn't believe it would happen.

Dorian lay stiff as a board on his bed, staring up at the ceiling with morbid, vacant eyes. He said, "If no one is around to pay the contract, then the deal is over, yeah?"

Angelo nodded. "I got a few bullets with his name on 'em. Dumbass put the word on the street and told one of my boys he was gonna have my boss whacked. What the fuck did he think would happen?"

"Man, I'd love to have a crack at his head. I'd put that son of a bitch in the ground myself."

The excitement and anger in Dorian's voice scared Jansen. His lover was seriously talking about ending someone's life. And there he was, spying on him like a damn fool. God, he was in over his head with this one. Maybe he needed to get out before the shit turned bad for him too.

Jansen went to the shower, started the water, and climbed inside. Every inch of his body started to tremble. He was afraid again. In the back of his mind, he knew Dorian wouldn't hurt him, not now, not while he could still stand being around him, but he couldn't help wondering how many people had once been the big guy's friends who happened to find an early grave at Grant's hand.

His back slid against the tiles until he sat in the bottom of the shower, hugging his own body. If he didn't, would the pieces tremble away and fall apart? Could he hold himself together? He was worried, genuinely worried, not only for his own safety, but Dorian's as well. Jansen's lover had a freaking contract on his head. Someone really wanted him dead.

AS ANGELO left the room, his last words were, "We'll get that son of a bitch, boss. Don't worry. Get back on your feet. Me and my boys will handle this shit."

Dorian nodded. There was one reason he tolerated Angelo's dumb ass: he knew the man would get the job done. He didn't need to look over his shoulder as long as he had Angelo behind him. For as many years as Dorian could remember, the man was always a step ahead of the enemy. Angelo had ears everywhere. He heard shit no one else heard.

And all would be peachy keen if Dorian himself could go out and just handle the one who had a hit on him. Who the hell did that crazy bastard think he was screwing with? Having his brother and cousin killed wasn't enough of a warning to him?

He settled back against the pillow. He was so pissed off he could feel his pulse pounding against his casts, which only pissed him off worse, of course. He needed the dancer to calm him down, but he could still hear the water running in the bathroom. It would be a minute before Jansen's sexy body popped out from behind the door. The best thing Dorian could do for himself was try to breathe and slow the shit down a bit.

Jansen killed the water, waited and listened for the deep rumble of Angelo's voice. He didn't hear him anymore, and Dorian wasn't screaming at the top of his lungs. It was safe again. Well, as safe as it could be around Dorian.

He dried his body, then wrapped the towel around his waist before going back into the bedroom, just in case Angelo was still there and he simply hadn't heard the big guy's deep baritone voice. He wasn't. Jansen silently thanked God for that little miracle.

When he stepped back into the bedroom, he couldn't bring himself to look at Dorian. Didn't know why exactly, he just knew he couldn't. He'd known the shit Dorian was into—or, at least he had an idea—before he'd ever signed up to be his....

What *exactly* was Jansen to him?

For Pete's sake, all this wondering and worrying would drive any sane person mad, he thought as he rubbed his fingers back and forth across his dampened brow. He went straight to the dresser, pulled out a pair of sleep pants, and had them halfway up his body when he heard Dorian say, "What are you doing?"

"Getting dressed."

Dorian's brow quirked and his face curled into a frown. "Why? You don't want to be naked with me anymore?" He watched Jansen turn around slowly; saw how his face had paled and how his hands shook, how Jansen looked completely terrified now. "What the fuck is wrong?"

Jansen flinched, tried to play it off as a shrug.

"Come here," Dorian said, fingers wiggling around the cast.

Jansen went to him. He didn't think twice about doing it. He just went and he climbed in bed beside his sadistic lover but kept a safe distance. Jansen crossed his arms over his chest, guarded.

"What's wrong with you?" Dorian asked again.

"Just… nothing. Nothing, I swear." Dorian looked over at Jansen. He knew better. The kid had been caught in a lie. And all Jansen could say was, "I heard… about the hit. Someone wants to kill you?"

Dorian's head rolled back. Sighing, he stared up at the ceiling, hating that he couldn't rub the aggravation off his face. "Yeah," he said in a flat voice. "Nothing new there, babe." But Jansen wasn't satisfied. His body stayed stiff. He didn't move any closer and didn't bother looking over. "Jansen, lie down, please. Don't do this distance shit with me."

"I'm afraid to get close to you."

"Why?"

"Because I'm afraid to care too much. Everything about you scares me."

"Baby, please lie down. Let's talk about this. Let's talk about me."

Jansen finally lay back against the bed, his head on Dorian's chest. His hand only lightly lay against his lover's heart. There was no nestling, no nuzzling or cuddling. The tension made it painfully obvious Jansen didn't want to be there, that he didn't want to touch Dorian. "I'm not gonna force ya to stay, if ya don't want to. I hope ya will, but I understand if ya don't."

"I don't like the idea of someone trying to kill you. I really don't like the idea of you being involved in all the crime. I mean, I knew what I was getting into… sort of, I guess. But it's still hard to hear, hard to know what goes on in your world."

Jansen finally forced himself to look up at Dorian. He finally had the courage to be honest. "I don't want you to wake up one day and decide you want me dead."

26

DORIAN couldn't exactly say he wasn't shocked by what Jansen had said. To think he'd ever want that beautiful, caring man dead. It was ridiculous. Insane. Completely over the fucking top! He didn't know what to say. His first instinct was to fly off the handle, start yelling curses at the top of his lungs. That's how Dorian reacted to everything, but what good would that have done? The kid was already scared of him, like going the hell off would make things better.

No, Jansen obviously wasn't thinking clearly. He obviously had no clue.

Or he's lost his fucking mind.

Shifting in the bed as much as the casts and his feeble limbs would let him, Dorian turned toward Jansen with a wince. His face curled in pain. He took a deep breath, let it go, and tried to relax his body again.

"Baby," Dorian said as he looked the dancer in his scared brown eyes, "I'm not gonna want ya dead. That shit, that side of my life has nothin' to do with ya, okay?"

He watched Jansen's Adam's apple bob as he swallowed. Jansen might've been nodding, silently telling Dorian he believed he wouldn't harm him or possibly kill him, but nothing about Jansen's body language backed up his soundless story.

"I promise," Dorian whispered. "You're safe with me."

Jansen stared, like his mind couldn't decide if it wanted to believe Dorian. His body had already decided to stay the hell away, and his stomach had become the knotted rope in that emotional tug of war.

Dorian's expression softened. He wiggled his fingers, batted his lashes, and melted Jansen's heart. The dancer laid his head back on

Dorian's chest. Every scant touch felt tense, forced even, like he was taking care—too much care—not to make any mistakes.

"Jansen?" Dorian whispered. The dancer lifted his head and stared up at him with a hard frown on his face. "If I tell you something, promise it won't leave this bed, okay?"

"I promise," Jansen breathed, gently rubbing his hand back and forth across Dorian's hard, bare abs.

Taking another slow, deep breath, Dorian arranged his racing thoughts. He licked his lips and said, "I don't like that part of my life. I wish I could wave a wand and make it go away, but the thing is, I can't. I don't have a choice."

Jansen looked up. Dorian's dark, empty eyes sent tingles down his spine.

"First," Dorian continued, "it was people screwin' Pops out of money or business. He would send Angelo and me out to 'take care' of the problem. We busted knees, ransacked a few businesses, that was it. Then someone put a contract out on my father's head. Pops wanted the bastard dead, and he told me if I didn't kill him, he'd kill me himself. My father and I didn't speak much after that. Not that we ever really had a relationship to begin with. I hated his fuckin' ass. But anyway, he put the fear of God in me. So, I did it. I killed the fucker—the uh, guy with the contract—and… well, I guess I never really had a desire or reason to stop. Seemed like the easiest way to solve a problem, ya know?" He shrugged his massive shoulders.

Dorian pressed his cheek to the top of Jansen's head. He wanted to touch him so bad, wanted to hold him so Jansen knew everything he was saying was truth and the dancer meant more to him than anyone had in a long time.

"I told myself, after you found me in the parkin' lot at Sin, then stayed by my side in the hospital, that I wanted to take care of you, like you did for me. I kinda wanted to make things safe for you. I wanted to keep ya around. Had Angelo not found out about the contract on my head, I…." Dorian closed his eyes, brushed his cheek over Jansen's head. His voice softened. "I didn't want to get ya mixed up in this shit. Baby, if I let that motherfucker live and someone picks up his contract, I'm gone. I'm dead. I can't keep ya safe if I'm dead."

Tears started to burn in Jansen's eyes. He touched his hand over Dorian's heart. Honestly, he wasn't sure what to say. He wanted to tell Dorian that he loved him and accepted him for everything he was. He wanted to tell him he'd been falling in love with him from the moment they met, but Dorian wasn't the kind of man to say shit like that to. He wasn't in a place where "love" was an option, not yet.

Jansen stroked his hand up and down the line of Dorian's chest. He pressed his lips to Dorian's pec, and the tears began to fall hard and fast. He saw their little droplets glisten on his lover's tanned, tattered, tattooed skin.

"I can't lie to you and say I'm not terrified. I am," Jansen said. "I'm scared of your temper, of your lifestyle. I'm absolutely fucking freaked, but part of me needs you. I need to be close to you, and I need to know you're okay. Maybe one day the fear will pass, but right now, that's the best I can give you."

Dorian instinctively tried to raise his arm so he could brush the tears from Jansen's cheek. "Goddamn cast," he muttered. See, that's why he got so pissed. Those assholes had immobilized him, and the one time he really wanted to hold and comfort someone, he couldn't. "I can accept that, Jansen. I know better than anyone that trust doesn't happen overnight." Dorian let out a hard sigh as he rolled his head back against his pillow. He had a burning, incessant need inside him to say something to Jansen, something that sounded a lot like "love," but he couldn't do it. He couldn't bring himself to say the word.

Fuck me.

He was being such a sap, and where in the hell had these *feelings* come from? What happened to being hard and not giving a shit?

"Look," Dorian said. "Just know you're safe here. As long as I'm here, you'll be safe. If anyone, and I do mean anyone, tries to fuck with you, they're dead. Period."

"Dorian, people mess with me. People have always messed with me and always will. I don't need some mafia-style hit man killing people to avenge me. And it's that very mentality that will keep you killing. Nothing is going to stop until you truly decide to change."

Jansen heard a low, rumbling growl in Dorian's chest. The sound made him tense again. "See! It's those kinds of responses that make me afraid of you. When I say something you don't like and you do the growling thing, I freak. I shouldn't freak. I should find that aggravation to be nothing more than an adorable part of who you are, but I don't. I think it's the beginnings of a death sentence."

"Baby, I'll never... *never* sign a 'death warrant' for you, I swear. You're all I have right now, and frankly, you're all I want, okay?"

"I want to start dancing again," Jansen said with his lips pressed to Dorian's chest and his body carefully woven around flesh and plastered legs.

The words stroked that nerve in Dorian's brain that made his eye twitch. Any kind of rational thought he might've had flew right the fuck out the window. Yeah, those few little words stroked that nerve in a major way. He tried to keep calm, but....

"I don't fuckin' think so," Dorian said, though the words were meant for his head only. What he'd planned to say wasn't so crass.

Jansen lifted his head from Dorian's chest. He arched a brow. It meant WTF without actually saying "What the fuck?"

"Why do you want to go back to that place?" Dorian asked as soon as the dancer's eyes met his.

"Um, maybe because I just want to," Jansen said as he hefted himself from the bed. "Not that I need to explain, but I need to do something with my life, and I make enough money at the club to put myself through school."

Dorian frowned. It was times like this Jansen wished he knew what Dorian was thinking. The guy was almost impossible to read unless he was pissed off.

"Okay," Dorian said with a slight nod. "I get wanting to go to school, wanting to do something with your life, but you don't need to work at the club to do it. I can afford to put you through Ivy League schools for the rest of your life, if that's what you want to do."

He watched Jansen pace back and forth at the foot of the bed. The kid's face gave nothing away. To the left. To the right. Back and forth. He kept pacing without saying a damn word. Dorian was already a ball of raw nerves, and this silent march wasn't helping.

Jansen turned the TV off and the lights on. The sudden brightness made the big man's eyes burn. He had to blink a few times before squinting even allowed him to see just how frustrated Jansen was with him.

"I don't want you to pay for my school. I want to earn it on my own. I want to do this for myself."

"You're being ridiculous," Dorian said, which flew all over Jansen the wrong way.

It wasn't ridiculous. He'd always taken care of himself. He'd always earned everything. That didn't need to change now. What if Dorian decided to toss his ass? Jansen wasn't so blinded by infatuation that he couldn't feel that day coming. He'd been with Dorian for months now, had pretty much fallen head over heels for him, and Dorian was still as cold as the day they'd left the hospital together. Sure, he admitted he cared, but beyond that, it was sex and silence and Jansen taking care of him.

"It's not ridiculous, and I'm going to do it."

"The fuck you are, not like that. If you want to earn the money, fine, but not in that club, you're not. I'll be damned."

Jansen crossed his arms over his bare chest and opened his mouth to say something, when a knock at the door stopped him.

It was Angelo. "Got bad news, boss."

Of fucking course, he did. Jansen rolled his eyes, stormed toward the door, and wrenched the damn thing open. He shoved past Angelo, feet pounding down the hall.

"God damn it," Dorian bit out beneath his breath. "Ya couldn't give me ten fuckin' minutes, could ya?" Angelo shrugged and stepped into the bedroom, closing the door behind him. "Can ya at least help me sit up?"

Dorian's mammoth of a security guard came to the bed, hooked his hands under his boss's arms, and lifted his body so he could lean against the pillows. "So what? What's the bad news this time?"

"The contractor who wants your head, apparently he knew you'd be looking for him, and he bailed. Word is, the contract has some damn good money on it. He wants you bad, boss."

Big fucking shocker there.

"Double it," he said. "Whatever the price of the contract is, double it. I want that one."

27

JANSEN stomped all the way down the stairs and out to the back patio of Dorian's mansion, grumbling curses with every exaggerated footfall. *How dare that man try to tell someone how to run their lives? He could barely manage his own!*

Slamming the French door behind him, he stomped toward the lounge and pulled up a chair. He fished a lighter and a pack of Camel Lights from his pocket. That pesky smoking habit still reared its nasty little head from time to time. He wasn't *really* a smoker, but he'd picked it back up since he'd been with, or near, or… whatever with Dorian. That man had a way of working Jansen's nerves. He loved him, God help him, he did. And yeah, that made him a glutton, but he couldn't help it.

Seriously, how dare Dorian tell him where he could and couldn't work?

Who the hell does he think he is?

That jealous, possessive bullshit wasn't going to work. He couldn't stand it and wouldn't put up with it.

He took one long drag after another from the cig, let the pissed off well up until it nearly boiled over. Part of him wanted to leave, wanted to go back to Jason's place and start living the life he'd become accustomed to. It might've been a crap life with shitty food and shitty accommodations, but at least it was his. At least he'd earned it honestly.

Then he had the part of him that wouldn't stop screaming for him to run back to Dorian, to accept that man and all his faults, love him, and be there for him. That part beat inside his chest and warmed every time he saw Dorian's face or heard his voice. That part yearned for the man Dorian Grant was deep inside his soul, not the façade he hid behind.

"Hey," Angelo's thick voice called from behind him. "Boss wants you."

"'Boss' can kiss my ass," Jansen said.

A huge shadow suddenly blocked out the sun that had been burning his eyes. It was Angelo, standing over him with his arms crossed and a tic in his jaw. "Watch it, boy," he said. "I'd choose your words a little fuckin' better, if ya know what's good for ya."

"And what are you gonna do?"

"You might not always be a protected asset," Angelo said with a disgusted snarl as he leaned in closer. "Now," he began again, "get your ass upstairs before I drag you up there."

DORIAN'S jaw clenched as he stared up at the ceiling. Two million dollars. Two. Mother. Fucking. Million. Dollars. He'd just agreed to pay that heinously huge amount for someone to bring him the head of the son of a bitch who wanted him dead. On top of all of that, he'd pissed Jansen off just because he didn't want *his* dancer in that nasty-ass club. It wasn't merely jealousy—partly, but not entirely. Jansen had it wrong. If someone like Dorian could be beaten within an inch of his life, what the fuck could happen to the kid?

The bedroom door slammed. Dorian rolled his eyes toward the commotion. "Don't start like this," he said as calmly as he could. "Let's talk about this for a minute."

"Talk about what?" Jansen bit out, slinging his arms into the air. "How you want to control my life? You don't own me, Dorian. We're not even fucking together! I live here and take care of you. Right? That's all I am, right?"

"Goddammit!" Dorian slammed his cast-covered arm down on the bed. It hurt. He deserved that painful reminder to watch his temper. "Why? Because I haven't told ya that I love you? Ya think ya don't mean shit to me? Is that what's goin' on? I fuckin' told ya I needed time with this shit. I fuckin' warned ya, didn't I?"

Jansen rolled his eyes, crossed his arms over his chest, and looked away. Dorian had made him feel like he was being completely childish, and he knew better. He wasn't. Dorian had no right to tell him where he could and couldn't work. He didn't want to be anyone's kept boy. He could take care of himself, had been doing a fine job all these years. There was no need to stop now, right?

Without being able to look at his mysterious new love interest, whether it was for being pissed off or utterly in love, Jansen finally said, "I'm leaving. I'm going to go back to my house. We both seem to need a little time and space, because this isn't working anymore."

"What the fuck do you mean 'this isn't workin'?'" Dorian tried to sit up in the bed. The damn casts made it impossible to move. The absolute discontent was clearly written all over his face. He growled out a thunderous, "Fuck!" Then he stopped, sighed, and lowered his voice. "Come here, please."

He let out a hard breath as he pressed his head against the pillow. It was the only thing he could do with his aggravation. He wanted so badly to wipe the tired from his eyes, but he couldn't. He couldn't stand up and go to the man walking out of his life. Dorian couldn't hold him and ask him not to go. He couldn't do shit, and if his mood wasn't bad enough, that made it worse.

"Will you please come here? Please?" Dorian begged with the last of his patience.

This time, Jansen didn't go to him. He stood at the foot of the bed with his arms crossed over his chest and stared down at him. He knew the shit Dorian was going through, and yeah, it might've been a lame move to leave him when he needed someone the most, but Jansen couldn't take it anymore. The smothering, possessive, jealous, controlling bullshit was too much. The sudden mood swings were too much. The threats to Dorian's life were too much. Jansen cared too damn much, and if he didn't get out now, he knew this relationship would destroy him.

"You're not going to change my mind, Dorian. I need to leave. I need to do this for me, because if I don't do it now, I might never do it. I need to take care of myself. I need to have control of my own life. I need to be on that stage dancing in the limelight, not someone's submissive shadow."

"I'm not askin' ya to be my fuckin' shadow!" Dorian growled. He didn't mean for the words to come out like that, but he was about to go insane in that bed with those damn casts, and the only person he'd cared about since his mom stood there threatening to walk out on him. "Don't go. Just stay here and let me take care of you. I don't mind. I have the money. You don't have to dance."

"You don't get it. I love dancing. I love being on stage—"

"You love fuckin' men in that club," Dorian interrupted.

Jansen's heart sunk down into his feet.

"Admit it. That's why ya want to go back. That's how ya picked me up. What, now that I am all broken and helpless and shit ya want to move onto the next sucker in line? Fine. Whatever."

It felt like Dorian had just driven a spear straight through Jansen's heart. It sucked the life and the wind and the hard resolve right out of him. "That shit hurt," he said in a soft, defeated tone. He went straight to the closet and grabbed the bag he'd brought with him, furiously stuffed the few clothes he had inside of it. He didn't bother folding anything, didn't give a shit if anything was a wrinkled mess when he got home. He just needed to get out of there… now!

With a sigh, Dorian hung his head and closed his eyes. He knew he'd just messed up the best thing that ever happened to him; and all because he'd let feelings he wouldn't admit make him jealous and insecure.

"I'm sorry, Jansen." It took a lot, but Dorian managed to hold out an arm for him. The pain tore through his broken limb and into his chest, but he did his best not to let it show. "Please, come here. Talk to me."

For a long, uncomfortable moment, their eyes met in a showdown of steely-eyed stares. Who would look away? Who had the strongest will? Who was wrong and who was right?

Jansen dropped his arms to his sides, jaw clenching. He took a deep breath, then let it go slowly. Finally he said, "What *exactly* do you want from me? Better yet, what do you expect? You want me to be your lap dog, your boy toy?" Tears filled Jansen's dark brown eyes. He tried like hell to blink them away so Dorian wouldn't see how much he truly cared, but he couldn't. Maybe Dorian needed to see it. Maybe he needed to know just how much Jansen felt for him and how badly this hurt. Dorian needed to know how terrified he was.

Eyes cast downward, Jansen said in a soft, broken voice, "You want me to sit around here and blindly pretend half of New Orleans doesn't want to see you dead?"

"Baby," Dorian implored, "please sit down with me so we can talk about this. Don't storm out of here because you're mad at me. Can ya give me that? Can ya give me a chance?"

Jansen slowly approached him and laid his hand over Dorian's cast-covered palm as he sat down on the edge of the bed. His gaze didn't shift back to his battered lover. If it did, Jansen's will would've broken, and he might give in to everything Dorian wanted or required. His heart would take over.

Dorian wiggled his fingers against Jansen's palm. He knew—God help him—he knew the pain showed in his eyes. It wasn't just the physical pain, but the emotional pain of knowing how bad he'd hurt the man who had seriously complicated his life… in a not-so-bad way.

"I didn't mean that shit, Jansen, I swear I didn't. I'm fucked up. I'm in a fucked up place right now, and I know that's a lame excuse, but it's true. I want to give ya everything ya could possibly want or need." Jansen finally looked back at him. Dorian's gaze searched his face. "I want to be able to tell ya I love you, but I can't. I don't know if I am capable of love, but by God, if there is anyone who comes close, it's you. Don't walk out on me. I know I keep askin' for chances and patience and time, but I really need it."

Jansen wanted to give him time and patience. He really wanted to be the one to bring Mr. Sadistic out of the hell he lived in. Jansen wanted to give him some sort of happiness, but he was seriously beginning to believe he wasn't the one who could fix him. Dorian Grant was too far gone to be saved.

"I thought I could, Dorian. I thought I could stay and put up with your shit and wait it out until things got better, but I'm either not strong enough or too strong to be under your thumb. I'm not saying I don't want to be with you, that there's no future for us. I'm saying I can't do this right now. I'm saying I need some space, and you need to realize you can trust me, that we're equals."

Dorian ripped his arm away from Jansen's hand as best as he could with the casts. "Well, what are ya waitin' for? Get the fuck out of my house," he said, filling his voice with all the false hatred he could find. It was hard. What Dorian felt for the dancer was far from hate, but no way in hell would he let Jansen know how much his leaving hurt his soul. He couldn't let him see that pain.

Tearing up from the edge of the bed, Jansen let out a low, aggravated growl, then went back to shoving his shit into the bag. He didn't say a word. His heart broke more and more with every item he crammed into that horrible little testament to how lame his life had turned out. He loved Dorian, more than he should have, but sometimes it was just better to walk away.

He hoisted the bag on his shoulder, then started for the door, but something stopped him. He turned around and looked at Dorian one last time. "Despite what you believe, I love you. I'm in love with you whether you can love me or not. Walking away from you isn't easy, but it's something I have to do for me. I only hope one day you'll understand, and maybe one day, you'll be able to love me too. Until then, we're both better off this way."

Jansen waited for a moment, hoping Dorian would say something to make him change his mind, but he didn't. Dorian didn't even open his eyes, didn't open his mouth, didn't ask Jansen to stay. That's how Jansen knew—beyond a shadow of doubt—he'd made the right decision.

Leaving the room he'd lived in for months felt like walking the final mile of his life. He took the last steps toward his heart's death sentence, knowing the pain of leaving the man who'd slammed into his life and stolen his heart would be indefinite. It took everything he had not to run back and throw himself at Dorian's mercy. It took every ounce of willpower in his soul not to beg Dorian to love him back. And when he left Dorian Grant's mansion, he swore it would be for good. God simply didn't make the kind of miracles it would take to turn the sadistic, narcissistic Mr. Grant around.

28

MONTHS had passed since Dorian saw Jansen. It seemed like a lifetime ago since they met, since Jansen had stormed out of his home and out of his life. He lay back against the passenger seat of his Mercedes sedan. Angelo had driven him back to the hospital to finally get the last two casts removed: one leg and one arm. The other limbs had healed, and Dorian had been doing physical therapy pretty regularly, but all that seemed to do was wear him down and piss him off.

Something had to give.

Something had to change before he lost his damn mind.

"I wanna see if he's at the club," Dorian said without looking over at Angelo.

Meathead knew exactly who his boss was talking about without having to ask silly questions. Jansen was a subject they religiously avoided. The excessive coke habit Dorian had picked up was another. Unfortunately, drugs had been his only way of numbing all the bullshit away. He couldn't escape it any other way. The shit they gave him for the pain had stopped working a long damn time ago, and without Jansen there to occupy his time, he had nothing.

"Ya think that's wise, boss?"

"I don't fuckin' pay ya to ask questions. I pay ya to do what the fuck you're told. Now, shut up and do what I said."

"Alright, then," Angelo said as he shook his head.

He took a hard right, then turned down Decatur, past Jackson Square and the drunken tourists stumbling around the French Quarter. Then he headed straight into the warehouse district. Sin & Seduction was the first big building on the right once they rounded the corner.

Luckily, the owners had been smart and put it far enough away from the Quarter that it hadn't become a tourist trap.

Dorian hated tourists.

The valet lifted his eyes, expression perking up a bit as soon as the Mercedes pull to the curb. He opened the door to the sleek black sedan and greeted Dorian with a smile. "Mr. Grant," he said as he hooked his arm in offering. "It's been a while."

It was considerate and maybe even genuine, but that didn't stop the big guy from snapping. "Back the fuck off. I'm not helpless," he growled as he white-knuckled the cane he'd been forced to use since the first leg cast had been removed. The other door slammed, and Dorian's head whipped back. "You ain't goin' in there," he barked at Angelo. "You wait right here. If I come down and you're gone, it's your ass."

That flew all over Angelo, but he wouldn't say a damn word. He'd stand there like a good little puppy, because he knew if he didn't, Dorian had enough money and enough connections—since he didn't have the strength right now—to end him.

Dorian hobbled up the stairs to the VIP section. The bouncer gave him a smile and a nod as he removed the velvet rope. "Good to see you again, Mr. Grant."

Dorian nodded.

Nothing in the club had changed, not that he'd honestly expected it to. His table was still there, cleaner than it had ever been, just waiting for its old, reliable friend to return. The dancers were the same, average and not what he'd come looking for. Sometimes he wondered why he ever darkened the door of that place. Or was he just being a grumpy-ass old man who saw fault in everything because nothing had been right since his dancer had left him?

Yeah, the latter was probably right.

Finally, the waiter brought his regular bottle of Johnny Walker Blue. "Just like old times," he muttered with a devious grin as he watched the half-naked waiter set down his bottle, the glass, and a few white bar napkins. With a hard, unwavering stare, Dorian watched the muscles flex beneath the kid's tan body. Sure, he was hot, and Dorian had always been the kind of man who appreciated physical beauty, but some ass-kissing waiter wasn't the reason he'd gone out.

The kid started back toward the bar.

"Hey," Dorian said, giving a two finger wave to call his eager friend back. "Is Sweet Heat dancing tonight?"

The guy nodded. He said the dancer would be on the stage in about twenty minutes.

"Good."

Reaching in his pocket, Dorian pulled out a stogie and a bag of powder. He dumped a little pile on the table, then cut three lines through the granules. He stared down at those three thick, white, mouth-watering lines and bit his teeth together. His nose curled as he took a swig from the bottle. Then he took a puff off the stogie before snorting back two lines like they were nothing.

He laid his head back against the leather booth. The lights flashed in their same red, blue, and green. Fog filled the air. Smoke wafted up from his hundred-dollar Cuban cigar. He let the bass from the music below pound his senses while he embraced one fucked up cocktail of depressants and speed. God, that was a heady mix, but it did exactly what he needed it to. He didn't feel a damn thing, not the throbbing in his legs or the pain in his heart.

Then he heard Jansen's song start. Dorian leaned forward and snorted that last line. He rubbed his hand over his nose to wipe away the evidence, then steepled his arms on the table so he could watch for his dancer to make an entrance.

Jansen sauntered onto the stage, looking a hundred times more confident than he had been the first few times Dorian saw him dance. The crowd cheered his name as he ripped away his clothes. He wore the same gold G-string he'd apparently become famous for. Dorian had a moment of weakness. He wondered if he could send a note down to him, invite him up to the booth, and start all over again.

Nah, fuck that. Dorian had messed up. He'd have to enjoy the view from the darkness.

Jansen ground himself against the pole. His muscles flexed and curled as his hips rolled. Sweat glistened in the spotlight. Sweet Heat fisted his own chocolate-colored hair, biting down on his bottom lip as he stalked around the pole and to the edge of the stage. The music stopped. Everyone screamed. And with the first sonic boom of the bass, he dropped to his knees, thrusting his cock out for all the eager hands.

"So fuckin' confident." Dorian laughed. A smirk fell over his face. He licked his lips, keeping his eyes trained on the dancer. "So fuckin' hot."

The longer he watched Jansen slam his cock against the air and all those begging hands, the harder his own business started to throb. Fuck, he wanted to be inside him, stroking that perfectly rounded ass until they both came. He wanted to spend hours filling the kid's body with warmth, feeling the kid's warmth.

Dorian reached down and grabbed a handful. He was rock hard already and wanted Jansen's hand to be there instead of his own, rubbing until he shot his load into the curl of the dancer's fisted fingers. He wanted to watch Jansen make him come.

He fumbled with the zipper of his designer jeans. The fly fell open, relieving the pressure against his hardened shaft and tightened sac. Dorian slipped his hand inside his pants and gripped his cock hard, slowly stroking. It wasn't the same, but damn, if he kept watching that sexy-ass dancer work his shit all over the stage like that, it would be close enough to the fantasy to do the job.

He curled his fingers, waving them over his shaft as he picked up the pace, stroking faster and faster. He almost met the club music's hundred and eighty beats per minute. Dorian was going at it pretty hard when Jansen's eyes shifted up to the booth. The dancer had done that a few times. It seemed like they were searching for each other, but they knew getting together again was a bad idea. Dorian also knew he appeared to be nothing more than a black, empty silhouette to Jansen's eyes, but Jansen never looked away. It was like Jansen knew Dorian was there, watching, getting off to his dance.

Just as the music started to wind down, Dorian's cock pulsed harder and his sac tightened more. Pressure built at the base, then started easing down to the head. He bit down harder on his bottom lip as his shaft thickened against his palm. Jansen blew a kiss in his direction, and Dorian came, nutted all over his own damn hand.

His heart raced. His head felt like it was going to explode. Dorian's high was hitting its peak, and somehow he'd managed to suck down half the bottle of JW Blue. But at least he felt good, better than he had in awhile. Tonight, Dorian could go home and maybe sleep… for a change.

Raking his hand over the napkins the waiter had brought with his bottle, Dorian gave the stage one last look. It was do or die now. Call the dancer up to his booth or go home.

He tucked his spent business away, then zipped his pants with a disappointed sigh. He'd let it go tonight. Now just wasn't the time.

Dorian grabbed that stupid damn cane and started for the door. He wobbled, stumbled, jerked back and forth. The bouncer had to keep him from falling on his face. He said, "I gotcha, Mr. Grant," and this time, Dorian let someone help. He wasn't so stupid to think he was invincible. Last thing he needed to do was tumble down the stairs and end up back in casts.

They made it to the bottom of the steps, where Angelo waited like a good little lapdog. "Get me the fuck outta here," Dorian barked, and of course, Angelo did without hesitation.

Dorian climbed into the car. He let his head sink back against the headrest. Then he felt the phone in his pocket vibrate. It was Jansen. The text said, "I miss you."

Fuck me.

Dorian missed him too.

29

JANSEN knew Dorian had been there, at Sin & Seduction, watching him dance. He couldn't make out his face, but he did see the outline of a body he'd become well familiar with, that he was damn sure of. Jansen knew when he saw the figure lean forward as he stepped to the edge of the stage; it was Dorian keeping an eye on him. He half expected a little green slip of paper to be handed to him backstage, but it never came. Something about that moment of waiting for Dorian, and him never sending for Jansen, broke the dancer's heart.

In all those months they'd been apart, Jansen had never stopped loving him, never stopped thinking about him. Men had requested private dances, all of which Jansen had respectfully declined. It didn't hurt his reputation or make him any less desirable. If anything, they tried harder, offered more money. They all wanted to see "Sweet Heat" up close and personal, but he only had eyes for one man.

And that man had walked out without even saying hello.

So, of course, Jansen couldn't let it go. He sent the elusive Mr. Grant a text telling him only that he missed him. God, did he miss him. He wanted to be close to Dorian again, wanted everything to be perfect between them. But those were silly daydreams. He knew the kind of man Dorian was, and he knew they would never have a relationship, not until Dorian decided to make the first move.

By falling for the one man he felt pretty certain he'd never have, he'd set himself up for heartbreak. Pain had become as natural as breathing, and the only drug that would take that pain away had just walked out of the club without so much as a "hello."

Jansen stared down at his phone, waiting for a text from his beloved Mr. Grant. His thumb brushed back and forth across the screen as though he could conjure the words he wanted to see. Jason had pulled up beside him, and apparently he'd been so lost, he hadn't heard the rattle of his roommate's old beater car.

Jason honked the horn, then yelled from the opened passenger window, "You coming?"

Jansen's head darted up, and he choked out a soft, "Yeah."

Climbing into Jason's car, Jansen kept his phone in his hand. He occasionally checked for messages he sort of knew would never come. Pathetic. Truly freaking pathetic, but he couldn't help who he'd fallen in love with. He couldn't help the unrelenting need in his heart, and he couldn't explain it either. Maybe he really was a glutton for punishment.

"You got class in the morning?" Jason asked. As if bringing up something that didn't revolve around Dorian Grant would take away the morose attitude Jansen had been rocking.

"No. Well, I do, but I don't need to be there. Comp One, people are reading their shitty stories. I'd rather not go through the torture."

"I hear ya. What are you waiting for?" Jason asked, nodding down at the phone.

"A miracle, I guess." Jason's brow quirked. He wouldn't stop looking over. If Jansen didn't confess something, his best friend would pry. That's just how Jason was. "Dorian was at the club tonight. He watched my dance, then left. He didn't even invite me to his booth."

"Did you think he would?"

Not really. But he'd hoped he would. Jansen shrugged. "I don't know. I miss him, man. I mean, I really fucking miss him, more than I should. For all the bullshit, life with him was… it was good."

"So why don't you call him?"

"You don't call men like Dorian. That makes you clingy and needy, and men like Dorian don't appreciate needy and clingy. He likes his solitude. He likes being a loner. It works for him, I guess."

Jansen turned his head away and stared out of the passenger window. The guy could never hide his emotions well, and the last thing he needed was Jason seeing how upset he was. He would handle this mess in his own time, in his own way. He didn't need his best friend nudging him along.

That night, when Jansen climbed into bed, he pulled a pillow into his arms and buried his face against the balled heap. He imagined Dorian there with him, holding him, loving him and being loved by him. Jansen cried seemingly endless tears into that pillow while he fought the urge to text Dorian again.

In the back of his mind, he'd accepted that he and Dorian would probably never be together. He'd accepted that Dorian could never love him, and the stronger, less selfish side of him hoped and prayed Dorian found someone who would love him for him, someone who could accept him the way he was and take all the bullshit he dished out. Jansen apparently wasn't the one, and knowing that—truly accepting that—broke a little piece of his soul.

Eyes fluttering, he fought off sleep as he white-knuckled the cell phone, hoping and praying for something, anything, even if it was a "Fuck off!" or "I don't want to see you anymore."

The phone vibrated, and when he looked down and saw Dorian's name, his heart stopped. The text said, "I miss you too."

30

DURING the last class of the day, Jansen sat twirling a pen between his lips and daydreaming of a life he doubted he would ever have. It was perfect; living with Dorian in a home they'd chosen together. Jansen had actually become a journalist who spent his free time dancing in small, local productions of classics, not filthy nightclubs. Dorian had stopped killing and ran his businesses like an honest man. They were both so damn happy, and when Dorian's big brown eyes looked Jansen's way, they held nothing but adoration.

Dorian finally said, "I love you."

Of course, Jansen said it back.

The scraping of metal legs against linoleum tore Jansen away from his perfect dream, back to the bleak reality of the life he had now. So, what was he left with? They had both admitted they missed each other. Whoopty-fucking-do. Where did that leave them? They were both too stubborn to take the first step, although it might have been Jansen's place to do so, since he had been the one to leave.

He fished the phone from his pocket and punched out a simple text to Dorian. "I want to see you."

Assuming Dorian wouldn't respond right away, Jansen shoved the phone back in his pocket, but no sooner than he had, it started to vibrate. He got that hand shaking, palm sweating, heart fluttering rush of excitement even before he read the message. And part of him was too afraid to look, afraid Dorian might not want to see him.

Jansen looked down at the phone and a smile spread across his face.

"Come to the house," Dorian had responded from the comfort of his satin-covered bed, which had now been moved back into his room even though the stairs still kicked his ass.

His body ached from that sadistic physical therapist he'd hired. If that asshole didn't watch it, Dorian was going to break his nose first, then fire his ass just to add salt to the wound. The guy had been pushing him hard, damn hard, and Dorian Grant wasn't the kind of man who showed weakness, even at the sacrifice of his own body.

Dorian Grant hated weakness.

"Maria," he called out as he eased up from the bed. Clenching the cane tight, he put most of his weight onto it. He wanted to get down to the hot tub and let the heated jets beat against his tense muscles. The housekeeper came running. She looked up the staircase and her steely brown *madre loca* eyes locked on him. She put her hands on her hips and pinched her lips.

Dorian asked softly, "Can ya just stay close? Don't wanna try the stairs alone."

Maria muttered something in Spanish as she climbed the stairs. She stood by him, matching each step he took. They made it about halfway down until Dorian had to stop. It was too much, too fast. He leaned against the wall and took a few deep breaths. His legs quivered and his chest burned. He didn't know if he'd be able to make it down another flight already, but Dorian Grant wasn't a quitter.

"Fuck it. Let's do this." He gripped the handrail and took the steps one at a time.

As soon as he hit the bottom step, the phone vibrated again. The text from Jansen read, "You sure that's a good idea?"

Well, fuckin' duh!

Dorian dialed the dancer's number, put the phone to his ear, and waited for him to answer.

Jansen finally said a quiet, "Hello?"

"Ya wanna see me. I wanna see you. Why would comin' to my house be a bad idea?"

"I don't know. It's not neutral territory? You're my weakness?" Jansen said nervously. An equally nervous laugh followed as he raked his fingers through his windblown hair. He'd started across the parking lot of the campus, heading for the public bus stop, eyes shifting about, looking to see if anyone was watching. "But I *have* to see you. I miss you... a lot."

"Where are ya?" Dorian asked. "I'll send the car."

Jansen's heart jumped, fingers shaking as he tried to hold the phone. "At school. Just got out of my last class."

"Perfect. I assume ya don't have to work tonight."

"No, I have a couple nights off."

"Even better. My driver will bring you back to my place. I'll be in the hot tub."

Dorian hung up the phone, looked over at Maria, and said, "Send the car to the community college. I want Jansen brought here. Tell the driver to take him anywhere he needs. If he wants food, it's on me. But bring him here after."

Maria nodded.

He went out to the hot tub, stripped away every inch of clothing he had on, and lowered himself down into the water. The sore muscles started to relax. His heart and mind even calmed. Somehow, he'd make this better for Jansen. He'd figure out a way to take care of him and make him happy, even if he died trying. That, Dorian could vow to himself, because being away from Jansen hurt more than any broken bones could ever hurt.

31

STEPPING to the French doors that led out to the patio where Dorian had been relaxing in his hot tub, Jansen's gaze collided with the most drool-worthy thing he'd ever seen. Dorian's arms spread wide, like muscled wings resting against the tub's edge. His head lay back, thick chocolate hair in moist, messy sprigs. The setting sun painted the curves of his body a perfect shade of gold.

My God!

Jansen's mouth watered at the sight of him. His pulse raced at the idea of being near him again. He was still so madly in love with that man and honestly didn't have the first clue why. Seriously, what had Dorian Grant done to deserve his heart? It wasn't like he earned or asked for it. The dancer had just given it to him without thought of consequence or fear of repercussion.

He gently closed the French doors behind him.

"Hey," Dorian said without lifting his head.

Jansen couldn't take another step. Hell, he could barely take a deep breath. In his wildest dreams, he never thought he would be back in this place, with this man. He never thought Dorian would take him back, not after the way he'd acted.

"Hey," he finally said, after a long moment of uncomfortable silence.

Dorian turned in the hot tub, looked up and grinned. "No more casts," he said, waving a dripping hand in the air. "Still have to do therapy, but I can... kinda get around on my own."

Standing there, hugging himself like a starstruck fool, Jansen kept his distance. He acted like he was still terrified of being close to Dorian, and Dorian knew he deserved that. He was an asshole, and he'd been the bad guy. He'd treated Jansen like shit, but couldn't people change? Could he not be reformed, or something like that?

Dorian eased out of the hot tub, grabbed the cane, and started toward him. His dancer closed the distance between them, reaching out to offer help. "I can make it," Dorian said in a low voice.

Jansen dropped his hands and bowed his head slightly.

Dorian took a few more steps, reached out and gripped Jansen's chin. Their soft stares met, and all the confidence the big guy had broken into a million little pieces like a mirror that had been slammed against the ground, because the truth was too hard to face.

Licking his lips, Dorian lowered his head. In a soft voice, he said, "I'm a bastard, Jansen. I know I am. And I know I don't deserve you, but I'd like another chance, if you'll let me."

It was the same lip service Dorian had given Jansen a thousand times before. "Be patient." "Give me a chance." He'd run out of chances. Despite loving that man with every inch of his being, the patience well had run dry. He knew he couldn't stop loving that hard-nosed, narcissistic, utterly gorgeous piece of work, but damn it, he could put up a good fight... or maybe he couldn't.

Jansen took a deep breath and lowered his eyes. "As long as you can accept me dancing at Sin & Seduction," he said in a calm voice. "As long as you let me take care of myself and give me the space I need when I ask for it, I think I can give you a chance."

Pressing his lips to Jansen's forehead, Dorian leaned his wet, naked, utterly gorgeous, utterly desirable body against him, and Jansen wrapped his arms around his lover's waist. It felt so undeniably good to have Dorian in his arms again. It felt even better to have Dorian hug him back.

"Thank you," Dorian finally said, though his voice sounded strained. He lowered his head and tightened his arms around Jansen's body.

This time, it was Jansen who lifted Dorian's head. He looked him in the eyes as their lips pressed together. Dorian's tongue slipped inside his mouth, eyes closed as Dorian splayed his hand over the small of Jansen's back and held them together.

For the first time in his life, Dorian felt like he was floating, like—no shit—ascending to heaven and all that romantic crap. It was something he never expected to feel, something he never thought would come true for him. He never imagined having a happily ever anything in his future, but Jansen seemed to make the impossible... possible. He was falling for Jansen, or maybe he *had* fallen for him.

He broke the kiss, grabbed Jansen's hand, and placed it over his own heart. "I feel you here. While you were gone, I felt empty. If that's what it means to be in love with someone, then I... I think I'm in love with you."

Jansen's eyes widened, heart pounding harder. "Did you... just say you were... in love with me?"

"I think I did." Dorian gave him a nervous smile.

Jansen covered his gaping mouth with his shaking hand. A tear hit his cheek. He couldn't believe his ears, couldn't believe that Dorian Grant—of all people—had finally used the big, bad "L" word. It was his best dream and worst fear wrapped up in one beautiful gift.

He threw his arms around Dorian's neck, and the poor guy hissed as they stumbled backward. Jansen locked his lips over Dorian's, kissing him with every ounce of passion he had in his soul.

"Dorian Grant, I love you. God, help me, I do."

With a stupid grin stretched across Dorian's face, he held his sexy dancer with one arm as he reached up with the other and thumbed the tear from Jansen's cheek. Being close to Jansen again was incredible. Being able to hold his sweet and caring lover was the most amazing thing Dorian had felt in a long fucking time, and he wasn't even high. Dorian wanted to be sober whenever he saw Jansen from now on. He wanted to make sure everything he felt was real and not some drug-induced trance that made him love everyone he looked at. No, these things he felt, they were all Jansen, and that's the way he wanted to keep it.

"I want to make love to you... under the stars," Dorian said, but his gruff Cajun voice didn't quite have the airy, whimsical romantic affect.

Jansen stifled a tiny laugh.

32

"'MAKE love'?" Jansen grinned. Dorian could tell Jansen was still fighting the urge to snicker. And when Jansen spoke again, his voice quivered with restrained laughter. "'Under the stars', huh?"

"Isn't that romantic or something, the kinda shit guys like you want?"

"Guys like me?"

Dorian nodded. A goofy half smile curled his lips. That smile had a way of melting Jansen's heart. He brushed his thumbs back and forth across Jansen's knuckles, slowly easing him closer to the hot tub with every soft stroke.

"Yeah," Jansen said in a low, breathy voice. A dreamy-eyed smile parted his plump pink lips. "Romantic... or something. What every guy *like me* wants."

Dorian kept his fascinated brown stare on the man holding his hand, then let his gaze wander down his dancer's body, down the ratty, green T-shirt that clung to every mound and ridge of Jansen's nicely kept chest. It kept winding down to the preppy-chic, factory-faded jeans that hugged Jansen's slender thighs and flared a little below the knees.

With a guttural growl and a primal reaction to a near-explosive desire, Dorian reached out and ripped away his dancer's shirt. One hand splayed at the small of his lover's back while his lips and teeth toyed with the smooth flesh at the curve of Jansen's delicious neck.

Dorian tenderly caressed the firm expanse of Jansen's utterly kissable chest with his strong fingers, then worked his way down to the zipper of Jansen's mall-bought denims. Jansen gave a little wiggle, and the jeans slid down to his ankles. He'd gone without underwear today, and damn if that didn't make Dorian's cock give a little twitch. He looked down at their hardening erections, both reaching out for a touch. And when he looked back up, Jansen was eyeing him with that same voracious gleam in his eyes.

But God, Dorian was so gorgeous: all hard, tattooed, muscled body. The few scars he had here and there only added to the wonderment of the complete package. Despite the weakness Dorian saw in himself, Jansen saw strength—both physical and emotional—in ways Jansen knew he would never be.

Dorian sat down in the water, then pulled the delicate dancer down to his lap. Bare flesh to bare flesh, nothing but a thin sheet of bubbling water separated their bodies.

Jansen straddled his thighs, hands cradling either side of Dorian's neck. "You're so hot," he breathed against his lover's moist cheek.

"Hot, huh? Hot for you, baby." Dorian leaned forward. Warm water splashed up between them. "Ya gonna relax for me?" he whispered as he reached down. He brushed his hand over Jansen's cock, over his sac, reaching further down to his lover's warm, puckered opening. Dorian slipped one finger inside, and Jansen moaned. "Kiss me and I'll give ya more," he purred against the hollow of the dancer's throat.

Before Dorian could take another breath, Jansen lifted his head and their lips locked. He slipped his tongue into Dorian's mouth just as the big guy eased another finger inside his body. Those fingers worked back and forth, loosening him up. That's when Dorian felt Jansen's hand slip around his cock.

"I want this inside me now," Jansen said breathlessly.

Gripping his hips, Dorian spun him around until Jansen's ass pressed against his crotch. He spread his hand over the dancer's bare chest, finger stroking his nipple. As Dorian eased the head of his cock inside Jansen's body, he trailed kisses down his lover's spine. He used his other hand to gently massage Jansen's sac.

"I'm going to make love to you," Dorian whispered against his skin. "I'm going to treat you the way you deserve."

As Dorian lowered his lips to Jansen's shoulder, he felt a hand wrap around his. Their fingers laced together, stroking Jansen's erection. There was something… more about the way they held hands this time. It was symbolic, holy, and beautiful. Loving.

"Jansen, I get it now," he whispered as he slowly, carefully slid his erection inside his lover's tight, warm body. Dorian cradled him against his chest, lips pressed to his shoulder. Jansen rolled his hips, rode him nice and slow. "I'm sorry. I was a dick to ya, and I'm so fuckin' sorry for that."

With the hot water splashing around them and the night hovering above, Jansen felt like he'd suddenly found his place in heaven. Jansen arched his back, and he leaned his head against Dorian's shoulder as their hips rolled in unison. Dorian took care not to hurt Jansen again, to be tender.

"Shh…. It's okay," Jansen panted. "I'm okay. We're okay."

Dorian gripped Jansen's erection, stroked up and down that thick, hardened shaft, and the dancer met his rhythm, stroke for stroke.

Teeth pressed against the flesh of Jansen's neck. Tingles erupted all over his body. Dorian kept one of his hands woven with his, massaging and stroking his erection, while he reached down with the other and locked it over his bare ass. Dorian squeezed hard. Jansen picked up the pace of his hand and Dorian picked up the pace of his thrusts.

"Ah. Ah. Oh. Fuck! Oh, God!" Jansen cried out. He bit down on his lip as hard moans rumbled through his body.

Dorian tightened his arms around his lover's chest as Jansen rode his body. The kid had moves, moves that didn't only exist on the stage. He moved his hips with a rhythm that made Dorian drive his hardened cock deep inside all that wonderful, undulating tightness. Dorian bit down harder on Jansen's back as his orgasm exploded inside the dancer's body.

"Oh God!" Jansen cried one last time before his own release tightened his sac and pulsed down his shaft. Pearly streams burst onto Dorian's hand and left Jansen's heart pounding. "Oh, fuck!"

Cock now soft and spent, Dorian wrapped his arms around Jansen and held him tight, pressing kisses along his dancer's moist skin. He still wanted to be inside of him. Damn it, he'd never wanted that before. Normally, he'd pull a hit and run, then send 'em packin' after he'd had his fix, but not this time. He wanted to keep Jansen close.

The beautiful dancer leaned back against Dorian's chest. He hoped to God Jansen understood what all this meant. Dorian Grant didn't love people. People were expendable. He didn't let anyone in, because the closer they got, the more they could hurt him. It took a major leap of faith to admit his feelings for Jansen. It took the kind of courage he didn't think he had, but now that Dorian had said those three horrifying words to him, he would've sworn he was the happiest man in the world.

33

DESPITE better judgment, Jansen had let Dorian convince him to stay for the night. No sense in fighting it, anyway. Jansen couldn't deny that he loved being close to that beautiful, stubborn man. He couldn't deny thinking about Dorian every waking moment when they weren't together, that he uncontrollably craved even the slightest touch when they were apart. So yeah, being in Dorian's bed, in his arms, as close to him as possible, was exactly where Jansen wanted to be, and that's exactly where he would be... despite better judgment.

An uneasy smile spread across his face. Post-orgasmic bliss hooded his eyes. Jansen rose from the hot tub, waiting for Dorian to come with him, but from the look in his eyes, Dorian was somewhere else.

Water clung to Jansen's slender, sinewy body. It glistened in the soft light of the gas torches surrounding the patio. The image was a work of art. Proudly, Dorian had claimed that treasure for his own. Another man would never come between them. He would gladly spend a lifetime loving, embracing, and revering that treasure. He would never make Jansen question his feelings again.

"Are you coming?" Jansen said with a euphoric lilt as he offered a hand.

Licking his lips, Dorian stared up at the man he'd claimed as his own. "Oh, I plan to be." A crooked grin lifted his cheek as he stood from the water and reached for Jansen's hand. "You gonna let an old man rest before we go another round?"

"You know what I meant." Jansen rolled his eyes and shook his head. "And who says you're old, anyway? I like to think of it as... mature. Definitely mature."

"Mature, huh?" Dorian wrapped his arms around Jansen's waist and pulled him tight against his body. Jansen's back pressed against

Dorian's chest as he ran the firm tip of his tongue up the side of his dancer's neck until his mouth reached Jansen's ear. As he whispered, his lips fluttered across his lover's flesh. "I'll show ya mature."

Dorian slipped his hand down, farther along the muscled curve of Jansen's stomach, down until his fingers brushed the thin patch of coarse hair at the base of the kid's cock.

Jansen hissed as he arched back against Dorian's body. "Again? Already?" he whimpered.

A low, throaty laugh rumbled up from Dorian's parted lips. He started moving their bodies closer to the French doors, closer to the inside of the house, closer to his bed. "What, you too young to hang with someone so 'mature'? You gonna let an old man outdo ya?"

"I can barely walk as it is, baby. My legs are all Jell-O, and my bottom is all…." Heat flushed Jansen's face and turned it fire engine red. "Well, you know."

Dorian let out another bassy chuckle as they made their way into the house.

Feet stumbled forward, legs twisting, arms holding their naked bodies close together. They laughed their way toward the grand staircase, but as soon as Dorian's gaze landed on the steps, the laughter died. That was the one hurdle that still gave him hell. Climbing that staircase continued to remind him he wasn't whole, not yet. He still had a long road to travel before he became the man he once was.

"Take it slow," Dorian said.

Jansen heard the absolute shame in his voice. "I know, baby. I'm right here, and I won't let go. I promise."

Getting Dorian back up to his second floor bedroom was a pain in the ass. Together, they conquered each step one at a time, making sure Dorian had each foot firmly planted before going any farther. He'd left the cane out by the hot tub. It didn't really help when it came to climbing the mountain of a staircase, anyway. Besides, the damn thing embarrassed the hell out of him.

"You okay?" Jansen asked.

Dorian nodded. He wasn't, but he didn't want anything spoiling the good mood they'd both been in all night. They needed it. They both needed to have fun and let go and laugh. Even though Dorian sort of had the feeling Jansen spent the majority of that time secretly waiting for a bomb to drop. Dorian was well aware of his temper, as was Jansen, and they both knew how badly Dorian lost his temper when he became frustrated. If anything, the stairs would've been the catalyst to ruin their special evening.

Jansen obviously braced himself. His body stiffened so much his shoulders squared. The heaving of Jansen's chest suddenly stilled.

Dorian huffed and puffed, but he never blew up. He never yelled or cursed. He never bitched about being weak, never looked embarrassed or aggravated that he'd needed help. He carefully, quietly made his way upstairs, occasionally giving Jansen a thankful smile as they held hands.

God, this had to be a dream, Jansen thought. He must have entered the freaking Twilight Zone or something. This so wasn't the Dorian Grant he'd met all those months ago. This guy was perfect. A little too perfect.

After helping Dorian into the bed and tucking the blankets around his body, Jansen kissed his forehead and said, "I should probably let my roommate know I won't be home tonight. He might freak if I don't."

"You do that," Dorian said with a smile as he rolled over in the bed. "I gotta spot right here for ya."

"Then I'll be right back."

Jansen grabbed the phone from the nightstand, then padded over to the bathroom. Dorian kept his stare glued on him, obviously watching his every step, every movement. And before Jansen disappeared beyond the bathroom door, he shot a sincere, loving smile over his shoulder. Dorian finally closed his eyes and settled into the bed.

The phone rang forever, it seemed. What in the hell could Jason possibly be doing that he didn't answer immediately? Finally, the background noise of Sin & Seduction wailed through the phone, followed by the sound of Jason's voice yelling, "Hello?"

"It's Jansen."

"What?"

"Jansen! I'm not…."

"Hang on."

Jansen sighed, rolled his eyes and slumped down on the toilet. He gripped the phone, waiting for his best friend to come back. The noise on the other end died away.

"Hello?" Jason said.

"Hey, I'm not coming home tonight."

"Why not?"

"Dorian asked me to stay the night." Jansen chewed his bottom lip.

"Sweetie, I hope you know what you're getting into. Jansen, he's not the guy who settles down and falls in love. He's the kind of guy you fuck and forget about. He'll break your heart."

Scrubbing his hand over his hair, Jansen let out a hard sigh. He stared at the back of the bathroom door. Maybe Jason was right, but that didn't change the fact that this had been one of the best nights of his adult life. He finally said, "He told me he loved me and I… I owe it to myself to see what happens."

"I hope things work out the way you want. God knows you deserve a break. Have a good night, sweetie. Call me if you need me."

"You too. I'll see you at work tomorrow."

What if Jason was right? What if this was just a fantasy?

He'd survive, that's what. Jansen would put on his best ambivalent face and walk away, hopefully with his heart intact. But for now, he wanted to have a fairytale with that beautiful, elusive man. Even if it was for one night or one week or one month, Jansen would have his perfect romance.

Returning to the bed, he smiled at the sight of his lover, the strength of his gorgeous tattooed man, the peace Dorian seemed to finally have. Jansen curled his naked body against Dorian, closed his eyes, and pressed his lips to his lover's heart. Jason had to be wrong. This felt too right. It felt too perfect. Surely Dorian had changed. Surely Dorian wouldn't hurt him, not after all this time.

Arms wrapped around his body. Lips kissed his forehead. Jansen opened his eyes and found Dorian staring down at him with something that resembled adoration. He smiled.

"I like this," Dorian said in a soft voice. "I like knowing you'll be here when I wake up in the morning."

Jansen swallowed hard. Those words contradicted everything Jason had said. They were the words of someone with a heart, someone capable of falling in love. "I like it too," he whispered.

That night, they fell asleep in each other's arms, naked bodies pressed together. Dorian cradled Jansen's thigh between his legs. He splayed his hand over his dancer's heart. He listened to every even breath Jansen took as sleep carried his consciousness off to a place where his life had turned out much different.

In that world, Dorian had been able to love Jansen from the start. There was no violence, no need for second chances. In that world, Dorian had grown up in a loving home. He hadn't lost his mother, and his father had been his hero, his perfect version of the American dream. He'd become a man capable of the kind of love he wanted to give Jansen. Life was perfect.

34

THE next morning, the smell of sausage and eggs, pancakes and warm maple syrup, and the sound of Maria tapping at the door with a tray in her hand woke Dorian and his lover. Jansen grumbled about sleep as he buried his face between the bed and Dorian's side.

"Just set it down over there," Dorian said, waving his hand toward the dresser.

Maria did as he asked before gathering his laundry and linens from the floor. "Shall I plan for lunch as well, Mr. Grant?"

"Please, Maria," he said. "Thank you so much."

Maria paused, brows furrowed as she stared at her employer. Mr. Grant usually said a small "thanks" in passing, but nothing ever so heartfelt or sincere. "You are most welcome, sir," she said with a slight bow before leaving his room.

Dorian rolled slightly, pulling Jansen up to his chest. He smoothed his hand up and down his lover's back as he pressed his lips against Jansen's forehead. He could spend the entire day like that. It was Saturday, after all. Jansen didn't have class, and Dorian's businesses could wait until Monday. The only thing he had on his schedule for the day was physical therapy, but that wasn't for a few hours. No reason to rush from the bed.

"Is that coffee I smell?" Jansen grumbled.

"Among other things."

"I just want coffee."

"Stay here. I'll get it for ya," Dorian said with a soft smile as he eased out from beneath Jansen's warm, naked body.

Jansen frowned, brow arched. He flipped over in the bed and propped himself up on his elbows so he could watch this alien in

Dorian Grant's body. Things had been pretty dreamlike last night, but this... this was straight up unbelievable. "Are you okay?" he finally asked.

"Yeah, why?" Dorian said as he handed over a fresh cup of coffee and a plate of food.

"You're acting strange."

"How?"

"This." Jansen nodded toward the plate and coffee mug Dorian had just handed him. "Why are you waiting on me like this?"

Dorian shrugged. "I don't know. I felt like it."

"Okay...." Jansen sucked down a gulp of coffee, then inhaled a piece of sausage. Maria sure knew what she was doing when it came to food. It was so good, in fact, he set down the mug just so he could scarf down the rest.

"I have to work tonight," he said after swallowing a mouthful of pancakes. He waited and watched for a tic or a twitch. He knew Dorian hated the thought of him going back to the club, and they'd carefully avoided the subject since his return. It just seemed safer for their fairytale that way, but at some point, they both had to face reality. Dorian had to face the fact that Jansen would be going back to the club, and Jansen had to face the fact that Dorian would never accept him dancing in that disgusting place.

It didn't surprise him when Dorian changed the subject.

"The therapist should be here soon. You gonna come down with me or stay up here?"

"No. I'll go with you. I told you I wouldn't make you do it alone."

THEY went downstairs to wait for the therapist. The silent moments on the couch were uncomfortable at best. That always seemed to happen when Sin & Seduction came into the picture, or better still, Jansen dancing for all those high, horny bodies. Jansen just couldn't quit the place. He truly loved being on stage, and, unfortunately, that was his best chance at dancing for the masses.

But that didn't change the fact that Dorian hated the idea of him going there, let alone going by himself. He couldn't protect his lover like that. He couldn't make sure that nothing ever hurt Jansen if the kid refused to let him.

So there they sat, quietly avoiding the uncomfortable stuff in hopes of keeping the good time they'd been having going at least until the therapist arrived.

"If he pushes you too hard," Jansen said in a quiet voice, "you won't blow up, will you?"

"I'll try not to."

"Please." Jansen laced his fingers with Dorian's. He looked down at the knot of hands, then back up to Dorian's deep brown eyes. "For me, will you promise not to get upset?"

"Baby," Dorian said as he shifted in the seat. He stared straight at his dancer and gave him the most honest answer he had. "I can only promise to try, and I promise to try for you."

"I can accept that."

Jansen leaned in for a kiss just as the doorbell rang. Maria tore through the room, averting her eyes so it didn't seem like she was watching them. She yelled "I will answer it, Mr. Grant" in passing. A minute later she brought a man into the room, and both Dorian and Jansen groaned in unison.

They hefted themselves up from the couch, keeping their hands locked together as they followed the blabbering therapist to the weight room. He kept going on and on about what he planned to put Dorian through today. A warning really didn't matter; he would put Dorian through hell anyway, even if Dorian protested. The therapist mumbled about something else as he pointed Dorian straight to the free weights.

Now, Dorian used to be able to bench press his own weight and then some. He wasn't weak by any stretch, but both his arms had been broken, so he didn't have the strength he once had. It frustrated him to no end that he could barely press eighty pounds. He cursed and growled as his arms wobbled and strained.

Jansen took a deep breath, calmed his mounting worry, and kept cheering on his lover.

Then the therapist made Dorian get on the treadmill.

He walked at a slow pace, about a mile an hour. Dorian kept that speed for about thirty minutes before his thighs began to quiver and his legs started to burn. He just couldn't do it anymore. The therapist yelled, and Dorian raised his fist like he was going to deck the man.

Jansen backed against the wall. Fear filled his big brown eyes; not *he might lose his life* fear, but the kind that came whenever Dorian's temper started to show its nasty face. That brand of fear made Jansen's heart beat a little faster. It made his hands shake slightly and his palms dampen with clammy sweat. It made Jansen feel like a teenager who'd just got caught doing something not too horrible by parents who might have blown an innocent misdeed out of proportion.

Dorian looked his way, saw the ghostly shade of pale Jansen's face had turned.

Jansen cut his eyes sideways, afraid to meet the devil's gaze.

"I'm sorry," Dorian said to the therapist. He sighed. "I can't keep going today. You might as well go."

The man started to argue, but Dorian gave him that blood-chilling, arched brow glare of his. He could've commanded armies with that glare. It almost had more bite than his mouth did.

"Very well," the therapist said, gathering his things before heading toward the door.

Therapy was over.

Somehow, Jansen had managed to calm the beast. They shared a quick shower in one of the downstairs bathrooms before returning to the living room. Jansen had him sitting on the couch again, watching TV and cuddling against each other like true lovers would do.

They spent the next few hours like that. The conversation was good, the laughs even better. The occasional kisses for no particular reason were amazing. The fairytale had survived.

Then Jansen looked down at his watch.

It was *that* time. Jansen had to get to the club or he'd be late.

He kissed Dorian's forehead and said, "I have to go."

"I'm going with you."

Silly boy. Jansen laughed and said, "No, you're not. You're going to relax, and I'll be back when I get off work."

"No. I'm going with you. I'll be damned if you're going to that place alone."

All hell broke loose then. Dorian yelled. Jansen yelled. The word "whore" trembled on the tight curve of Dorian's lips as he snarled, but he knew better than to let that word find life. Jansen called him a jealous bastard, told him that nothing had changed and that shit *still* wouldn't work. Dorian Grant had a thing or two to learn about trust, and this was the best damn lesson he'd get.

"At least let Angelo go with you," Dorian said through clenched teeth.

"Goddammit, no! And that's it. You can deal with what I do, or deal with being alone. Take your pick!"

Dorian crossed his arms over his chest and cut his eyes. Ultimatums were never good friends of his. That might as well have been a threat.

Finally, he said, "Go, and don't worry about coming back tonight. I'll catch up with you when I can."

35

NO MATTER what Dorian said or did, it always came out wrong. Yeah, he didn't want Jansen dancing in that shithole nightclub. Jansen belonged to someone now. He belonged to Dorian. They'd said they loved each other. They were together now, right? Dorian didn't want other men or even women groping and ogling his dancer's goods.

Fuck that!

But this time it wasn't just about jealousy. Dorian genuinely worried about his safety. Fuck, if a dude like him could get the shit beat out of him at that club, then Jansen, they'd....

No fucking way. They're not getting my *dancer.*

The bottom line—Dorian had enemies. People who would kill someone he loved just to get at him, and he didn't want to put Jansen in harm's way. But somehow, he kept failing to show the kid that he just wanted to protect him and keep him from the monsters hiding in the dark. He'd thought loving him, telling him he loved him, would be enough to make Jansen stop messing with that place.

So now the dancer was pissed, and Dorian's stubborn ass hadn't made it any better.

Looking down at his watch, he realized hours had passed, many hours. He'd been sitting there staring at the television, stewing over the situation with Jansen, and nearly piddled away an entire night. The upside to all of that was Jansen would be getting off work in about two hours. Which meant Dorian had a chance to fix this mess. Come hell or high water, he would make this right.

He called Maria into the living room and asked her to grab one of his nicer suits: a black one with a deep red button-down. He asked her to get his driver. Dorian wanted to take the sedan out tonight. "Oh, and grab one of the smaller suits, one that might fit Jansen." She nodded before scurrying off to find everything he asked for.

Honestly, Dorian couldn't believe he was doing this. There was a time in his life that he would've let the kid go and not thought twice about him, but damn, Jansen did something for him no one else had done. He made Dorian feel. He touched something inside his soul that had been closed down to the world. He made Dorian want to be a better man.

And he'd be damned if Jansen ended up being the one that got away.

He changed into the suit, had Maria hang the spare in the car, fixed his hair, and sprayed on some of the cologne he'd been wearing the first night they met: Armani Gio. Then he had his driver take him to the club. He didn't go inside. He didn't bother with the booze or the drugs or the invite to the private booth. Dorian just wanted to wait in the car and watch for Jansen to leave.

His dancer came out through the back door, just as Dorian knew he would. A streetlamp poured a stream of gold down upon Jansen's delicate form. The light glistened on his sweat-moistened face. It highlighted his plump pink lips and firm jaw, sparkled in his soft chocolate eyes, and painted serene waves of honey-like light along his slender throat.

Dorian popped a high-dollar Cuban stogie between his pursed lips. One cheek rose with his hungry grin. His own brown eyes softened as a heady mix of lust and love spread like butterfly wings through his body and fluttered beneath his flesh.

"Mmm… dancer," purred from his curled lips.

He stepped out of his sleek black Mercedes, ran his hands down the front of his Armani suit, then started toward him.

Jansen's eyes widened.

Dorian's knees knocked with the excitement of seeing him again. "I want to take you on a date," he said as he held out his splayed fingers to hold Jansen's hand.

The dancer's brow arched, lips pinched into a smirk. He crossed his arms over his chest. "A date, huh?"

"Yeah, a date. I think I owe ya that, right?"

"Thought you didn't want to see me tonight."

Dorian took a deep breath, reached out to curl his fingers around Jansen's hand. He took a step closer as he pulled his sexy dancer toward him. "I always want to see ya. And I think we really need to talk."

"Yeah, we do, but I don't have anything to wear on a date."

"I brought a suit for ya. Will ya please go with me? We'll have dinner and talk about... ya know, things."

Jansen nodded. "Okay, I'll go. We can talk."

"Thank you," Dorian said with a slight nod. He gave Jansen the most sincere, thankful kiss he'd ever given anyone before.

Their lips met, mouths tangled in a tender caress. Dorian gripped Jansen's hip with one hand while the other touched his dancer's cheek. He stroked his thumb back and forth, and when the kiss broke, it left them both locked in a starry-eyed stare.

36

"I'LL wait here," Dorian said, thumbing away the remnants of Jansen's delicious kiss from the edge of his lips. He waited in the car while his dancer went back in the club to change into the black Brooks Brothers suit Dorian had brought for him to wear on their date.

A date? Really? The thought made him laugh. Dorian Grant didn't date.

Dorian laid his head back against the smooth leather headrest while his gut continued to twist and turn and knot. He didn't do well with feelings. Never had. Being numb to them had worked well for a very long time. Now he had Jansen, and suddenly he's supposed to have a heart or some shit. To top that off, this whole dating mess had him so far out of his element he didn't know how to act.

"It'll end in a fight," he whispered, keeping his eyes trained on the cloth-covered roof of his Benz. "It always ends in a fight."

A lot of subjects were still touchy between the two of them, and he was never really sure which subject might be the minefield on any given day, but it almost always seemed to revolve around Jansen dancing at Sin & Seduction.

Okay. Okay. Sure, Dorian could admit it. He didn't like those men groping *his* dancer. He could own up to a certain level of jealousy, but that wasn't where the story ended. He needed Jansen to realize what being with him meant. A world of trouble followed him, and he didn't want a stupid association with the wrong man to cause Jansen a moment of pain, or worse, cost him his life.

Jansen stood in the backstage area, staring at himself in a suit that cost more than his entire freaking wardrobe. It was a little large, but he expected it to be. Dorian was a lot bigger than him, but he made it work. It looked good. The cobalt blue button-down looked great against his now mediocre tan. It made the brown in his eyes not so bland and the chestnut color of his loose, flowing hair a little less boring.

With a sigh, he looked himself over in the mirror, then tilted his head left and right. He only saw a façade, a charade, something that wasn't him and would probably never be him. *Dorian's adorable clone,* he thought. At least he could pull it off and make it believable.

"Since when can you afford Brooks Brothers?" Jason asked as his arms came around Jansen's sides. He reached up and began to knot the black silk tie Dorian had thrown in with the suit.

Jansen rolled his eyes. "You know good and damn well I would *never* pay that kind of money for a suit."

"You look nice."

Jansen shrugged.

"So where is he?"

"Waiting in the car."

"What's going on?" Jason raked his fingers through Jansen's hair, trying to form it into some sort of style.

"He wants to take me on a real date. We need to 'talk'." Jansen's fingers formed air quotes around the word "talk."

"Well, now. That Neanderthal is capable of intelligent thought?"

"Alright, smart ass, you're talking about the man I love."

Shaking his head, Jason gripped Jansen's shoulders, turned him around until they faced each other. "You be careful. He hurts you, you know I'll go after him, Jansen, and you know I'll end up dead. Right?"

"Yeah. Yeah, I know."

"I'm not kidding." Jason leaned in and kissed Jansen's cheek. He gave his best friend a worried smile. "Call me and let me know if you decide not to come home so I don't end up worrying about you all night."

"I will," Jansen said as he patted Jason's shoulder.

Walking toward the exit, with Jason's worry tapping at his frontal lobe, Jansen finally started having his own reservations about date night with his hunky, sadistic possible boyfriend thing. He honestly had no clue what was up with Dorian. The guy had to have a chemical imbalance or something. One minute he was happy and in love. The next minute, he says, "Don't call me. I'll call you." Then shows up at his job with a suit and expects a date. Jansen would go, because he loved Dorian. He would go, because he wanted them to work out, but Dorian had to understand Jansen wouldn't be under his thumb, and honestly, this back and forth shit was getting old.

Dorian was waiting inside the car when he saw the streetlights hit Jansen's face. The kid looked worried, maybe even afraid. Dorian hated that. He wished he could change it, or maybe at the very least, take some of that fear away.

Dorian stepped out of the car and met Jansen on the passenger side.

"You look nice," Dorian said as he leaned in for a kiss. He touched Jansen's forearm, and he felt the muscle flex against his palm, like that simple, innocent touch unnerved him.

"Thanks," Jansen said flatly before he pressed his lips to Dorian's.

Dorian opened the back passenger door, smiled, and made a sweeping bow as he said, "After you."

Jansen gave him a tight-lipped half smile. His gaze kept darting away from Dorian's, like he was ashamed or maybe he was hiding something or maybe he was genuinely afraid to be in Dorian's presence. Whatever the reason, Dorian didn't like that the man he loved wouldn't look him in the eye. Without saying a word, Jansen climbed into the backseat of the Benz. Dorian took a deep breath, scrubbed his hand over his face, then sat down beside him.

The driver knew exactly where to take them. Maria had set everything up, because Dorian just wasn't romantic enough not to screw things up. She made reservations at some swanky restaurant where they would have a candlelit dinner. The place had a waiting list a mile long. Reservations normally had to be made a month in advance to get in, but enough money opened doors most people didn't have access to.

Fresh baked bread and the scent of fine wine filled the air. Candles flickered in nearly every corner of the room. The waiter guided them through a maze of red-covered tables, back to a dark, candlelit corner hidden in the quietest part of the place. It was nice and private, a place where they could really talk.

They took their seats. Dorian waited for Jansen to sit first. He looked up at the waiter and said, "Can you bring a bottle of Moscato, something nice? And maybe some bread and seasoned butter?" The waiter nodded, then made an about-face.

"Look, I gotta get some stuff off my chest," Dorian said, watching the pimple-faced, ginger-haired waiter saunter away.

"So talk."

"I know you want to work at the club," Dorian said. Jansen arched his brow and crossed his arms over his chest. Dorian pressed his palms to the air. "Hear me out, okay?"

Jansen nodded. The waiter reappeared with everything Dorian had asked for. He served the wine, then laid out the spread of different breads and butters. Dorian glared. Jansen smirked. The waiter shifted uncomfortably.

"Give us two specials," Dorian barked, but immediately calmed himself long enough to look at his lover and ask, "Is that okay with you, baby?"

Jansen nodded again, gave the waiter an uneasy smile that screamed "I'm sorry" louder than any words he could've said. The poor innocent waiter jotted down the specials and bolted from the table as fast as he could.

"Where was I?" Dorian asked.

"I'm supposed to be 'hearing you out'."

"Right. Because you've been seen with me, because you're involved with me, you're not safe. People will try to hurt ya just to get back at me. I wouldn't be able to live with myself if I knew something I did—or just knowing me—endangered ya. So all I ask is that ya let me protect ya the only way I know how." Dorian sat up in the chair and reached across the table. He touched Jansen's hand. Their eyes locked. "I can admit that I am a stubborn asshole. I can admit to sayin' mean things just because I know I can, but I don't say things that don't have a valid point."

"If you're so concerned about my safety," Jansen said, "then it would appear you have two choices. You can give up your lifestyle or you can give up being with me."

Dorian could already feel the heat on his skin. His temper kicked up, and it took a few deep, solid breaths to keep it in check. By God, he was putting in a lot of effort for this kid, and Jansen didn't seem to care.

"Jansen," he said as calmly as he could, though he felt the tension in his ticking jaw. "It ain't that easy. I have enemies, and I have businesses to protect. Unfortunately, people don't appreciate anything other than ball-crackin' violence. It gets the point across."

"Then you're choosing to give me up?"

A hard fist slammed down on the table, and Jansen jumped. "I'm sorry. I didn't mean…." Dorian said with a sigh. He lowered his head. "Baby, I'm really tryin' here. I don't want to give ya up either. You're the only person—besides my fuckin' mother—I've ever told I loved. Can't ya see I mean it? Can't ya make this a little easier for me, please?"

God, Jansen wanted to. He wanted to wave a magic wand and make everything perfect, but he wouldn't be changed. Jansen was who he was, and he wanted what he wanted. "Like you, I'm doing what makes the biggest impact." He stood, pulled the napkin from his lap and tossed it on the table. "Dorian, I love you. Oh my God, I love you a lot, but this—" His hand waffled between the two of them. "—isn't going to work out. We're from two different worlds. We have two different lives. People like us don't make happy families."

"Don't do this, baby," Dorian said as he stood from his seat. He took Jansen's hands and pulled him close. He could feel his throat starting to fist. His breath burned as he inhaled. "I've done a lot of changin' for ya. I've done a shit-ton of soul searchin' and tryin' for ya. Don't run out on me now."

"I need to think about things, Dorian. I gave you time. Now I need you to give me time. I need you to let me be me."

"So, what? We're done? We're not going to see each other?"

"Just give me a little time to think, okay? You love me? You can do that for me."

"Fine. If you want time, you got it. I'll... I'll give you time and space and whatever else you need."

"Thank you." Jansen leaned in and kissed his lips, brushed his hand over Dorian's hot cheek. What he was about to do was probably the most painful thing he'd done in a very long time. He left him standing there, just as the waiter brought out the first course of their meals.

Dorian didn't sit down to eat. He only watched Jansen walk away.

37

SHOVING through the restaurant's front doors, Jansen hit the street with a hard footfall against moist pavement. The sounds of jazz and drunken tourists screamed from the other end of the French Quarter. At least the cops kept watch over the crowds, like guardian angels to all the oblivious humans. If there was a safe side, it was down there, with the tourists.

This end of the Quarter was dark and, for the most part, quiet... deserted. It wasn't the safest place to be, but Jansen didn't care. Safety was the last thing on his mind. Yeah, Dorian had warned him, but what did he care? He felt empty now, alone.

He kept walking, thinking maybe he would pick up a cab somewhere along the way. Right now, he just needed to feel the cool air on his face. He wanted to smell the spicy scent of New Orleans as it wafted through the night. Air was freedom. The weight of Dorian Grant's innocent oppression had been lifted from his shoulders, but now he found himself with a heavy heart.

Damn it!

And that fucking suit still smelled like Dorian. Was it Calvin Klein or Armani that wrapped his senses in the ghost of the lover he'd just walked out on?

So much for fairytales.

Okay. Sure, it was partially his fault, but it was also Dorian's fault. That ultimatum should've been a no-brainer, if Dorian truly loved him as much as he'd claimed to. Maybe the feelings weren't there. Maybe they were one sided, and Dorian had been blinded by... something. Maybe Dorian truly didn't know what it meant to love someone, and Jansen had been so thrilled to hear the words, he'd absently accepted them.

"What the hell am I doing?" Jansen mumbled as he turned back around to face the restaurant. He knew good and damn well Dorian was the only person who could fill that emptiness inside of him. Despite all the possessiveness and attitude, Dorian seemed to genuinely want to make him happy. They had their good days and bad, just like any real couple. It was normal, healthy.

As Jansen stood staring at the windows to the restaurant where his lover sat alone, a black SUV with pitch-black tinted windows pulled up beside him, and someone yelled out the window, "You Dorian Grant's boy?"

A frown curled his face as he turned back around. He said "Who wants to know?"

The barrel of a gun poked out from the glass. "Eye for a fucking eye," the voice growled from the darkness of the backseat. Jansen heard the bang long before he felt the pain. It felt like a hot spear had been plunged into his body and lava exploding onto his skin. The impact doubled him over. He touched his hand to the wound, and when he looked down, glistening red fluid coated his fingers.

His body hit the ground.

Rubber tires squealed across the asphalt, leaving a trail of red taillights cutting through the darkness.

Lying on the concrete sidewalk, he stared up at the night sky. Stars twinkled above him. The city around him fell silent, and that silence could only mean he would die in the middle of a filthy French Quarter street, alone, with no one there to save him.

Everything around him started to go dark. The stars faded one by one.

"H-help m-me, p-please," he choked out with the last ragged breath he could breathe.

DORIAN sank back down in the chair. He didn't have an appetite anymore. The food had made his stomach turn. He asked the waiter for the check and tossed down a credit card, thinking he would go home and just.... What the hell would he do? Something. Anything to get his mind off Jansen.

Then he heard the gunshot.

Normally, he wouldn't have cared. Gunshots in New Orleans were nothing new, but Jansen was out there, walking the streets. Unprotected. Alone.

He jumped from the table, forgetting the cane he'd been relegated to using, and he ran as fast as his gimpy bones would let him. He was out the door and down the street faster than he could've dreamed. But when he saw a crumpled Brooks Brothers suit and sprigs of chocolate-brown hair lying on the sidewalk, his stomach sunk to his feet.

"Jansen!" He dove down beside him, screaming for someone to call an ambulance as he pressed his trembling hand over the wound in the dancer's abdomen, but it wouldn't stop bleeding. "Wake up, baby. God, please fuckin' wake up," he cried, lightly patting Jansen's cheek.

The few people who'd been in the bars and restaurants flooded out into the street. They stood and stared, gawked and gaped. Whispers of disbelief soiled the air. Not one of the rubberneckers had a phone in his hand. Not one of them offered to help.

"Call the goddamn cops!" Dorian yelled over his shoulder as tears filled his eyes. One soggy, wet, desperate tear dripped down to land on Jansen's pale cheek, then another.

Jansen's eyes fluttered, lashes slowly parting and closing again. He was still alive. Holy hell, he had a chance! "Wake up, baby. Help is comin', I promise."

Jansen slowly opened his eyes. He met Dorian's gaze in a terrified, almost lifeless stare. He tried to move his lips, but he couldn't make the first sound. Tears formed in his eyes, clinging to his fluttering lashes. He just wanted to tell Dorian he really did love him and always would, but he couldn't. He was dying, and he couldn't confess his soul to the man he loved.

"Hang on, baby," Dorian said. "You're not gonna die on me. Just hang in there, okay?"

Tears fell faster from Dorian's eyes, and he realized there wasn't a single moment in his life when he'd been more terrified of losing someone he cared about, the only person who somehow managed to make him happy.

He carefully slid his arm under Jansen's neck, pressed his lips to his forehead and whispered, "I fuckin' love you! Don't ya die on me! Don't ya fuckin' die on me, kid! I can't be without ya, baby." Dorian turned his watery brown eyes heavenward. He cried out, "Please, God, don't let him die. Please."

38

THEY immediately took Jansen into surgery. The amount of blood he lost on the street and in the ambulance had turned Dorian's stomach. He never knew the body could hold so much blood, and seeing it all scared him even worse. It wasn't the blood itself. Dorian had seen a shitload of it in his lifetime. It was knowing that all the red, life-sustaining fluid wasn't in the body of the one man he loved. It was knowing that Jansen wouldn't survive without it. And the pain of that knowledge threatened to pull him into hysteria. He could feel the feeble threads of his sanity starting to break.

For hours and hours, Dorian paced the waiting room. He walked circles until he couldn't move another inch. His legs ached. His chest ached. His heart pounded as badly as the top of his skull. He didn't know what was happening, if they had saved Jansen or not. No one bothered to tell him shit. The whole situation put Dorian on the verge of losing control.

"Dorian Grant," an old man in a white coat called from the edge of the waiting room. The doctor pulled off his glasses, then rubbed his forefinger and thumb against his eye sockets. The guy looked completely exhausted. He called out Dorian Grant's name again, and Dorian nearly fell on his face trying to get to him.

He stumbled forward.

The old man grabbed his arms. "Dorian Grant?" he asked.

Dorian nodded.

"We were able to save Jansen. The bullet missed his stomach. It put a rather big fracture in one of his ribs, which wasn't a major concern. The problem we had was the bleeding. Poor kid had a lot of internal bleeding, and we had a hard time finding the source, but eventually, we found it and stopped it. I believe he's going to be okay."

Dorian's heart stopped beating. The relief brought a tear to his eye. He thanked the doctor repeatedly, nodding as the old man spoke, though he didn't really hear the words... not until the doctor said "coma."

"Wait. What? Did you say 'coma'?"

"Yes, sir. It isn't unlikely for that kind of blood loss to cause a coma. We're going to keep a close watch on him. I'm sure he'll be okay, Mr. Grant."

"Can I see him?"

"Absolutely."

The doctor led him to Jansen's room. The walk was hard, not only because of his mending legs, but because of the sick feeling in his gut. He didn't know how he would react to seeing the man he loved in a coma. Oh, he knew he would freak, maybe even get a little pissed off... or a lot pissed off, but he wasn't sure he would be able to keep his hysteria in check long enough to make the right decisions for either of them.

"Don't be concerned. He doesn't look good, but trust me, he's going to be okay," the doctor said as he reached out for the doorknob. Dorian nodded, staring at the cruel white surface that separated him from the man who had a firm lock on his heart. The doctor opened the door, and Dorian stepped inside the room. He moved like a zombie, afraid to really look up at Jansen, afraid to accept his hand in the dancer's fate. "The nurse should be by shortly," the old man said before closing the door behind him.

Dorian's knees weakened as soon as he saw Jansen with all the tubes and shit. His skin was so pale and the circles around his eyes so dark, hair knotted and wet. His dry, parched lips were slightly parted, and his head hung to the side. He looked dead. Had it not been for the almost unnoticeable rise and fall of his chest, Dorian wouldn't have believed his lover was actually alive.

He took Jansen's limp hand and pressed his lips to the knuckles. "I'm so fuckin' sorry, baby. I didn't mean to get ya mixed up in this shit. I...." The tears choked his voice. He was coming unglued. And he wanted to kill the guy who had put Jansen's life in jeopardy.

Sniffling back the tears, Dorian pulled a chair over to the side of the bed and sat down. He immediately fished the cell phone out of his pocket and punched in Angelo's number. He waited and waited, and the more the phone rang, the more pissed he got. "Answer the motherfuckin' phone, ya asshole," he bit out through clenched teeth.

"Hello?" Angelo said in a gravelly voice.

"What the fuck took ya so long?"

"Dorian, it's four in the morning. I was sleeping."

"Well, get up. This *won't* wait. Someone tried to kill Jansen." Complete silence. "Did ya hear me? Get the fuck out of the bed, wake ya dumbass up, and find out who tried to kill him!"

"Boss, no offense, but I won't find out shit this early in the morning."

"I don't care!" Dorian growled. "Pretend like you're workin' on it! I don't fuckin' care, just do something!"

He slammed the phone down on the table so hard it cracked the screen. It didn't matter. The phone didn't matter, and Angelo's lazy ass didn't matter. The only thing that mattered right now was the man lying in the bed.

Bile rose in the back of his throat, and he had to swallow it down before he hurled all over the hospital's sterile white floors. He pressed his head to the mattress and held Jansen's hand as he listened to the beeping of the heart monitor. He silently swore he wouldn't leave Jansen's side until he saw his dancer's big, beautiful brown eyes again, until he knew his lover was safe and sound again.

NURSES came and went so often he couldn't relax even if he'd wanted to. Jansen still hadn't woken up, hadn't even batted an eye. Dorian was losing hope, despite the doctors saying Jansen would be fine. He couldn't help thinking how differently things could've worked out had they both approached the topic of their relationship a little differently.

Dorian started running down his life's list, wondering what all he would willingly give up for Jansen. The drugs were a no-brainer. He could do without them. Going to the nightclub, again, a no-brainer. The mafia-style life he'd been living would be much harder to undo. Maybe he could take a step back. Maybe he could let Angelo handle the more violent side of his business. But truth be told, this wasn't all Dorian's doing. Sure, he'd take the blame for some of it, but he'd tried to warn Jansen. He'd tried to protect him, but his dancer seemed to be just as stubborn as he was.

The door to the private room creaked open. Dorian didn't bother raising his head. He thought it was just another nurse coming to check the machines and jot down their little notes, but then he heard Angelo's voice behind him, saying, "Hey, boss." He sounded careful, solemn even.

"What the fuck do ya want?" Dorian choked out. Five hours had passed since he called that useless fat ass and told him to get info on whoever tried to kill Jansen, and this was the first he'd heard from him since.

"Have you ever heard of the Cabrezzi family?" Angelo asked as he closed the door behind him.

The name made Dorian finally lift his head from the bed. Fuck yeah, he knew that family. He'd had Marco Cabrezzi offed for trying to put one of Dorian's warehouses out of business by stealing money and cooking the books. The whole mess got Dorian in some hefty shit with the IRS, brought down a lot of unneeded heat, and had the authorities watching Dorian real close for a long while. Cabrezzi had really rubbed him the wrong way with that one. That Cabrezzi boy *had* to be executed, and it wasn't Dorian or Angelo that had done the deed. Yeah, he'd hired outside help for that one. Didn't want that death to be associated with him *at all*.

"What about 'em?"

"They're the ones who hit Jansen."

"I want 'em all fuckin' dead! The men, the women, the kids… I don't give a fuck. I want 'em dead!"

"Boss—"

"No!" Dorian's head whipped back. "No. Fuck you!" He stumbled out of the chair, stabbed his finger against Angelo's sternum. "I don't want to hear any lip from you. Ya do what the hell I say!"

Angelo grabbed his hand and looked his boss in the eyes. It was the only time Dorian had ever been remotely intimidated by the bigger man, but he sure wouldn't let Angelo see it.

"Boss, your head's all messed up right now. You're worried about Jansen and not thinkin' clearly. Why don't ya take a step back and think about how Dorian Grant the smart businessman would handle this."

He had a point, but fuck his point.

"I want every Cabrezzi male dead, and I don't mean maybe," Dorian bit out between his clenched teeth. "Ya start with the one who pulled the trigger."

Angelo nodded.

Dorian stumbled back to his chair and started staring at the monitors again.

Angelo said, "Can I get ya anything before I go?"

He shook his head. "No. I just need him to wake up."

And that was the most honest-to-God, deep-from-the-soul answer Dorian could've given the only person he'd allowed himself to get close to before Jansen came along. He never let anyone in his affairs if it didn't involve the businesses. Angelo knew more about his boss than most, but Dorian sure as hell had never let him see inside his heart.

Right now, though, his heart hurt so bad he didn't know what to do. Dorian felt like that scared little boy again; the one who clung to his mom's hand and cried as she lay lifeless in a casket. He was afraid if he lost Jansen, nothing would ever be the same again. He would be ten times more cruel and ruthless and vicious. He knew if he lost Jansen, he would die a lonely, angry old man, because his heart didn't have the strength to let anyone else in, let alone love anyone else.

39

THE sound of the heart monitor, though a welcomed sound for the most part, was about to drive Dorian insane. Jansen still hadn't woken up. Dorian still hadn't left his side. Angelo kept calling, updating him on the Cabrezzi situation every hour on the hour, just like the boss had instructed him to. Nurses and doctors came in just as often. They'd expressed concern that Jansen was still under. That sure as hell didn't help Dorian Grant's less-than-sunny disposition, that's for damn sure.

Add to all that, aching legs and arms, and he was a walking recipe for a time bomb.

With a sigh, Dorian sat back in the chair and rubbed his palms up and down his legs. He wanted a shower and a meal that wasn't processed chicken and gravy with a side of green Jell-O. He wanted real food and a real bed, but by God, he wanted Jansen more. He wanted to see those big brown puppy-dog eyes, wanted to hold his hand and actually feel like Jansen was still alive.

He pulled his dancer's soft, limp hand to his mouth and bowed his head until his lips pressed against Jansen's knuckles. He closed his eyes and started to pray. For the first time since he was thirteen years old, he had a sincere conversation with the big man upstairs, and he begged God to do him a solid, not for him, but for the innocent man lying in that bed, fighting for his life.

The silent prayer ended with a desperate, "Baby, please wake up."

Jansen felt warm hands wrap around his. He smelled a faint hint of Dorian's cologne, but then he heard his voice. He didn't know what had happened after leaving the restaurant, save for seeing the barrel of a gun pointed at his gut. The rest was history.

"I'm awake," Jansen said in a hoarse voice as he tried to sit up in the bed. Pain shot through his gut. He hissed as gravity pulled him back down to the pillow. "W-what happened?"

Dorian's head shot up. His eyes widened. "Jansen?" he gasped.

Jansen nodded slowly.

"Holy… fuck me!" Dorian came out of the chair and nearly threw himself on top of the bed, but better sense came over him. He reached down and brushed his hand over Jansen's messy brown hair. The smile on his face was so wide it made his cheeks hurt. He could barely contain his excitement. "Baby, you're alive. That's what happened."

"No, w-what happened to m-me?" Jansen asked, and despite the gravelly sound of his voice, it was music to Dorian's ears.

"You were shot in the stomach. They fixed ya up, but you'd lost a lot of blood by the time ya got here. You're okay now, baby. You're fuckin' alive!"

The absolute happiness on Dorian's face made Jansen's heart melt. He gripped Dorian's hand with all the strength he had and said, "I l-love you, Dorian G-Grant. And I'm s-sorry."

"I love you, too, baby, but ya don't owe me any apologies. It's my fault you're here."

Dorian sat back down in the chair but didn't let go of Jansen's hand. He lowered his head, scrubbed his other hand through his own hair, guilt kicking his ass something fierce.

"You know w-who did this, d-don't you?" Jansen asked.

Without lifting his head, Dorian nodded and said, "Yeah, I do. It's being handled."

Jansen knew what Dorian meant by "being handled," and it wasn't through legal, official channels. He sighed. It wasn't the time or place to bring it up, and maybe he wouldn't, because the way he felt, he wanted the asshole who did this to pay. He swallowed, closed his eyes, and tried not to remember the gun poking out the window, firing a bullet into his gut.

40

A FEW days passed, and the doctor finally released Jansen to go home. Of course, he went straight to Dorian's place, where he would get the best care possible. People waited on the dancer hand and foot. If it wasn't Dorian running to his side, it was Maria or Angelo or any one of the many people Dorian had on his payroll. The way he saw it, he owed the kid… not to mention the fact that he loved Jansen with his heart and soul, and wanted to take care of him more than anything.

Dorian had been sitting in the bed with Jansen's head in his lap, fingers drawing lines in his dancer's soft hair, when the phone rang. He cursed that damn contraption, but as soon as he saw Angelo's name on the caller ID, the curses stopped. He needed to take the call.

Patting Jansen's shoulder, he said, "I need up, baby. Gotta take this."

Jansen raised his head from Dorian's lap. Dorian eased out of the bed, neglecting the cane as he made his way into the hall. He knew why Angelo was calling, and he knew Jansen didn't need to hear the shit.

"What?" Dorian barked. He could practically see Wide-ass flinch, despite there being miles and miles of information superhighway between them.

"We got him, boss. I'm heading to your place now."

"Good. I'll be downstairs waitin'."

Dorian went back into the bedroom. Jansen was lying on his side, cradling his stomach. He leaned down and kissed his lover's forehead. "I have to go out for a bit. Make sure ya call Maria if ya need anything."

Jansen didn't say a word. Dorian assumed he'd heard him. Should've heard him, hell, he was wide awake and staring at the TV.

Dorian headed to the closet to grab a pair of black boots, black jeans, and a black shirt. Last thing he wanted was for anyone to see his clothes coated in blood when he came back.

"What are you doing?" Jansen said in a soft voice.

"Gettin' dressed," Dorian replied from inside the closet.

"No, I mean, what are you going to do?"

Dorian's hands stilled about the same time his heart hit his chest with a hard thud. "I'm goin' out, baby."

"Angelo found him, didn't he?"

Eyes closed, Dorian lowered his head. Trembling hands fought to pull a shirt over his head. The combination of adrenaline and guilt was kicking his ass. He couldn't lie. He physically couldn't do it, couldn't bring himself to do it. That was not only one fucked up realization, but a fucked up feeling, since he'd had to lie his way out of almost everything his entire life.

Dorian stepped out of the closet, grabbed his jacket, and approached the bed. He sat down on the corner and said, "I love you, Jansen. I gotta go handle some business, but I'll be back. If ya need anything… anything at all, call Maria, okay?"

As Jansen shifted his eyes away, he nodded slowly, but he never said a word. He didn't like that "business," and Dorian knew it. No sense in rehashing old news. No sense in playing a broken record. But Dorian *had* to handle this one.

No one… no fuckin' one, shoots the person I love and lives to tell about it.

He kissed Jansen's forehead, then started down the stairs. For the first time in his life, he felt guilty, truly miserable, about the life he'd been living. Would he change it? Probably not. People screwed up when they thought the scary ones weren't watching, but he might try to take a step back just for Jansen's peace of mind.

Angelo was waiting by the front door when Dorian finally made it downstairs. The black sedan waited in the driveway. Angelo leaned over and opened the passenger door. Mr. Louisville Slugger rested in the backseat.

Dorian climbed in and bit out, "Let's get this fuckin' done."

The sedan hit the highway, doing about eighty. They headed toward Slidell, tearing down I-90 like a sinner from the flames of hell. They could get to the swamps faster that way. What they did, the "business" they handled, it was best handled in the swamps. The gators always ate the evidence, and most of the local cops wouldn't bother going down there because of the gators. *Fuckin' city folk.* They were great about not meddling. It was those crazy, bug-eyed swamp dwellers they had to watch out for.

Angelo pulled off the highway and onto a gravel road. It led back to a piece of property that had been in the family for close to two centuries, but no one ever bothered to go out there anymore because the place had become nothing more than a messy ruin.

Dorian reached in the glove box and grabbed the Walther .45, tucked it into the waist of his black jeans, then followed Angelo to the back of the car. "What the fu...." Wide-ass popped the trunk, and Dorian almost fell into hysterics when he saw Tony Cabrezzi hog-tied in the back. "Oh, this is gonna be fuckin' great."

Angelo yanked Tony up by the rope that bound his arms and legs behind his back.

Dorian grabbed the Louisville Slugger, and they headed down to the edge of the swamps. "Ya know why you're here, Tony?"

He mumbled something around the gag Angelo had stuffed in his mouth.

Dorian said, "What, asshole? I can't hear ya."

Tony mumbled again, and for some reason, just the sound pissed Dorian off even more. He ripped the gag out of Tony Cabrezzi's mouth.

"Fuck you, Dorian!" Tony barked.

Dorian punched him in the jaw. "I'm sorry. I don't think I heard ya correctly. Can ya say that again?"

"Fuck you!" Cabrezzi spat back and literally spat blood in Dorian's face.

Looking up at Angelo, Dorian's face was nothing less than calm. He said, "Put him down." Angelo let go of Tony's arms, untied his legs, and left the dumbass standing there all wide-eyed and cocky, like he could actually do something still half tied up. Dorian gripped the Louisville Slugger between his fists, swung like major league hitter, and popped that bastard right in the face. "Ya wanna try that again?"

Tony started laughing.

Angelo shook his head.

Dorian swung the bat again.

41

THE Louisville Slugger came down across the side of Tony's knee with a vengeance, and the guy dropped to the ground with an ear-splitting scream. His leg was toast. He crumpled to the ground like an accordion, fell to his side with his good leg open for a brutal free-for-all.

No way in hell would he be standing back up again. No way in hell would he be able to put up a fight, but that didn't stop Dorian from taking the bat to the other knee. He hit Tony's kneecap hard enough the bone cracked on impact.

Tony screamed again.

"Please don't...." he cried out, but he couldn't finish his sentence before Dorian swung the bat again. This time, the Slugger connected with the side of Tony's scalp and split his skin wide open.

Dorian honestly thought he didn't have that kind of strength after both his arms had been broken. But as sure as he stood there, the side of Tony Cabrezzi's face had busted open and blood had erupted all over the place. As sick as it sounded, it felt good... damn good.

After that, Dorian lost all logical thought. Seeing Tony's blood forced him to remember Jansen, lying in his arms, bleeding to death while he cried out for help while everyone ignored him. A bullet from one of Tony's goons' guns had put Jansen down on a filthy French Quarter sidewalk. As Dorian remembered holding Jansen, watching the life bleed out of his body, he lost the will to stop himself from beating Tony to a bloody pulp.

"Ya think ya can take from me?" Dorian growled as he reared the baseball bat back again. "This wasn't his fuckin' fight! He was innocent!"

The bat came down on Tony's head: once, twice, again and again. His face had become completely indistinguishable by the time Dorian had finished pulverizing it. Bubbles of blood hung at the end of Tony's crooked nose. Blood rolled out of his mouth. Dorian could hear the gargled breaths in the back of his throat that said he was still alive enough to be saved.

"Fuck you, Tony!" Dorian brought the bat down across his chest, his legs, and his face again. "Ain't nobody gonna save ya now! You're dead! Ya fucked up, Tony!"

And when that wasn't enough to extinguish the flames of Dorian's rage, when the need for revenge still burned in his soul but he'd lost the strength to keep holding the bat, he pulled the .45 from his waistband, and started firing rounds into Tony's battered body.

The first shot coated Dorian's face with blood and bits of something he'd rather not think about. The second shot blew a hole in the middle of Tony's face. He couldn't stop himself. He kept thinking about how close he'd come to losing Jansen, the days he'd spent praying the kid would wake up, the pain his dancer had to have been in. It was all this asshole's fault. He had to pay.

"Die, you sorry son of bitch! Die!" Dorian yelled over the boom of his gun. The louder he screamed and cursed, the more he wanted to collapse. He felt the tears burning in his eyes, but he wouldn't cry. Not in front of Angelo, not in front of Tony's mutilated corpse, not in front of anyone.

By the time Dorian was done, there wasn't much left of Tony Cabrezzi. He'd emptied a seven-round magazine into the motherfucker's body, kept pulling the trigger, but nothing happened. No bang. Just a clicking noise. That's when he realized the tears he'd wanted to hide had won the battle for their freedom. He'd been crying the whole damn time. "I hate you! I fuckin' hate you!" He pulled the trigger again and again and again.

Angelo grabbed Dorian, throwing his entire big-ass body around his boss, and he pulled Dorian back. "You got 'em, boss," he said in a calm, even tone. "It's over."

No, the fuck it wasn't over.

Pulling away from Angelo's grip, he swung the gun in his hand until his fingers wrapped around the hot barrel, but he didn't feel it. Rage had taken over. Dorian had lost control of himself.

He dropped to his knees beside Tony's mangled form and slammed the butt of the gun's grip down on what used to be the face of his most hated enemy. "I hope ya burn in hell!" he growled as he continued to beat Tony's corpse. He just didn't feel like Tony had suffered enough. He hadn't gotten his vengeance for Jansen, and goddammit, he wanted more.

Angelo wrapped his arms around his boss again, hefted him up from the ground, pulling him away from the swiss-cheesed corpse lying in the mud. "He's dead, Dorian. Let it go."

"Fuck you and fuck him!"

"Get it together, man!" Angelo gave his boss a hard shake, swung him around and shoved him away from Tony Cabrezzi's vapid body. "He's dead! There ain't nothin' left. Ya got him!"

Dorian stumbled backward, his legs a tangled mess as his feet fought to keep on course. Had it not been for the massive tree he backed into, he would've ass-planted right in the mud. Normally, he would've chewed Angelo up one side and down the other for that little stunt, but Dorian was neither in the frame of mind nor did he have the energy to go after his hired hand.

They stared silently at each other, Angelo daring his boss to try something out of line, Dorian trying to take stock of what had just happened. Rational thought had stepped out on him the first time he swung the bat against Cabrezzi's face. His brain was on hiatus, and his voice had followed right along with it.

Something had to give, though. They had to get out of that swamp.

"Strip," Angelo finally said.

"What the...?"

"You got too much blood on ya. I'm gettin' a blanket from the trunk. We're gonna destroy your clothes, then I'm takin' you back home." Angelo's jaw clenched. He narrowed his serious eyes on his boss, daring him to try his patience. If he had to knock Dorian over the head and haul his ass out of the swamps, he would. Thankfully, it wouldn't come to that.

Absently, Dorian did what Angelo told him to. His hands were shaking, and his mind was gone. He honestly couldn't feel a thing anymore. He couldn't even feel the love for Jansen that had driven him to go completely insane. He was there, and that was it. And then he stood naked in a marshy field while Angelo rolled Tony Cabrezzi's body toward the swamp. The gators would finish the rest.

They rode back to the mansion without saying as much as two words to each other. Dorian stared zombielike from the passenger window as the city flew by in a stream of bright colors. He could still smell Tony's blood on his body, even though they'd tossed his clothes into the swamp for the gators to eat. They would shred the blood-soaked fabric until there wasn't a single thread left.

Angelo helped Dorian out of the car and into the house. The man moved like he was half comatose, but Angelo wouldn't leave until he knew his boss was safe and sound. After all, that's what Dorian Grant paid him to do, never mind the fact that he almost considered Dorian a friend. They'd been pullin' jobs together for close to twenty years now; of course they'd formed a bond. Who wouldn't?

He helped his boss up the stairs, but stopped at Dorian's bedroom door. What went on beyond that wasn't Angelo's business. He said, "You're home, boss."

Dorian nodded but didn't say a damn word.

Jansen, Dorian's beautiful, innocent dancer, his peace and his sanity, lay on his side in the bed with his head propped up on a pillow. The white bandage at his stomach jarred Dorian's sight. If it hadn't been for that stark white reminder of the heinous crime committed against that gorgeous, miraculous man, he would've appeared absolutely perfect.

A low light cast a soft golden glow over Jansen's tan skin. Shadows accented his muscles. The light bathed each and every ridge and sinew with a magical glow. The flashing light of the television reflected in his deep brown eyes as he stared at the TV with so much focus and intensity.

But then there was that damn bandage. Dorian just couldn't look at him anymore. It hurt. All he saw was blood and death. Emptiness consumed him. He turned his glaring eyes away, ground his teeth together, and wished like hell he could go back and kill Tony Cabrezzi again.

When Angelo shut the door, Jansen turned his head and his eyes widened. Silently, he stared at his lover, his strong, commanding, stubborn, but oh so beautiful lover whose face had been spattered with blood, whose eyes looked so empty and desperate.

"Dorian?" he whispered, brow furrowing, nose flaring. "What the…?"

Dorian collapsed right there, fell to his knees with his back bowed and his head hanging. He began to sob. Like a fucking baby, he cried so hard his whole body shook. He hated the look on Jansen's face, hated what his dancer obviously saw. Jansen clearly saw a murderer, covered in a victim's blood. He saw a monster. Dorian could tell by the expression on Jansen's shocked face.

"I…." Dorian shook his head back and forth, the movement slow and miserable. "Don't look at me. Please, don't look at me." The sound of his voice was nothing more than a quivering timbre of broken words. "I'm a… a monster."

"No," Jansen breathed, shaking his head as he climbed down from his perch on his lover's bed. He couldn't watch the suffering anymore. He couldn't stand to see Dorian's pain.

Wrapping his arms around Dorian's head, he pulled him against his stomach and held on tight while the man who'd stolen his heart sobbed against his body. Jansen pressed his lips to the top of Dorian's head. In that sweet, beautiful, compassionate voice of his, he said, "It's okay, baby. It's over now. You're home."

42

DORIAN held Jansen's legs tight, face buried against his stomach, and while the pressure against Jansen's wound wasn't very comfortable, he let it go. Dorian obviously needed him. Jansen had never seen his mysterious lover break down so badly, had never seen him completely fall apart. But right there, as sure as he lived and breathed, Dorian Grant sobbed the most painful tears Jansen had ever seen in his life. And there wasn't a damn thing he could do to take that pain away, to heal whatever had broken in Dorian's soul to make him fall apart like that.

"Baby?" he whispered.

Dorian didn't loosen his hold, didn't utter the first sound.

Jansen brushed Dorian's hair, and when he pulled his hand back, his palm was coated with blood and tiny bits of… gross. "Baby, why don't we get you cleaned up?" he said. Dorian nodded against his stomach. The movement made Jansen wince, but he tried to hide the discomfort. Now simply wasn't the time for his pain. Now was about Dorian and fixing whatever had broken in his mind. "Come on, baby, let's get you in the tub. Maybe it'll make you feel better."

With Jansen's help, Dorian lifted from his knees and wavered on his feet. He dropped the blanket from his body, and had it not been for the blood all over his face and neck, he may not have made it to the bathtub. Jansen would've had his beautiful tattooed body on the bed, straddling him while they fucked their way into oblivion.

Jansen clenched his jaw and he swallowed hard. Just thinking about Dorian lying on the bed, thrusting all that beautiful, hardened length into Jansen's tight, puckered opening made his dick twitch. He shook his head and averted his eyes so he could *try* to compose himself. Not now. He had to help snap Dorian back to reality. He had to get his lover cleaned up and half aware of where he was, what he was doing, and who he was with.

"Walk with me," Jansen croaked, voice hoarse with a heady mix of fear and desire.

They laced their hands together, fingers bound and knotted like living stitches to hold the fabric of their lives together. If only it were that easy. If only the simple act of holding hands really did have the power to cement a relationship and make it unbreakable.

Jansen led Dorian to the bathroom, sat him down on the toilet, and brushed the top of his free hand over his cheek. He didn't want to let go, didn't want to leave Dorian sitting alone on the toilet long enough to cross the few feet to the bathtub, but he really didn't have much choice if he wanted to clean the blood and bits of body out of Dorian's hair. He shuddered at the thought. "Just sit here, okay? I'm going to draw a hot bath."

Dorian lowered his head and nodded slowly.

Jansen went to the giant tub, then started running warm water. It trickled over his fingertips and splashed down to the huge porcelain basin of the Jacuzzi. Too bad he couldn't climb inside and bathe with Dorian, maybe just relax against his body and hold him. Doctor's orders, no bathing with the stitches in his gut.

He looked back at Dorian's huddled form and said, "You okay, baby?"

Absently, Dorian nodded, though truthfully, he was far from okay. He opened his mouth to say something but stopped. Jansen frowned. With those dark, caring eyes staring at him, Dorian couldn't bring himself to make a sound, and it wasn't until Jansen turned back to the tub that he actually spoke. Voice soft, full of fear and disappointment, full of sorrow and sadness, he said, "I saw the way ya looked at me when I walked into the bedroom. Ya saw a monster, didn't ya?"

"No, baby," Jansen said as he lifted away from the tub. He went back to Dorian, knelt down in front of him and held his hands. "I didn't. I saw the man I love covered in blood, and I freaked. I didn't know if you were hurt or not. I just…." He shook his head and sighed, set his dark gaze on Dorian, let his stare yo-yo back and forth across his lover's face. "I just saw the blood, and I guess I panicked."

"It was Cabrezzi's blood," Dorian mumbled, not that saying it or having Jansen know the truth could make the situation any better. It just felt relieving to get it off his chest. "The guy who shot ya, I killed him. He won't ever hurt ya again. I swear to God, no fuckin' body will ever hurt ya again."

"I know, baby. Let's not talk about that right now, okay? Let's just get this mess off of you," Jansen said as he urged Dorian from the toilet seat. He guided his lover over to the tub, helped him ease down in the water. As Dorian's body became completely submerged, his muscles relaxed and his head lay back. "That's it," Jansen said with a soft smile. "Just relax. Let me take care of you."

Jansen soaped a rag, then started cleaning the blood away from Dorian's face and neck.

Dorian kept his eyes closed, completely trusting, completely at ease. It was like he'd never left the house, never mutilated the man who put his delicate dancer in the hospital. Everything felt normal again, as normal as it ever had been, anyway. Maybe in time, if Jansen stayed with him, if his dancer never abandoned him, things could truly be normal. Maybe Dorian could leave the life he'd been living and settle down into a new happy, healthy life.

Maybe.

"Thank you for takin' care of me," Dorian whispered.

"Of course I'm going to take care of you. Why wouldn't I?"

"I don't know. Just not used to it, I guess. Don't really feel like I deserve it."

"You do. Trust me, you do."

Jansen brushed his soapy hands over Dorian's chest, drawing foamy white circles over the tattooed expanse of his lover's flesh. A smile curled the corner of his lips as the soapy water ran down Dorian's pecs and his hard abs. He worked the suds into a thick lather as he slowly washed down Dorian's muscled thighs. Then his eyes caught sight of the flaccid cock lying on the crease of Dorian's pressed thighs.

Jansen's mouth watered as he dipped his hands in the water to wash away the soap. He couldn't resist the urge to stroke his palm back and forth across all that soft, sensitive flesh. Leaning down, he swirled his tongue around Dorian's nipple while he tightened his hand around his lover's cock.

"Please, God, don't stop," Dorian rasped, eyes clenched tight as he pulled his lower lip between his teeth and arched into Jansen's fist.

Fingers waved, loosened, then tightened again as Jansen's palm rode up and down Dorian's hardened shaft. He pulled the puckered nipple between his teeth.

Dorian moaned and arched a little more so Jansen could get his hand all the way down to the base of his erection. He threaded his fingers through Jansen's hair as the dancer teased and toyed with his nipple.

Picking up the pace and tightening his hand, Jansen felt Dorian's shaft pulse and thicken. Then suddenly, Jansen felt a warm explosion erupt over his fingers.

Dorian's body tensed, and he cried out to thank the God he'd lost faith in a long time ago.

43

"I'VE never let anyone see any kind of weakness in me," Dorian said as he climbed in bed next to Jansen's naked body. He pressed kisses up the line of his dancer's chest as he pressed himself against Jansen's lean, muscled form. Dorian slid his leg between Jansen's thighs, brushed back and forth against his cock. His last kiss landed at the hollow of his lover's throat. "I think that means something. I think I trust ya more than I've ever trusted anyone in my life." Dorian's deep brown gaze traveled up Jansen's body until it landed on Jansen's intrigued eyes. He whispered, "I hope ya never use that against me."

"I wouldn't do anything to hurt you, Dorian. I love you."

Rolling onto his side, Jansen nestled against Dorian. He felt the stiffened length of a renewed erection press against the valley between his cheeks. The sensation made him roll his hips so his bare skin brushed over Dorian's firm shaft. Dorian wrapped his arms around him, then rolled his body until Jansen lay on his stomach.

Dorian kissed his shoulder blade, then ran his tongue down the length of Jansen's back, bypassing the bandage covering the bullet's exit wound. He tried like hell to pretend it wasn't there. "I want you," he whispered as his fingers slipped between those beautifully rounded cheeks. He toyed with Jansen's warm opening as he kissed his way back up. At his ear, Dorian whispered, "Can I have you?"

"Yes," Jansen said hoarsely. He was already rock hard from the simple, gentle foreplay. "Take me."

And Jansen thought he would, thought he'd slam him down on the bed and fuck him hard like he normally did, but instead Dorian said, "No, I want to make love to you."

One finger slid inside, and Jansen's back arched. Every place Dorian's lips touched made Jansen's skin warm, but the way he teased him with a hint of teeth made everything tingle. Dorian slowly slid his finger in and out of Jansen's body. His lips never left Jansen's shoulder.

The nightstand drawer opened. Jansen knew Dorian was reaching for the lube, and that made his body come alive with a new excitement.

Jansen hissed as Dorian took his fingers away, but he had a much better gift to give his dancer. He squeezed the lube onto his palm, then rubbed it up and down his hardened shaft. Sure, Jansen had gotten him off in the bathtub, but he was ready to go again. He wanted to give his lover the same pleasure.

Dorian eased the tip of his cock inside Jansen's waiting opening as he kissed the side of his lover's throat. Fuck, Dorian loved him so much it scared him. There was so much he was willing to do, and give, and be for Jansen. And now, with his lean body stretched out and waiting, Dorian only wanted to be gentle and caring.

Jansen relaxed, moaning as Dorian slowly stroked, in and out, in and out again. Jansen's breath became short, ragged pants. His eyes closed. His back arched, pushing his ass farther into the air. Dorian rolled his torso, glided in, then pulled out. He teased Jansen's opening before sliding in again. Jansen reached back, fingers biting into Dorian's hip.

Christ, Dorian didn't think he could get any harder, but the sensations of it all made his cock start to thicken against all that tight, muscled warmth. Pushing deeper, Dorian gently kissed down Jansen's shoulder. The caressing and taking care, it felt pretty damn good, better than Dorian could've ever expected.

"Oh God," Jansen rasped. Dorian worked his cock back and forth across that smooth, happy little nub buried deep inside Jansen's body. Dorian always managed to find that spot, always managed to stroke it just right.

"I want us to come together," Jansen breathed.

Dorian started stroking a little faster. Jansen's back bowed against him. One arm came across his shoulder, and Dorian's fingers started toying with his nipple. Jansen didn't think he would last. Every way Dorian touched him, loved him, fondled him, and fucked him, made tingles shoot down his spine. His sac tightened. The pressure became too intense. The throbbing became almost unbearable.

Then he felt the throbbing inside him, and he knew Dorian was about to come too.

In and out, up and down. Dorian worked his lover's body. His hand was relentless, plucking and teasing sensitive nipples. Then his other hand reached across the dancer's hip and down between his firm thighs, palm riding over his tightened sac.

A shiver rumbled through Dorian's body. It exploded in his cock. He came inside his delicious dancer, and that only made him pump harder and harder, until he felt Jansen's creamy warmth against his palm. He pressed his lips against the back of Jansen's neck. Dorian didn't pull out. He liked the warmth around his cock, liked the feeling of being so connected to another man, a man he sincerely loved.

Using a handful of the sheets, he cleaned his hand as much as he could, then he wrapped his arms around Jansen's chest, careful not to catch his wound, and he held him tight, so tight he wondered if the kid could even breathe. But Dorian needed this. He needed the closeness, the togetherness. He needed Jansen. Like this, Dorian didn't feel like a monster. He finally felt like someone who deserved to be loved.

44

JANSEN sat in bed, legs hugged against his chest, watching Dorian sleep. He'd been like that for a few hours, watching the slow rise and fall of that gorgeous, tattooed chest, watching the way the edge of his lover's mouth curled as though he really enjoyed the movie his mind played for him. He listened to every little grumble and every breath Dorian took, and Jansen couldn't get over how completely peaceful he felt now.

The only problem he still had was that whole mess about Dorian being a criminal. It completely freaked Jansen out that he could just kill someone—end a human being's life—as if it were no big deal. It honestly made him question his morals and his integrity, but ironically, it never made him question Dorian's love for him. Did he think Dorian would kill him? Not anymore, but that could change, depending on his temper, he guessed.

A night or… many nights of mind-blowing sex couldn't just wash those fears away.

Jansen knew he needed to talk to Dorian about his worries. He knew if he kept silently harping on them, it would make him crazy and maybe even drive him to resent Dorian, if even a little. But, God help him, he was so afraid that if he did mention his lover's appetite for murder, Dorian would get mad. Maybe even mad enough to kick him out of his life. He didn't want that. He never wanted that. Despite all the bullshit, Dorian made him happy, happier than he'd been in a long time, and he didn't want to lose that.

Dorian made another little grumbling sound. His eyes started to flutter. He brushed his hand up and down Jansen's bare leg, smiled, and said a raspy, "Hey, baby," nodding like he wanted Jansen to kiss him.

Jansen leaned down, pressed his lips to Dorian's, and the big guy locked his arms around Jansen's body. Of course, Jansen gasped when he did it, which made his chest constrict. It made the healing wound in his stomach hurt, and he winced.

Dorian eased off, whispering a soft apology as he pulled his arms away.

"I'm okay," Jansen breathed, failing to hide that bit of pain.

But he wasn't okay, not really.

Dorian knew his dancer, and he knew that distant look in his eyes. He gently rolled their bodies so Jansen could lie down beside him; so Dorian could kiss him, touch him, be near him. He pressed his lips to the rounded edge of Jansen's shoulder while he cradled the side of his lover's throat with his hand. Jansen only stared at the ceiling, albeit with a slight grin on his face, but something was wrong. Something was different.

"What's on your mind, baby?" Dorian asked, voice soft and husky from the few hours he'd been asleep.

"Nothing much." Jansen shrugged. God help him, he was such a horrible liar, and Dorian knew it. Jansen knew he could see right through him. He just didn't have the guts to say anything. So, what, he would live their relationship in a lie?

"C'mon," Dorian said, looking up with those beautiful, soft brown eyes. He looked like a freakin' puppy dog when he did that, and there was no way Jansen could not be honest.

"I love you," Jansen finally said, and he felt Dorian's body tense. That had to freak him out a bit, and yeah, that was never the best way to start a "we need to talk" type of conversation. "I don't want you to get mad at me...."

"And it's never a good sign when 'don't get mad' comes directly after 'I love you'." Dorian sat up beside him, wrapped his arm around Jansen, and pulled him closer. Jansen laid his head on Dorian's shoulder. Dorian rested his cheek against the top of Jansen's head. "What's wrong, baby?" Dorian asked in a soft, concerned voice. "Ya need to know ya can talk to me, Jansen. I ain't some irrational monster."

"I do. I mean...." Jansen sighed as he relaxed in the hold of Dorian's strong arms. "Dorian, I.... Sometimes, you scare me."

Dorian raised his head. He looked a little shocked, like he couldn't believe Jansen could ever be afraid of him. Which was really pretty ridiculous, all things considered. He'd given Jansen plenty of reasons to be afraid or worried or whatever. Hell, these days, it seemed to be normal for anyone and everyone to be bothered by his presence.

"Not you, not exactly," Jansen quickly offered when he saw the conflict on his lover's gorgeous face. "Your killing scares the shit out of me. It freaks me out that you can just kill and not feel anything or even be remorseful for what you've done."

Dorian stiffened, brow arched. "Not remorseful? Ya think I don't feel bad about the shit I do?" His voice had started to rise, but he quickly reeled it back in. This wasn't the time for anger, and anger damn sure wouldn't insure his dancer stayed in his life.

"Jansen, I do feel guilty, even more so now that I have a reason to live and a reason to care. Their faces have haunted me since the beginning, since the first one my father'd had me off for him. I wanted to stop a long damn time ago, before I ever met ya, even. I hated killin', but I couldn't stop. I still don't think I can stop. It ain't that I'm numb to it. It's more a means to survive a life I was forced into."

"What about Tony Cabrezzi?" Jansen asked.

Dorian straightened his spine, shoulder squared. He took a deep breath, scrubbed his hand over his head, then slowly exhaled. "He was different. I'll admit that, but that fucker had it comin'. He tried to kill ya. He almost did fuckin' kill ya. Ya think I could sit back and let that happen to ya? Ya think I want a message goin' out to the thugs that they can mess with mine and not expect retaliation?"

"So, you killed him because you wanted to send a message."

"No!" Dorian sighed, lowered his head. "No, that wasn't it, not exactly."

"Then what was it?"

Swallowing hard, Dorian sat up on the bed, eased his way to the edge, and swung his legs over the side. He steepled his arms against his knees, locked his fists under his chin. Did he need to confess how crazy he'd gone over Tony, or would that just make Jansen fear him even more? In all honesty, if had it been anyone other than Jansen, Dorian would've let Angelo handle it, and nothing more would've been said about it.

"If I tell ya something, ya gotta promise to stay calm. Promise ya won't freak out and run away from me again, because, Jansen, I gotta be honest. I need ya like I ain't never needed anyone before."

With a frown on his face, Jansen watched Dorian's back muscles flex and tense. He climbed up on his knees and eased across the bed. He lightly touched Dorian's back, laying his palm on his lover's shoulder blade. "I promise," Jansen said in a soft voice. The words fell so easily from his lips. Jansen had never been the sort of man to give away promises, but that—for some reason—felt like a promise he could keep.

"When I saw that man, I wanted to kill him. I wanted him to feel every ounce of pain his gunshot caused ya. I thought I would beat him a little, then let Angelo finish him up. I didn't want to be the one to end his life, but I wanted him to know the same pain you'd felt. I swear to God, baby, I was fine until I saw the blood. The fat lady fuckin' sang her song. It was all over. I saw the blood, and I remembered holdin' ya in the middle of that dirty fuckin' street while ya tried to die, and nothin', I mean *nothin'* could've stopped me. Angelo couldn't even drag me off of Tony. I beat his ass with the bat until I didn't have the strength to keep goin'. Then I pulled the gun outta my waistband, and I emptied the clip in that son of a bitch. And when the bullets were gone, I kept shootin'."

Dorian's hands had begun to tremble, his face pale. A thin sheen of sweat clung to his brow. His eyes turned red and glassy. Each breath he took seemed to be shorter and shorter. He was on the verge of a panic attack. Jansen knew the signs all too well.

He climbed down off the bed and knelt down in front of Dorian, taking his lover's clenched fists into the cradle of his warm, caring hands. Jansen met Dorian's hard brown stare and softly said, "Calm down, baby. You're pale, and you're shaking. You don't have to keep talking about it."

"No. I do. I need to get this off my chest."

"Okay." Jansen nodded slowly. He didn't take his hands or eyes off Dorian. "Okay. I'm listening."

Licking his lips, Dorian stared down at the floor. He took a deep breath, cleared his throat, then slowly found his voice again. "When I came back home, the way ya looked at me, Jansen, my heart sunk. I knew ya saw the blood, and I knew, in your eyes, I was nothing but a fuckin' murderer. I didn't want ya to see me that way. I never want ya to see me that way. It was hard enough knowin' how bad I'd flipped out on Cabrezzi, but seein' ya starin' at me, like—"

"Hey," Jansen interrupted. He kept his voice calm and steady. "I was worried about you, baby. Yeah, I saw the blood, but I didn't know if it was yours or...." He pulled Dorian's hands to his lips, kissed the rounded, scarred edge of his lover's knuckles.

One tear dropped from Jansen's cheek, then another. When Dorian felt the third drop, he raised his head. Brow furrowed, he stared at Jansen for a moment. He absolutely hated the sadness and pain in his lover's dark brown eyes. Dorian would've bargained with the devil himself to give Jansen back his happiness.

"Don't cry for me, okay?" Dorian whispered. "I'm not worth your tears." Because watching Jansen cry hurt too damn bad, and knowing the tears were his fault made it that much worse. *So this is what love feels like*, Dorian thought.

"Yeah, you are, Dorian. You really are," Jansen said as he brushed his hands across his watery eyes. He sniffled back the remaining tears. "You also deserve to be loved, to be happy. And I promise, I will try my best to give that to you."

Dorian pulled his dancer up into his lap, threaded his arms around the kid's waist, and he held Jansen tight, burying his head in the curve of the dancer's firm chest. Taking slow, deep breaths, he clung to the most treasured person in his life. Dorian held on to him with ferocity, like if he didn't, the world would come in and steal the love of his life away from him.

45

"JANSEN," Dorian said as he shifted his dancer out of his lap onto the edge of the bed. He knelt down in front of Jansen, kept their fingers woven together, because even that slight touch kept them connected. It made everything look and smell and feel perfect. Even if, at the moment, it was an illusion.

The soft light of the room cast a golden glow on Jansen's sun-kissed skin. It reflected in his loving brown eyes and shimmered against his moist pink lips. Seeing him sitting on the bed, watching and waiting with bated breath, did something to Dorian's heart. For the first time in a lifetime, he felt warm inside, maybe even genuinely happy. Dorian knew he still had a lot to say, a lot of things he needed to make right with his dancer, but he would stop at nothing to give Jansen everything he deserved. In that moment, he knew he would happily spend a lifetime making Jansen the happiest man the world had ever seen.

"I need ya to listen to me, okay?"

Jansen looked down at his lover, saw the crease in his brow and the worry in his dark brown eyes, the way Dorian's shoulders squared, and the uneven rise and fall of his chest as he breathed. Then Jansen noticed Dorian's fingers trembling around his. "What is it, baby?" he asked in a concerned voice. He had to fight the urge to climb down onto the floor and pull Dorian into his arms.

"I know how ya feel about dancin', and ya gotta trust me when I tell ya I want ya to keep doin' it, but, baby, I don't want ya dancin' at Sin & Seduction no more." Jansen started to open his mouth, but a palm thrust into the air stopped the inevitable argument that topic always caused. "Hear me out, please."

"Okay," Jansen nodded, keeping his eyes on Dorian.

SIN & SEDUCTION | 203

"I want ya to live with me in the mansion." Dorian paused, waited for the protest, but it never came. Jansen didn't so much as open his mouth or raise his brow. His face remained stoic and attentive. Maybe that was a good sign... maybe not.

"I wanna put ya through school," Dorian continued. "Ya don't have to work. I'll take care of everything: food, clothes, a new car, whatever ya need. And as far as the dancin' goes, I'll pull some strings to get ya an audition with one of the local dance groups. If ya want or need a private coach, I'll even pay for it. Please, just please, stop dancin' at that club, okay? I don't want to worry about ya every time ya leave for work. I don't want to worry that someone's gonna try to hurt ya again." Dorian lowered his head, and with it, his voice. "I wouldn't be able to live with myself if someone tried to hurt ya again."

Those last words went straight to Jansen's heart. The sorrowful sound of Dorian's voice cradled that pounding, pumping vessel of life and gave it a solid tug. He brought their woven fists to his lips and kissed the top of Dorian's shaky hand.

"Baby," Jansen whispered. "It happened and we dealt with it. I survived and I'm okay. You didn't shoot me. You saved my life. Dorian, I could've died in the street, but I didn't because you saved me. Stop blaming yourself."

Dorian's head shot up, eyes narrowed, jaw clenched. How in the hell Jansen had forgiven him for pulling him into the wreck of a life Dorian had been living was a mystery. One he'd try not to question, but the kid needed to understand. He needed to know that being with Dorian Grant would never be a walk in the park.

"But it was my fault. I made the enemies myself, and my enemies came after ya because you're with me. That's not acceptable." He broke his hands free of Jansen's grip, touched either side of his face, and kissed his lover's forehead. "You'll always have to look over your shoulder. You'll always have to wonder if someone is waitin' in the darkness, behind the bushes or around the corner. That's why I have Angelo. I can't keep my eyes and ears on everything. I can give ya the same protection, but baby, ya gotta let me."

And Dorian would. That man, his dancer, meant the world to him. Thinking about what had been done to him, the way Jansen had been so helpless, clinging to the edge of life and death, it made him realize there wasn't anything he wouldn't do to keep his dancer safe. He'd put Jansen's life before his own, and that alone scared him enough to make him get down on his knees and beg Jansen to quit the club.

Keeping his lips against his dancer's soft skin, he whispered. "Please do this for me, baby. I need the peace of mind."

"Okay," Jansen said with a slight nod. He reached up and laid his hand over Dorian's, nestling his cheek against his lover's warm palm. "Okay. I'll quit the club. Honestly, I haven't wanted to go back since the gunshot. I've been a little scared." He cast his eyes away as he pulled his bottom lip between his teeth. He had more than ample reason to be afraid, though he'd never shared the full story with Dorian. "Remember when I asked you to be careful with me, back when we first met?"

"Yeah."

"I never really told you the whole story."

"No," Dorian shook his head. "No, ya didn't."

"When I first moved to New Orleans, I worked at a tiny club in Slidell. Occasionally I'd climb up on the bar and shake my ass. It was the only way I made enough money to make ends meet, well, barely make ends meet. Anyway, there was this guy who would come in and pay the bartender a hundred dollars to get me on the bar. I would climb up there and shake my shit for him. By the end of the night, I usually had close to two hundred bucks tucked in my jeans. The guy never came off as creepy or anything. He was actually sort of charming and pretty handsome in a reserved sort of way. I never thought anything of it. I mean, he seemed nice enough. A few months later, he attacked me."

Jansen took a deep breath, licked his lips, and turned his face away so Dorian wouldn't see the pain in his eyes. He let the breath go, and when he started to speak again, his voice was shaky with the tears he'd been fighting.

"He followed me out to the parking lot one night after the club had closed down. The bouncer was supposed to stay until we all left, but he didn't. Nothing ever happened there anyway, so normally, it wasn't a big deal. The parking lot was dark and empty, except for a few cars. The owner had been warned about the lights being out months before, but he never did anything about them. I was almost to my car when I felt the hand lock around my wrist. It was him. He pulled me back and asked me to go to his house with him. I didn't want to. I told him no, but...."

Closing his eyes, Jansen took another breath. He clenched Dorian's hand a little tighter. This was the one story he never thought he'd have to tell again. It was the one thing that had happened to him that he'd worked damn hard to forget about, but there he sat, digging into the furthest depths of his mind just to share his deepest, darkest secret with the man he loved.

"I don't remember the attack. I only remember him pulling me into my car and tearing my jeans off. I'm thankful for that, that I don't remember. When I felt him... you know, I blacked out and...."

"Stop," Dorian interrupted. "I don't wanna know. He'll be the next motherfucker on my hit list. Just.... Yeah, don't tell me anymore. No more nightclubs okay? Not unless we go together and it's just for fun."

"Yeah, I, um, I didn't want to relive that whole incident. It took close to a year for the nightmares to go away." Jansen gave Dorian a wry smile as he wiped the brewing tears from his eyes. "I guess the point is, I'll take whatever protection I can get. If I get attacked again, odds are I probably won't survive. So, I'll stop dancing at the nightclubs, but I have to keep dancing. It's all I've ever had going for me, and I can't give it up completely."

"That's fine. I'm okay with that." Dorian pulled him into a hug. He held on tight, burying his head in the curve of Jansen's neck, splaying his hand over his lover's back, holding him against his body. "Ya don't know what ya just gave me," he breathed.

"I do, Dorian. It shows in your eyes and the way you touch me." Jansen leaned back. He lifted Dorian's face and their gazes met again. "You really want me to live here? You want to pay my way for everything, really?"

"I do. I really do."

"Why?"

"Because I love you. Because ya deserve it, and I have the means to give ya what ya want. You can do or be anything ya want."

"And what do you want in return?"

"Nothin'. Ya don't even have to love me back. I just want ya to have the things ya want. I want to see ya do something with yourself, because I know your potential. You're smart, baby. Too smart for that club. Ya deserve to have the best life has to offer, and by God, if I can give it to ya, I will."

Tears filled Jansen's eyes again, and this time, he couldn't stop them from rolling down his cheeks and coating his lips. He threw his arms around Dorian's neck. "No one has ever said anything so kind to me, Dorian. No one has ever wanted to make my dreams come true. And I do love you. I fell in love with you a long time ago. I only wanted you to love me back."

Dorian threaded his arms around Jansen's smaller body. He licked his dancer's lips, eyes closing. Dorian took a deep, contented breath, the first of many in the arms of the man he truly loved more than anything. He spoke in the softest, most sincere voice when he said, "I do love you, with all my heart, baby."

It all started with a dream that made her heart wrench and set of mesmerizing eyes that begged to be seen, and ALLISON CASSATTA the writer was born. A techie by trade, the daydreamer in her wanted to sail away from the mundane, while the hopeless romantic in her searched for the perfect love story. Many poems and short stories were written before her first attempt at a novel, and once that piece of her soul spilled onto paper, there was no stopping it.

She has an eye for the visually stunning and a mind that screams to bring that beauty to life. She gives her readers something they can feel in the depth of their hearts, creates worlds they can touch, and characters who become your best friend or worst enemy.

Born and raised in Memphis, Tennessee, big-city life was a rat race that kept her busy in her career. It took moving with her new husband to a sleepy Mississippi town to make her realize that dreams can come true, and did they ever. She found herself a published author. She found her perfect romance.

Visit Allison at

http://www.allisoncassatta.com

http://www.facebook.com/pages/Author-Allison-Cassatta/158938557051

http://www.goodreads.com/author/show/4417507.Allison_Cassatta.

Also from ALLISON CASSATTA

http://www.dreamspinnerpress.com